Second Sunday

Also by Michele Andrea Bowen

Church Folk

Michele Andrea Bowen

West Bloomfield, Michigan

WARNER BOOKS

An AOL Time Warner Company

This book is a work of fiction. Names, characters, places, and incidents are the product of the author's imagination or are used fictitiously. Any resemblance to actual events, locales, or persons, living or dead, is coincidental.

Published by Warner Books, Inc., with Walk Worthy Press™

Walk Worthy Press
Real Believers, Real Life, Real Answers in the Living God™

Walk Worthy Press, 33290 West Fourteen Mile Road, # 482, West Bloomfield, MI 48322
Warner Books, Inc., 1271 Avenue of the Americas, New York, NY 10020

Visit our Web sites at www.walkworthypress.net and www.twbookmark.com.

 An AOL Time Warner Company

Printed in the United States of America

First Printing: June 2003

10 9 8 7 6 5 4 3 2 1

ISBN: 0-446-53033-6
LCCN: 2003101824

This book is dedicated in loving memory to my cousin, Mack Earl Sanders (1955–2003). On hot St. Louis summer days, when I was six and Mack was eight, we watched the clouds as I told him some of my first stories.

Acknowledgments

Two years ago my first novel, *Church Folk*, was put on bookshelves across the country. What an incredibly joyous and blessed experience. And it didn't stop there. Because you, the readers, responded to my little ole country story about the folk at "chutch" in a remarkable way. Thank you with all of my heart.

Now I have been blessed with the release of my second novel, *Second Sunday*. And nothing as big as publishing a novel happens without the help and support of so many wonderful people. I know I can't name everybody, but I want to give a few shout outs to a few.

Thank you Denise Stinson, publisher of Walk Worthy Press, for believing in me and my projects. I know that I've given you some "heart attack" time. But you are a top notch publisher and our work together and friendship is truly a blessing in every way.

Elisa Petrini, my editor. Thank you so much, girl. I really appreciate your understanding of my work and what I try to accomplish with each story. I am very fortunate to be able to work with you. You are absolutely the best (and "good people," too).

Warner Books and the artist who creates my beautiful book covers—thank you.

My family. What can I say about y'all? You have been there for me through it all. I appreciate your help and support and ceaseless prayers.

Thank you, Mama, for helping me with the girls. I couldn't tour and travel without your help.

Thank you Laura and Janina for being so patient with all that Mommy has to do with work.

My friends in St. Louis (including the "Theodosia Girls" from back in the day), and in Durham, Richmond, and all the other cities where my loved ones live.

Thank you Valerie Ann Kaalund for taking my picture for this book. And thank you to my sweetie Harold, for reformatting the disk with the corrections on it at the eleventh hour, when my old dinosaur of a computer wasn't compatible with anything, let alone the computers of the folks who needed that information ASAP.

A special thank you to the extraordinary pastors in my life. My church home, St. Joseph A.M.E. Church, Durham, North Carolina, Rev. Phillip R. Cousins, Jr., Pastor. My home away from home, Mount Level Missionary Baptist Church, Durham, North Carolina, Rev. Dr. William C. Turner, Pastor. Bethlehem Temple Apostolic Church, Baltimore, Maryland, my uncle, Bishop James D. Nelson, Sr., Pastor.

And most of all, thank you, Lord, for letting me know what it feels like to be exceedingly and abundantly blessed.

Contents

Second Sunday

Part 1

A Little Women's Revolution, Right Up Here in the Church

1

In September 1975, just nine months before Gethsemane Missionary Baptist Church was to celebrate its hundredth anniversary, its pastor, Pastor Clydell Forbes, Sr., died. Some church members cried, others immediately started cooking food for the First Lady and her three boys, and Mr. Louis Loomis, one of the senior deacons in the congregation, said out loud what others were secretly thinking: "Why couldn't that cross-eyed, carrying-on stallion of a preacher hang on till the church was a hundred and one? If the boy had to up and die, at the very least he could have had the common decency to get us through the church's hundredth year."

Pastor Forbes was only in his fifties and hadn't occupied Gethsemane's pulpit all that long; just six years to be exact. No one expected that they'd lose him so soon, and at the worst possible time. A church anniversary without a pastor was like a Sunday worship service with no Hammond organ—the pastor was that central—and the centennial was the most momentous occasion in Gethsemane's history. The pastor was the one who would appoint and supervise the centennial committees, oversee fund-raising, and, most important of all, determine the celebration's theme, developing the sermons to herald and commemorate that special day which, for Gethsemane, was the Second Sunday in June.

Now all the planning was brought to a screeching halt until the Forbes family and the church family got through the man's funeral. And it was an ordeal—a long tear-jerking service that became a spectacle when three of his "special-interest" women fell out, crying and screaming with grief, and had to be removed by the ushers. Then the congregation pitched in to help his widow pack up the parsonage and get resettled with her children in a new home. So it was some time before Bert Green, the head of the Deacon Board, thought it appropriate to resume business and called a meeting of the church officers to discuss hiring a new pastor.

As they chewed over the list of potential preachers to interview, Bert's wife, Nettie, walked into the room, carrying a tray loaded down with sandwiches, potato salad, pickles and olives, caramel and pineapple coconut cakes and sweet potato pies cooked by one of the church's five missionary societies. Bert grabbed himself a thick, juicy, home-cooked ham sandwich as his fellow Deacon and Finance Board members heaped their plates high with food. Nettie had gotten an earful of their conversation on her way up from the kitchen, and it hadn't escaped her that the men had quit talking the moment they saw her struggling with that tray in the doorway.

Now they all sat there so self-satisfied, with that we-is-in-the-Upper Room look on their faces—the same men whose political head-butting had led to the appointment of Clydell Forbes, as spineless and weak a pastor as the church had ever seen. Helping them to their choice of iced tea or fresh coffee, Nettie pressed her lips together, mad enough to want to shake up these smug, never-did-know-how-to-pick-a-good-preacher men.

So she ignored Bert's signals that they were impatient for her to leave. Avoiding his eyes, she asked, as if butter wouldn't melt in her mouth, "So, who's on this list y'all talking about?"

No one seemed to hear her but Mr. Louis Loomis, the oldest member of both boards, who was chewing on the fat from his ham sandwich. He slipped his reading glasses down to the tip of his nose and resumed where he'd left off. "Like I said, some of these here preachers out of our price range."

Bert looked at the paper without acknowledging Nettie, picked up his pen, and asked, "Which ones?"

"Rev. Macy Jones, Rev. David O. Clemson, III, Rev. Joe Joseph, Jr. . . ."

Bert started drawing lines through those names until Cleavon Johnson, the head of the Finance Board, stopped him. "Keep Rev. Clemson on the list," he said.

"Why?" Mr. Louis Loomis shot back. He and Cleavon Johnson mixed like oil and water. Cleavon might be a business leader who had grabbed hold of the church's purse strings, but to Mr. Louis Loomis he was still the arrogant punk he used to belt-whip.

"Because—," Cleavon started to say, then slammed his mouth shut, staring pointedly at Nettie.

Pretending not to notice, Nettie grabbed one of the chairs

lined up against the wall, pulled it up to the conference table, and sat down like she belonged there. Then she looked straight at Cleavon and asked, still sounding innocent, "Just what is it that *we're* looking for in *our* new pastor?"

Cleavon Johnson glared at her, as if to say, "Woman, you way out of line." His "boys" on the Finance Board coughed and cleared their throats, Bert's cue to get his woman straightened out. But Bert locked eyes with Wendell Cates, who was married to Nettie's sister, Viola, and caught his smirking wink.

Wendell's expression told Bert, "Your girl on a roll. Let it be." Bert gave Wendell a sly smile that implied, "I hear you," and sat back to watch his wife give Cleavon a good dose of her down-home medicine.

When it became clear that Bert was not going to chastise his woman, Cleavon decided that he had to intervene. Puffing himself up to his full dignity as head of the Finance Board, he began authoritatively, "Sister Nettie, the senior men of this church, including your husband, have carefully formulated this list based on reliable recommendations . . ."

Nettie stole a glance at Mr. Louis Loomis, but all he did was adjust his glasses and crumple his napkin, as if to say, "My name is Bennett and I ain't in it."

Taking that as approval, she interrupted, "What I'm asking is, who—"

Cleavon tried to cut her off. "You'll meet our choices along with the rest of the congregation—"

"Or rather, what kind of men are being 'formulated' and 'recommended' to be *our* new pastor?" she continued, as if he were not talking.

"Sister Nettie," Cleavon scolded, "it's time for you to run along, like a good girl. You have your own proper duties as one of the church's handmaidens. We have ours, and you are stopping us from carrying them out." His voice grew stern. "You are not a duly appointed officer of this church, and until you are I think it would be wise on your part to let the heads of this godly house run this house."

Nettie pushed her chair away from the table, rose, and wiped her hands on her apron. Cleavon thought it was a gesture of defeat, that she was accepting his rebuke. But Nettie wasn't conceding defeat or retreating. She was retrenching as she stacked the dirty dishes and mustered up her sweetest, most chastised-woman-sounding voice to say, "Brother Cleavon, only the Lord knows what moves you. Only the Lord knows what makes you so forceful in what you do and say. But I am thankful that you express yourself so openly. Pray my strength."

As Nettie left, Cleavon nodded self-importantly to the group, not realizing she had just told him that he was in a class by himself and too dumb to try to keep it to himself.

Bert and Wendell stifled chuckles, but felt unsettled by Nettie's exit. She had to be up to something more than needling Cleavon Johnson. The encounter felt ominous, leaving them both with the impression that Nettie was throwing down a gauntlet, as a declaration of war.

When Nettie got back to the kitchen, she slammed her tray down on the counter so hard that she almost broke some of the heavy, mint green glass cups, plates, and saucers that were always in plentiful supply at church.

Her sister Viola jumped up, startled, and Nettie cussed, "I be doggoned and banned from heaven!"

"What's all this banging and ugly talking?" Sylvia Vicks demanded. "Nettie Green, you ain't out in them streets. You up in church. And you just best start remembering that."

"Sylvia, pray my strength, 'cause I am so mad at our men up in that room." Nettie pointed toward the ceiling, shaking her head in disgust. "I mean, they should have learned something worthwhile about hiring a preacher after Rev. Forbes. But they not even talking about character and morals—"

She stopped herself—"Forgive me, Jesus, for speaking ill of the dead"—then continued, "Lord only knows how much money they wasted bailing Clydell Forbes out of his women troubles—"

"What 'women troubles,' Nettie Green?" asked Cleavon's wife, Katie Mae Johnson. "I never heard about the church spending money like that. With Cleavon on the Deacon Board and being head of the Finance Board, I think I would have heard if he was making payoffs to errant women."

"Humph," Sylvia interjected. "Don't know how you missed all that, with the way Pastor Forbes had such a weakness for loose-tail women in booty-clutching dresses—bigger and fatter the booty, the better, I hear. And sad thing, Sister Forbes had a big fat rumpa-seat hangin' off the back of her. Don't know why he wanted all those other women, seeing what he had laying up next to him in his own house."

"Y'all, we should not be up in this church, talking all in Sister Forbes's business and up under her clothes like that. It ain't right, and it sho' ain't Christian."

Viola sighed out loud and raised her hands high in exasperation. "Katie Mae, it's Christian charity to tell the truth about the truth."

"And you should have known something, Katie Mae," Sylvia added. "We all keep telling you that Cleavon keep too much from you. He your husband, and all he ever tell you is that you think too much and read too much and always working your self up over some nonsense. Then he go out in the streets, and when he come home, be acting like he just got through passing out the two fish and five loaves of bread to the multitudes."

Katie Mae sneaked and wiped her eyes with the edge of her apron. Sometimes even your best friends didn't truly understand the magnitude of your pain. She sniffed once and put on a brave face before saying, "Aww, Sylvia, you can't judge my Cleavon by your Melvin. Melvin Sr. tells you pretty much everything and lets you run your house. But in Cleavon's home, the woman is beneath the man. He believe in the strict Bible ways."

Sylvia had to stop herself from quoting one of Mr. Louis Loomis's observations about Cleavon's "strict Bible ways" mess. "That boy always pontificating about a woman being beneath a man 'cause his tail always so intent on being on top of one."

"Well, it don't matter what Cleavon believe," Nettie said. "The fact is, he used church money to get the Reverend out of trouble. But it ain't just the money that makes me so mad—it's our men using they man pride and they man rules to pick our preachers, acting like I committed a sin just by asking them a question. Look at us down here in this hot kitchen, fixing food and washing dishes, while they upstairs eating, talking, laughing, and acting like they the Apostles. This is our church too. It just ain't right. And I ain't gone stand for it *no more.*"

"But what you propose to do?" Viola asked. "We not on any of those boards. So I don't see how we gone select a preacher."

"That's right," Katie Mae said. "You doing all this big bad talk and you don't even know how to go from A to B."

Nettie took off her apron and closed her eyes, praying for direction. When the inspiration came, she snapped her fingers.

"Viola, Sylvia, Katie Mae—here's what we'll do. Our mens thought they could put me in my place. So what we gone use is our women's place to make them do right. We're gone get us a woman's secret weapon."

"And what in the world would that be?" Sylvia asked.

"*Who* is more like it," Nettie stated. "We need someone who's an expert when it comes to sniffing out a man. Someone who can tell us which one of those preachers on they list is decent. And I know just the secret-weapon girl who can help us. My neighbor, Sheba Cochran."

"Sheba Cochran?" Katie Mae snapped, incensed that Nettie would even form her mouth to utter Sheba's name in her presence. "The heifer with all them baby daddies? Why that party-hearty club girl used to be one of Cleavon's women!"

For a moment, none of them breathed. Ever since high school, Cleavon had believed he was "fine as wine and every woman's kind,"and even though he was staring forty in the behind, he was still running around and chasing tail like his life depended on it. And no matter what Cleavon did, Katie

Mae defended him. It infuriated her friends, but if Katie Mae pretended he acted right, they felt obliged to hold their peace.

Now the truth was out.

"I didn't mean to hurt you," Nettie said softly. "And you have a right to be angry."

"Why would you or any other married woman even want to cut your eyes at that thang?"

"Katie Mae, there's something you should know. Cleavon lied to Sheba."

Katie Mae opened her mouth, but Nettie went on before she could speak. "Cleavon met Sheba over in East St. Louis at the Mothership Club. He claimed to be legally separated from you, and she honestly believed his marriage was over. So did I, until I learned he was still spending some nights with you. When I told Sheba, she broke it off. Remember Cleavon's black eye?"

Katie Mae nodded.

"Sheba did that, while she was cussing him out. I've known Sheba since we were kids, Katie Mae. She's never purposefully gone with a married man."

Tears streamed down Katie Mae's face. She was hurt, angry, and convicted in her heart all at the same time. She knew how Cleavon operated. And her grandmother constantly told her: "Baby, just a 'cause you let Cleavon run you, don't mean nobody else will. You better understand that there more folks than not who want to set his tail straight."

Sylvia handed Katie Mae a paper napkin and then gave Nettie the eye, hoping she could think of something to soften the blow she had just delivered. Nettie got the message and went to Katie Mae, taking both of her hands in her own. "I'm so sorry," she said.

When Katie Mae regained her composure, Nettie added, "Please trust me about Sheba. Cleavon picked Clydell Forbes, and he ain't picking our new pastor. But the fact is, none of these men—including Bert, Wendell, and Melvin Sr.—have the sense to find a man who can lead the church, bring us together for the anniversary, *and* do right by the women. It's got to be up to us."

Katie Mae sighed heavily. Nettie was right.

"And for that we need Sheba," Sylvia said.

"Yes," Viola chimed in. "That Sheba knows men like I know my name. If one of these preachers on they list is bad, she'll find him out."

"And if one is a good man?" Katie Mae asked.

"Then she'll know that, too," Nettie answered. "She the one always told me to quit worrying about Bert. Said, with a good man, if you take care of him right, he ain't going nowhere. But with a bad man, ain't nothing you can do. Whatever he looking to find out in the street ain't about you. It's just some of his own mess that he ain't ready to deal with."

Katie Mae sighed again, as if taking Nettie's words to heart.

"So, are we agreed?" Viola asked.

They all clasped hands to seal the bargain.

"Now how do we plan to get Sheba next to these preachers?" Sylvia said. "Some of them slick as slick oil and liable to slip from a tight spot. And what if our men catch her East St. Louis, love-to-party-self up in church? One of them bound to ask what got Sheba up so early on Sunday morning."

"Hmmm," Nettie said, turning it over in her mind. "I think we'll have to leave it to Sheba to get to the preachers, and we'll each have to find a way to handle our men ourselves."

"Okay, I can see that part. But, Nettie, will Sheba help us?"

"I bet she will. She'll see it as a challenge."

"Wait a minute!" said Katie Mae. "What if Sheba decides she wants to lay up with one of those preachers?"

She paused, and her eyes got big and round. "And, and what if one of those preachers real low-down and try to get some from her, when even *she* don't want to give it to him."

"Katie Mae, why you all of a sudden so worried about Sheba Cochran? I thought you said she was nothing but a party-hearty hussy."

"I did. But I don't want to have a hand in her sinful ways."

"You won't. If Sheba will help us, it'll be for her own good reasons. Look, the girl is tough—she's raised four kids alone. I've seen her box down her old men when she needed her child support payments. And do you think preachers are rougher than those men she meets out in the clubs?"

"Yeah," Viola said, laughing, "if she do want one of those old men, she can have him. And that'll be between her, her sheets, that man, and the Lord—and then we'll know for sure that preacher ain't worth a poot."

"Shoot, I say let the chile have her fun," Sylvia agreed. "It'll be worth it to keep some trifling no-good thang out of our pulpit."

Katie Mae closed her eyes and clasped her hands to her chest. She hoped that the Lord would understand and forgive their wayward souls.

Sylvia looked over at Katie Mae agonizing and praying over Sheba Cochran, when what she needed to pray and agonize over was that no-count, trouble-causing man of hers.

II

Nettie had good reason to be worried. Two weeks later, the search committee met again, only to discover that Cleavon Johnson had gone behind their backs and invited a Rev. Blue Patterson to interview for the pastorship. Blue Patterson had recently taken over what Cleavon claimed was an up-and-coming church in Pine Bluff, Arkansas, and was making quite a name for himself in that community. Bert, Wendell, Melvin Sr., and Mr. Louis Loomis had never even heard of Blue Patterson or his church, which seemed odd, considering his memorable first name.

"Cleavon," Melvin Sr. pointed out, after digesting as much of Cleavon's jibber-jabber as he could stand. "Sylvia's uncle belongs to one of the largest Church of God in Christ churches in Pine Bluff, and he does all the robes for the preachers and choirs in the area at his cleaners. If this Blue Patterson was that much of a top dog, Sylvia's uncle would surely know something about the man."

"I wasn't aware that your wife's kinfolks are so much in the mix that they know everything about everybody there is to know in Pine Bluff," Cleavon said in a nice-nasty voice.

"Maybe we need to put Sylvia's Uncle COGIC on the case to hire a preacher for our church, since he can tell everything about a man just from cleaning his funky clothes."

Melvin Sr. started to rise out of his seat, but checked himself when he felt Wendell's hand on his arm.

"Well, as for me," Mr. Louis Loomis said, "I don't know a soul down in Pine Bluff. But I do know that Blue boy ain't all you saying he is. I have his application right here in my hand, and he has been at his present church for only six months. Before that he was at a smaller church in Little Rock for four months. And now he want to move again? Cleavon, we need to leave Blue Patterson right where he is—somewhere out there in the blue."

"He's coming for an interview whether you or anybody else on this committee likes it or not," Cleavon snapped, slamming his hand on the table, hoping to make it clear that he wasn't playin'. Rev. Patterson has gone through all kinds of trouble to be able to come to St. Louis, and it will make the church look bad if we up and withdraw this invitation 'cause of something *you* don't like in his resume."

Mr. Louis Loomis snorted. Trouble getting to St. Louis? You could practically walk from Pine Bluff, Arkansas to St. Louis, Missouri. Mr. Louis Loomis was sick and tired of Cleavon Johnson and his whole family. It seemed that every black church had its resident big-shot family who wanted to run everything and got on everybody else's nerves. And the Johnsons, who owned a string of mom-and-pop convenience stores throughout North St. Louis called The Only Stop, were definitely Gethsemane's pain-in-the-butt, big-shot family.

"Cleavon," Mr. Louis Loomis countered, "that man ain't what we need for this church, and you doggone well know that. It worries me that you let the funk of your own mess overpower you to the point where you can't think straight enough to do right by your own church."

Cleavon bristled but composed himself enough to say, "There is nothing wrong with you, old man, but mad—mad because you like an old tree that has lost all of its sap. You need to step aside and let a young man do what you ain't got the stamina for."

Mr. Louis Loomis dropped his hand to his belt, moving in on Cleavon as if to say, "Boy, give me a reason to whip your tail."

Instead, he told him, very quietly, "Boy, a tree just reaching its prime at one hundred. At seventy-six, I got a ways to go. A short hard stroke ain't always what it take to get the job done right. But I'm sure you don't know what I'm talking 'bout, since you spend most of your waking hours wasting time with short, no-count strokes."

Cleavon stood up, stuck his chest out, and made a move toward Mr. Louis Loomis. Wendell and Melvin Sr. jumped up to intervene, but held back when they saw that Mr. Louis Loomis was not fazed one bit by Cleavon's posturing. He didn't move a muscle, but just said firmly, "You need to watch how you come at me, son, 'cause you know I don't play that."

At that point Bert, who was fed up with all the bickering, decided to exercise his authority as committee chairman and head of the Deacon Board. To show he meant business, he pushed his chair back from the table so hard that it wore through the threadbare gold carpet and scraped the dull wooden floor beneath it. Then he announced, "This meeting is adjourned," and stormed out of the room, forcing all of the other committee members to follow suit.

Wendell Cates and Melvin Vicks, Sr., were equally tired of all the dissension, but kept quiet until they all reached their cars. Then Melvin Sr. said, "That poot-butt Cleavon think he's so slick. I don't believe that Negro wants Rev. Blue Patterson any more than we do. We don't need all of this headache from Cleavon. It would solve a whole lot of problems if we could kick him off this committee."

"Yeah," Wendell agreed, "Cleavon keep up more mess than a little bit."

"Well, we can't get rid of him," Bert said flatly. "Being in charge of the Finance Board, he is entitled to help choose the pastor. I suppose that technically we could remove him from the Finance Board, but think what a ruckus that would raise. We have enough problems to deal with already in this church without going off and usurping church protocol."

Melvin Sr. shrugged and sighed heavily in frustration, even though he knew Bert was right. Bert was always on the money when it came to church—that's why he was head of the Deacon Board. They were stuck with Cleavon Johnson for the time being.

"I'm wondering," Wendell said, "if Cleavon is forcing this interview because he believes that Blue Patterson will make the preacher he *really* wants, at this church look good. Did you see how excited he got when somebody asked a question about Rev. David O. Clemson?"

"Yeah, I saw that," Bert answered. "At first I thought it was just me."

"Nah. It was me, too," Melvin Sr. chimed in. "Cleavon could hardly contain himself."

"Umm-hmm," Bert said. "He came close to showing his hand when Rev. Clemson's name was put on the table."

"Cleavon is gone do any and everything that he can to get around us and have his way," Wendell said. "Let us not forget to stay on our knees, 'cause we really gone need the Lord's help with this."

"Yep," Bert said with a heavy heart, as they got into their cars. How in the world were they going to find a decent preacher with all this intrigue and mess and with the biggest devil in town, Cleavon O'Rell Johnson, able to cast a crucial vote in the matter?

Two Sundays later Rev. Blue Patterson came to preach at Gethsemane. Twenty minutes before the service started, Bert Green eased his gold Cadillac Eldorado into the church's gravel parking lot and searched for a space, all the while wondering what kind of church they would be having this morning. He hadn't met Rev. Blue Patterson, but in his short phone conversation with the man the night before, Rev. Patterson struck him as pompous and ill-mannered.

So Bert had been relieved when Nettie had nagged him into changing his suit from the brown three-piece knit he had selected to an outfit complementing the cute blue knit minidress his wife had had the nerve to wear this morning. Nettie had insisted that Bert put on his navy blue leisure suit with his new cream and blue polyester shirt and the gold medallion necklace she'd bought him last Father's Day. Now they were running late, and mercifully, he'd barely have time to do his duty as head of the Deacon Board and extend their guest an official welcome.

The rocks crunched and popped under his brand-new whitewall tires as Bert spun the car slowly around in circles, trying to find the perfect parking space—one where nobody could hem him in. He hated having to wait when he was ready to go home from church, especially when there was a good baseball game coming on TV, like today.

Nettie, sitting quietly beside him, felt glad that their daughter, Bertha, didn't ride to church with them this morning. Bertha was twenty-seven, with her own business, house, and car, but she still wanted to ride to church with them. A big baby, that's what she was—a big spoiled baby. And today Nettie needed some private time with Bert, to try to pick his brain about Rev. Blue Patterson without Bertha all up in their business.

"Honey, do you think this man can preach?" she asked softly, knowing how discouraged Bert had been after talking to Rev. Patterson last night. She had wanted to ask about their phone conversation then but knew better than to press her husband, especially when he was already so upset over Cleavon's machinations. She also knew that Bert would take interviewing Rev. Patterson seriously. Her husband was a man of integrity, and if he agreed to do something, no matter how much he might have initially opposed it, he was going to do it right. Wisdom and prudence and twenty-eight years of marriage told her that she was going to have to handle Bert with care.

So Nettie placed her pink-pearl-painted fingertips gently on Bert's right knee and let them inch their way to that spot, *way* up on the inside of his thigh.

Bert grinned, watching Nettie out of the corner of his eye, and relaxed his leg a bit when he felt the perfect application of pressure from her hand. He saw her peeping at him from under the floppy brim of the ivory silk hat she was wearing, with that little look on her face that *always* got under his skin.

"Baby, why you giving me that yum-yum look of yours and asking about that preacher all in the same breath?"

Nettie stroked Bert's leg a few more seconds and then gave him the sweetest smile, while thinking about the trump card up her sleeve—Sheba Cochran. When Nettie had approached her about taking on the mission, Sheba had said, "Yes, I'll be glad to do it, because I've been itching for a way to get Cleavon Johnson back for playing me for a fool."

Then, all of a sudden, Sheba got distant and quiet, as if she was thinking about changing her mind.

"Sheba?" Nettie asked, a bit puzzled by the abrupt shift in her.

"On second thought, y'all on your own," Sheba said.

"But just a moment ago, you were all eager to help us."

"Nettie," Sheba stated matter-of-factly, "you never have and never will be seen by other women as the party-hearty girl. Humph, the women at your church got some nerve. Whole bunch of those biddies don't even speak to me when I come to church, and now they need me to do what most of y'all can't do. And you know that Katie Mae Johnson is the worst when it comes to me."

"But Sheba, Katie Mae is Clea—"

"She didn't speak to me *before* Cleavon, Nettie."

All Nettie could do was sigh. Sheba was right. Some of the women at church acted like they were so much better than Sheba because she liked to go to that hot and jumping disco, the Mothership Club, over in East St. Louis, Illinois. And Katie Mae could be the snootiest of all—not only to Sheba but to any woman who appeared to be the type Cleavon chased in the streets. Nettie was about to tell Sheba to just forget it when she felt a gentle nudge, deep down inside, to give it one more try.

"Sheba, me and Viola and Sylvia have always been your friends. We love you, my mama loves you, our children love you, and our husbands are like brothers to you. I'm asking you for our sake. We need to hire a good pastor, and it is going to take a lot more than Bert's Search Committee to beat Cleavon at his own game."

Nettie watched Sheba's face as her words sank in. Then she pleaded, "So please, Sheba, can you find it in your heart to help us? Forget those women who need a lesson on what it means to be Christian."

After a long moment, Sheba gave in. "Okay, I'll help you, Nettie. But you and Viola and Sylvia better tell them other stuck-up, wouldn't-know-Jesus-if-He-slapped-them-in-the-face heifers not to disrespect me. Alright, Nettie?"

"I will," Nettie promised, praying that the main culprit among the women, Katie Mae Johnson, would heed their advice and leave Sheba alone.

"Nettie," Bert said impatiently. "You gone answer my

question, Nettie Green? Or just sit there looking dumbstruck and make us even later for church?"

Nettie came back to earth with a jolt, but recovered quickly. "Well, Bert honey," she managed to say, "last night makes it mighty hard to stop thinking about you, even though I know I need to have my mind staying on Jesus and praying on the trouble plaguing our church." She rubbed his leg some more, only a little higher, and continued, "Ain't my fault you such a sweet thang, boy, that you distract me right up to the front door of the Lord's house."

At first Bert sat up all cocky-like, with his chest stuck out, grinning from ear to ear. But when he stole a look at Nettie, an alarm went off inside him.

"Miss Lady is *up* to something," he thought as he turned off the motor, stepped from the car, and walked around to Nettie's side to help her out. She had been furious over what happened at the first search committee meeting, and he should have been expecting her to zip something by him. He'd have to be on the lookout for anything that might tell him what Nettie was planning to do.

As soon as they walked into the sanctuary, Nettie tried her best to find Sheba Cochran without Bert's catching on. She let her eyes dart around the church, turning her body as slightly as possible, until she saw Sylvia sitting in her spot with Melvin Sr. Nettie waved at her friend, who quickly glanced over at Melvin Sr. before giving a nod toward the front of the church.

Bert watched Sylvia closely before turning back to his wife. "Nettie, why Sylvia jerking her head around like that?"

"Like what, Bert, honey?"

"Like she trying to give you some sort of secret message."

Nettie hated lying in church—even more than lying to Bert—but there were some things he didn't need to know. "Honey, you know how that crazy Sylvia is. She was trying to get me to see a woman wearing a feather hat that is so ugly, it looks like she killed a chicken on the way to church and stuck it right on her head."

Bert, a tall, husky, cocoa-colored man, with captivating black-brown eyes set in a round and boyish face, looked around the sanctuary, wondering why his cute, sexy, tiny, coffee-with-two-drops-of-cream wife would think he believed she could get all that information from just a nod. Sometimes Nettie thought she was so clever and smooth, but she'd just overplayed her hand.

He said, "Humph. Everybody look okay to me. I don't see one person in here wearing a hat that ugly."

"Well, maybe the woman left the sanctuary before you started looking for her, honey."

"Maybe," Bert answered, culling his eyes at Nettie to let her know she hadn't convinced him of a thing.

Nettie caught the look, read Bert's mind, and proceeded to give him the same bold smile she had given him in the car. Bert got embarrassed, and Nettie grinned on the inside of herself, thinking, "That'll teach Mr. Bert Green about trying to get *me* straight in church."

As Bert ushered her down to their regular seats next to Nettie's sister, Viola Cates, and her husband, Wendell, his eyes scanned the sanctuary to see if their daughter had made it to church. Lately she had been missing too many Sundays for his comfort, and he wondered what was going on with her. He checked the balcony where Bertha always sat with her cousin Phoebe and the other young adults. They had occupied that same spot since they were old enough to sit in church by themselves and had continued the tradition now that they were all grown, and some of them married with children of their own.

Phoebe was there in her seat next to Melvin Vicks, Jr., Melvin Jr.'s sister, Rosie, and their friend Jackson Williams. Rosie's husband, Latham Johnson, sat a bit off to the side, by himself. Bert thought that Latham was just like his uncle Cleavon—selfish, stuck on himself, and convinced that his wife was put on this earth to serve him. Latham didn't run around on Rosie like Cleavon did Katie Mae, but Bert and Wendell were certain that virtue wasn't the reason. Latham Johnson was a conceited tight-butt who probably thought he was too good to need a strong rap to pull a woman his way.

The seat next to Phoebe—Bertha's spot—was empty. Bertha always sat on one side of Phoebe and Melvin Jr. on the other. It had to be that way, because Bertha and Melvin Jr. had been fussing with each other since they were little. Many a Sunday morning, either Bert or Melvin Sr. had to go up in the balcony and separate those two at some point during the service. Poor Melvin Jr. would always look him in the eye and say, "Mr. Bert, she started it." And when Bert looked at Bertha, all pretty in her pink organza dress, hair ribbons, fancy lace socks, and black patent leather shoes, he knew that it was true. Bertha would tell all on herself, saying something stupid like, "Daddy, I just can't stand him." Then, when she thought Bert wasn't watching her, Bertha would stick out her tongue at Melvin Jr., who would make a fist and say, "We can finish this after church." To this day, Bertha complained that Melvin Jr. got on her "last nerve." As Bert looked at the empty space next to Phoebe, he made a mental note to ask Nettie if she knew what was up with that girl.

All throughout the service, Nettie kept trying to find Sheba Cochran without drawing Bert's attention to herself. She knew Sheba was in the sanctuary, but couldn't locate the girl for the life of her. She was looking for Sheba so hard that when the sermon began, she could barely concentrate on what Rev. Blue Patterson was saying. She, Viola, Sylvia, and even Katie Mae had promised to pay close attention to the content of each applicant's text. They agreed that they had to avoid getting carried away with the emotions raised by a sermon—by the man's voice, how he moved when he preached, how well his robe fit him—to the point that they forgot to think about whether or not the sermon was anything worth hearing.

When Nettie finally got her mind off finding Sheba long enough to listen to Rev. Blue Patterson's preaching, she noticed that he was doing a lot of hollering and screaming. And when Nettie fine-tuned her ears to the actual words, she heard Rev. Patterson say, "Ummm, chutch. When God woke me up this morning and started me on my way, He said, 'Blue, you tell these people that they are charged to obey you or else they's got to deal with *Me*.' "

Nettie couldn't believe that Blue Patterson would stand there and let that garbage spew out of his mouth and all over the congregation. He was, as Nettie's mother, MamaLouise, later described him, "determined to show his rusty behind to the whole church." But to Nettie's surprise, certain members of the congregation actually seemed to be caught up in the sermon, making her wonder what she must have missed. Cleavon Johnson, who seemed especially pleased, was wearing a self-satisfied smirk.

Blue Patterson dabbed at his bald spot with a handkerchief. It glistened with beads of sweat, highlighting its presence in the middle of the half-moon natural that wrapped around the bottom of his head. Then he pulled the microphone off the podium, pacing back and forth for dramatic effect, and in a voice he must have believed mimicked the voice of God, bellowed, "Geth-se-ma-ne. Geth-se-ma-ne. Blue is my ser-vant. Obey my ser-vant or else."

Up in the balcony, Phoebe, Melvin Jr., Rosie, and Jackson Williams were torn up with laughter. Nobody tried to shush them. Viola leaned toward Nettie and whispered, "Girl, the people on the front row show do need to move, so they don't get hit when that big bolt of lightning comes out of nowhere to strike him dead."

Nettie turned to Bert to ask what he thought about the sermon. But Bert was sound asleep, with his head back and his mouth open, snoring faintly. When the choir stood up and prepared to march out for the benediction, Nettie nudged him, whispering, "Thank you, Lord" when she had trouble waking him. She figured that if Bert was sleeping this hard, he would oppose doing anything for Rev. Blue Patterson, other than giving him a plate of food and enough gas money to drive back home.

She poked at him again, and Bert woke up in the middle of a snore, saying, "Wha . . . wha . . . inning is it?"

As soon as the benediction was given, Bert and Nettie got in the receiving line at the front of the church, where Rev. Patterson stood greeting the members. And it was there, after searching for her all morning, that Nettie finally found Sheba Cochran. She was the first one in line, glittering in a tight black rhinestone-studded dress with a scoop neck that was more suitable for the Mothership Club than church.

Sheba Cochran stood five-foot-five and had a deep cinnamon brown complexion. She wasn't beautiful like Katie Mae Johnson, but she was just as cute as she could be. Sylvia always said that Sheba's best asset was that big round, onion-shaped behind sitting up high on her "little thin-shaped self." And Sheba was funny, with a good heart and a whole lot of smarts. She was a devoted mother who took good care of her four children all by herself, thanks to her full-time job at the post office and a side gig doing taxes. She was a good neighbor and a loving friend.

With some maneuvering, Nettie landed a spot three people away from Sheba, who was chatting comfortably with Rev. Blue Patterson. Behind her, the people in line were growing restive, frowning and whispering, "That hussy in the hot-mama dress know she need to move on. And her self know she not saved." A little farther back, Cleavon Johnson stood scowling at the sight of Sheba in church, which made Nettie smile. "If you knew why Sheba is here, you'd be cussing," she thought.

Rev. Blue Patterson didn't seem inclined to have Sheba move on. For all his hollering at the congregation about sin and sinning, he was grinning and ogling Sheba, making Nettie wonder if Blue Patterson himself had even heard a word he said. As if to reward Rev. Patterson for indulging her in conversation, Sheba gave him a dazzling smile, put her black, satin-gloved hand daintily in his, and sighed deeply, as if the man and his sermon had really put something on her. When Nettie heard that old rascal tell Sheba the Lord had led him to instruct her to meet him in *his* office after the church dinner for prayer and private counseling, she said, "Thank you, Jesus," right out loud, before she could catch herself.

Bert frowned and said, "Why you acting like you getting the Holy Ghost, standing here watching that jackleg preacher act like the clown he is over Sheba, and service *been* over with?"

Nettie didn't blink an eye. She said, "Sometimes, when I think about how good the Lord has been to me, I just have to thank Him. Don't matter if I'm sitting in service or standing in line waiting to shake somebody's hand. I just have to forget where I am and praise Him."

Bert didn't say a word to Nettie. He simply narrowed his eyes at her again before grunting, "Humph," just to let her know she wasn't fooling *no-body.*

All during the dinner, Bert kept close watch on his wife and her friends, thinking that whatever was up, Sheba Cochran was right in the middle of it. For why else would Sheba be at church today? The girl only came to church on Christmas and Easter Sunday, dragging her four kids behind her, looking all uncomfortable in stiff new dress clothes and shoes she had bought solely for those holidays. But today wasn't Christmas or Easter. It was just a regular Sunday in September—more than three months in advance of one of Sheba's church days.

When the desserts were being set out on the serving tables, Nettie, Viola, Sylvia, and Katie Mae all got up and went to the bathroom together. Sheba, who was sitting at the guest pastor's table, saw them leave and followed, pausing for a second when she passed by Cleavon, just to slice right through him with her eyes. By the time Bert returned from the dessert table, carrying two big pieces of lemon coconut cake for himself and Nettie, the women had disappeared behind the rest room door.

The door had barely closed when Nettie blurted, "Tell us! What did you find out?"

"Yeah, Sheba," Katie Mae said in a nasty voice. "What can *you* tell us that is helpful for *our* church?"

Sheba resisted the urge to stab her eyes into Katie Mae as she had done her husband. She knew Katie Mae's little attitude wasn't about anything but Cleavon, with his jive, no-good, lying self. Sheba couldn't stand Cleavon Johnson. And if Katie Mae wasn't always snubbing her, she would have set the record straight on what really happened between herself and Cleavon—not that much of anything.

"So, you gone meet the Reverend up in the office?" Nettie asked, hoping that Katie Mae wouldn't keep talking and make Sheba so mad that she changed her mind about helping them.

"Nettie," Sheba said, looking at her like she was crazy, "did you see Blue Patterson's hair?"

Nettie nodded, as Sylvia broke out laughing, saying, "How could she not see *that*?"

"I know," Viola added. "His hair convinced me that he don't really listen to the Lord all that much. 'Cause I know the Lord has said *something* about his hair on many occasions."

"Blue, Blue," Sylvia said, imitating Rev. Patterson. "Your hair, son. It's *Me*. Your hair, your hair."

"Sylvia, you know you need to quit," Nettie said, laughing.

"No, this whole church need to quit," Sheba said very seriously. "Y'all need to quit fooling around with that trifling Negro, who here lying and acting like he's a big-shot preacher, when he know he ain't nowhere close to that. He did all that hollering and screaming, talking junk about how he been called to lead this church. And yet he didn't even think enough of this church to bother with how he looked. The hair said it all. Why, that Negro didn't even have the decency to put some grease on his hands."

Viola nodded. "Come to think of it, he did have some rough and ashy hands. Make you wonder about how bad his feet must look."

Katie Mae grimaced. "Ugh, don't make us think about his feet. We just got through eating."

"And the clothes," Sheba said. "The fool didn't even have on a decent suit or real leather shoes. Now, if his church was all that he saying it is, would it have a pastor running around looking like Bozo the Clown?"

Everybody shook their heads. Sheba was on target. No self-respecting congregation would want a pastor representing them who looked like that.

"So," Sheba continued, "I ain't wasting my time with that Negro. Because it don't take a whiff of church-fan-air to figure out that he ain't worth jack."

Sheba rolled her eyes as she asked Nettie, "Girl, what made Bert an' them bring Blue Patterson here for anyway? Gethsemane may not be a big fancy church, but it got enough going for it that y'all can do better than him."

"Well," Katie Mae answered, "Cleavon told me Rev. Patterson had good references."

Sheba just closed her eyes and sighed. Cleavon needed to be reined in before he ran this church so far into the ground, they would be looking right into the devil's living room. She said, "I don't care if he got a reference from the Rev. Jesse Jackson. Blue Patterson is a chump and a two-bit hustler playing church—and playing a very dangerous game with the Lord. Shoot, y'all let him up in here as y'all's preacher, I know *I* ain't coming here to worship no more for Christmas and Easter."

Sheba turned down her mouth in disgust. "Nettie, tell Bert to send him packing. And if I were y'all, I wouldn't even give him gas money."

III

Three weeks later, the second candidate came to spend his trial week at Gethsemane. The Rev. David O. Clemson, III, a handsome, light brown, expensively dressed man with a head full of dark brown, well-groomed, and naturally straight hair, was smooth as silk and charismatic. He had most of the members of the Deacon and Finance Boards practically eating out of his hand—with the notable exceptions of Bert, Wendell, Melvin Sr., and Mr. Louis Loomis. Mr. Louis Loomis took one look at Rev. Clemson's suit and declared loudly, "What y'all got him here for? We cain't afford this here boy. His suit cost most a month's salary."

Not wanting to scare Rev. Clemson off, Cleavon laughed nervously and said, "Now, what would Louis Loomis know about a good suit? He only shops at Sears," as if Mr. Louis Loomis wasn't even there.

At the Sunday service, Rev. Clemson won over the congregation as well, with his compelling sermon, "God Always Has a Ram in the Bush." It was lively, funny, provocative, and right on target with the concerns of the community. He impressed the women, especially, with the rhythmic cadence of his delivery and his frequent pauses to smile, eyes twinkling like diamonds, at certain sisters in the pews. A few found him so electrifying that they kept jumping up, hollering out, "Preach, preach" when Rev Clemson hit the "hot spots" in his sermon.

But as soon as Sheba Cochran laid eyes on Rev. Clemson, she detected a coarseness beneath his smooth ways and exquisitely tailored suits. Her suspicions were heightened when she noticed that during the service, Mrs. Clemson spent most of her time scrutinizing the women who were most intently focused on her husband while he preached. And the woman never so much as cracked a smile throughout her husband's entire fifty-minute sermon.

Sheba wasn't the only one worried about Rev. Clemson. Mr. Louis Loomis got very concerned when Cleavon Johnson started singing his praises after the Sunday morning service. When he overheard Cleavon's dumb cousin, Rufus, bragging that they had found the pastor for the job, he got scared and got to praying. Mr. Louis Loomis spent half of Tuesday praying on that man, petitioning the Lord with such intensity, he wore himself out and fell into a deep sleep.

When he woke up, the Lord led him straight to the telephone to call Sheba Cochran. As soon as she answered the phone, he said, "Why do you keep coming to church three months before you s'posed to, and without your children? You ain't got no bad news on your health or your job lately, has you, babygirl?"

"No, sir," Sheba answered politely, and then laughed softly into the telephone.

Mr. Louis Loomis listened to her laugh. He had seen Sheba in church over the years. But he didn't ever remember seeing her smile or hearing her laugh. He liked that old sassy laugh. It was the laugh of a woman who knew how to take care of a man right. Shame the girl was always alone whenever he saw her. She would make some man a good wife, if the man had sense enough to see her for the jewel she was.

"Well, Miss Sheba, you haven't answered my question. Used up two words to put my mind at rest about your health and your job. But I want to know why you been all up in Gethsemane acting like you a full-fledged member."

Sheba didn't know what to say. Mr. Louis Loomis was, after all, a member of the very committee the women were fighting against, and the last thing Sheba wanted to do was cause problems for her friends. She sighed heavily into the telephone.

"Babygirl?" Mr. Louis Loomis asked.

Sheba weighed her options. She could put Mr. Louis Loomis off with some vague excuse, but that might just make him nosier. If he started sniffing around, he might discover what the women were plotting, and even which women were the ringleaders. Then, if he tipped off their husbands on the search committee, the entire plan could backfire. Maybe the safest course would be to make him her ally, especially since her heart was telling her she could trust him. She took a deep breath, silently praying that whatever was leading her to talk was pushing her to say the right thing.

"Mr. Louis Loomis, some women in the church are not happy that they have been shut out of helping to hire a new pastor. A few think these men need to be checked out a bit more than your committee is doing right now. From what I've seen so far, it don't seem to me like you all are doing your math on the men you've interviewed. It adds up pretty quickly if you look at them right."

"I see," he said, wondering when this revolt began. He figured that it had to be sometime after the search committee practically ran Nettie Green out of the conference room, right after Pastor Forbes died.

"And to be honest, something tells me Rev. Clemson ain't right. I think I know how to flush him out, but I can't do it by myself. I need some help."

"Can't some of those churchwomen help you?" Mr. Louis Loomis asked, wanting badly to question Sheba on what he already knew in his gut—just who these busy women were.

"Not for this, Mr. Louis Loomis," Sheba answered him. "I need a man's help for what I've been studying on doing."

"Well, you show right. I know that Rev. Clemson got some of those jokers on the committee so bamboozled they want to hire him. So, I'd sure love to see you pull that wolf out of his sheep's clothing. Whatever you need from me, babygirl, you got it," Mr. Louis Loomis promised, a bit excited about this adventure Sheba was cooking up.

Rev. Clemson preached on a Sunday, and by Thursday Sheba had called Nettie to ask her to schedule a meeting so that she could give the women her report. Nettie suggested that this time they meet away from their men, because Bert kept asking her why Sheba had been at church two times, when it was barely October. They met for lunch at the White Castle on the corner of Kingshighway Boulevard and Martin Luther King, Jr. Avenue, piling up in Sylvia's Buick station wagon, after ordering and picking up their food, to get the lowdown on the man.

Sheba got comfortable in the front seat of the car, took a long sip of her Coke, and then said, "Viola, let me get a couple of your cheese fries before I get to talking. I knew I should have ordered me some of those things."

Viola passed the box of cheese fries over to Sheba. "Girl, take as many as you want. Sylvia got a whole extra box in her bag."

Sheba picked out some fries with the most cheese on them. "White Castle show do make the best fries."

Katie Mae got herself a couple of fries and said, "They make good orange soda, too."

Nettie said, "Girl, hurry up with those fries. I been on pins and needles ever since you called me, dying to find out what's up with Rev. Clemson."

"Yeah," Sylvia agreed. "I been wondering myself if he all he saying he is. Melvin Sr. liked his sermon a lot, but I'm kind of up in the air about him myself."

"Well, I thought his sermon was so much more sophisticated than what we've been hearing," Katie Mae said. "But I didn't like Mrs. Clemson all that much. She wasn't friendly and barely said two words when I tried to talk to her after service."

"I didn't care for him at all," Viola said. "And neither did Wendell. He said that Clemson was too much of a pretty boy for him. Nettie, what about Bert? Did he like Rev. Clemson?"

"He thought he looked good on paper, but he ain't all that excited about hiring him as a pastor."

"Cleavon can't wait to hire him," Katie Mae said brightly.

"Humph," Sheba said. "Ladies, that Rev. Clemson even farther from what he pretending to be than you can imagine."

She bit into her hamburger, drank some Coke, and then closed her eyes and sucked on her teeth. They all sat up, because they didn't want to miss a word of what she had to say.

"That man is a nasty, no-good, sneaky thang if I've met one, and I have certainly met my fair share of no-good men. But I have to tell you that the men I run into over at the Mothership Club ain't got nothin' on Rev. David O. Clemson, III At least they honest about being hound dogs, but Clemson is as slick and oily as the grease on my head."

"Well," Viola said, looking kind of confused, "we figured you got some good dirt on him, but when did you even get with the man? The only time I saw you near him was after prayer meeting on Tuesday, and all you did was shake his hand—though he did seem to hang on to it a little longer than normal."

"Viola, the reason he held my hand that long was because *his self* was slipping me a note to meet him at a friend's house over on Kossuth Avenue."

"He from Chicago," Katie Mae pointed out. "How he find a house to go to over on Kossuth Avenue? And what did he do with his wife? Wouldn't she think that something funny was going on if he left her to go off somewhere like that?"

Nettie looked hard at Katie Mae and said, "Mrs. Clemson was wherever Rev. Clemson told her she could be," all the while thinking, "Just like you are wherever Cleavon tells you to be when the church goes on a big trip and he ups and goes off to who-knows-where."

Katie Mae backed down, not wanting anyone to bring up Cleavon, and said, "So, how did he do all of this? Explain it to me, Sheba Cochran, since you the expert on no-good men."

Sheba chose to ignore the remark. She felt sorry for Katie Mae, having to deal with Cleavon's ways and all. But Sheba was not going to be her whipping post, either. She had now let Katie Mae get away with cuts on two occasions. But the very next time she struck, Sheba was getting the woman straight. She gave Katie Mae an I've-just-about-had-enough-of-you look and said, "Didn't I just tell you the

Negro was slick? And he slick enough to get rid of his wife long enough to make a play on me."

"You didn't 'play' with that man, did you, Sheba?" Sylvia demanded.

"Girl, please, I got standards. Okay? And don't you or anybody else in this car go off on me like that again," Sheba snapped, staring right at Katie Mae. "Don't forget that I am helping you'all out. Y'all asked me to do all of this stuff, not the other way around."

The car was silent. Because all four of them knew good and well that Sheba had been minding her own business until they asked her to get mixed up in their mess.

"Let me put it to you all this way," Sheba said, breaking the silence. "When I got to that house on Kossuth Avenue, Rev. Clemson had the drapes all closed up, blue bulbs in all the lamps, and he was playing some Muddy Waters 'I'm a Mahn' on the hi-fi. He was also wearing a fancy robe, and I know he didn't have on a stitch of clothes underneath. It made me nervous that I might accidentally see something I did not want to see."

"Oooh," Viola said with her mouth turned down. "That is downright raunchy—wearing your robe in front of somebody you don't even know, and naked underneath."

"Humph," Sheba said with her lips turned down, rolling her neck around and waving her hand in the air. "That ain't even the half of it."

David Clemson stared Sheba down from head to toe when she walked into the house. He licked his lips and pointed to the couch.

"Don't you want to sit down?"

"Naw, Rev. Clemson. I'm more comfortable standing."

"Oh, you like it on your feet, huh, girl?" he said with a soft laugh that didn't have a hint of warmth in it.

Unsettled by his steady gaze, Sheba tried to calm her nerves. He reminded Sheba of a wolf. Sheba was not afraid of many things, and on most occasions she could handle herself with a man trying to hit on her. But this man was out of her league. She had sensed a cruelty in him before, and now that she was alone with him behind closed doors, her instincts warned that he might be violent.

"Can I get you something to drink?" he asked, stroking his chin. "Hmmm, let me see. How about some Mad Dog 20/20 or some Rosie O'Grady?"

"You got some nerve, Negro," Sheba thought, "offering me wino wine like I was standing on a street corner." But she managed to say, "Please don't put yourself to any trouble, Rev. Clemson, because I don't drink."

"Oh really?" he answered. "That's awfully surprising, girl. You look like you could put the Rosie in the O'Grady."

"Well, contrary to how it looks, I can't," Sheba snapped, and then caught herself when his face hardened. "Reverend, I am a churchgirl. I don't think it's right for me to be drinking wine, and especially not in front of a preacher."

"Baby," he said, toying around with the belt on his robe, "drinking wine is all throughout the Bible. And some of those Bible-days folks could really chug it down."

"Jive-time punk," Sheba thought, "trying to use the Bible to get a woman drunk." She wished she knew the Scriptures better, so that she could quote an actual passage to rebuke this man, but ventured, "Rev. Clemson, weren't most of the drinking people in the Bible in the Old Testament under the Old Covenant?"

Rev. Clemson busted out laughing. "Baby, what Bible do you read? Jesus turned water into wine at that big party he was at in the *New* Testament, not the old one."

Sheba was confused. She remembered Jesus changing water into wine at a wedding, not at a party. But she tried again.

"Rev. Clemson, isn't there something in the New Testament saying church leaders shouldn't be heavy drinkers and neither should the people in their families? So you shouldn't even have anything like Mad Dog 20/20 or Rosie O'Grady, because that's heavy-drinker, drunk-people liquor."

David Clemson frowned. The tramp had some nerve, up in here arguing the Bible's teaching with a preacher.

"You are becoming very annoying with all of this so-called Bible talk," he snapped, and walked over to a wooden tripod with a black silk cloth thrown over it. "Sheba, whether you drink or not, you are so fine until I could get a buzz just standing here looking at you. And if you would indulge me a bit, I'd like to capture your fine self on film." Then he removed the cloth slowly, like he was undressing someone, to reveal a movie camera.

Sheba's mouth dropped wide open. She knew this fool was nasty, but she had no idea that she was dealing with a freaky-deaky man. "Why do you need that thing?" she asked carefully.

"Like I said, 'cause you such a sexy little thing," he said, looking through the camera and fussing with the lens, as

Sheba slipped off the couch and tried to edge toward the door.

"Going somewhere, Miss Lady?" Rev. Clemson asked, jumping out from behind the camera. He yanked at Sheba's arm and started to drag her roughly back to the couch.

"Let go of me, you nasty, freaky, two-timing mangy dog."

"What did you say to me, tramp?" he growled, and tried to push her back on the couch.

"I said . . . ," Sheba began, but couldn't hear her own words for the ringing in her ears from that slap he now gave her upside the head.

"One more word from you, and I am going beat you like I'm Massa and you the slave. Now get undressed and quit playin'. You know what you wanted when you came up in here."

"Help me, Lord," Sheba cried out.

Clemson slapped the air as Sheba dodged his hand while grabbing the lamp on the end table. Snatching it up, she swung it at his head.

Clemson ducked and lost his balance, but then quickly recovered his feet when he heard a loud banging on the door. "Open up," a menacing voice hollered. "If my wife in there, she better come on out, or I'm gone tear this house down to the ground."

"You're married?" Clemson asked Sheba, fear creeping into his voice.

"Open the dag-blasted door!"

Sheba moved to open it. "Hold it," Clemson told her. "You can't open the door on me dressed like this, with your husband out there."

"Uhh, Rev. Clemson, I have to open the door," Sheba said, "because my man kind of crazy."

The banging and yelling stopped momentarily. Rev. Clemson sighed in relief, but then the color drained from his face when the he heard a click, like the sound of a gun being cocked. The voice threatened, "I'm gonna shoot a bullet right through this door."

"JESUS! He has a gun!" Rev. Clemson exclaimed, yanking Sheba up in front of him like a shield.

"Don't you call on Jesus!" the voice bellowed. "Too late to call on Him when you already messin' with another man's wife!"

"Help me, Jesus," Clemson cried out.

The voice on the other side of the door said, "Jesus, if You in there, You better move, 'cause I don't want to have to answer for shooting through You when I get to heaven."

Rev. Clemson shoved Sheba to the floor and ran for the back of the house, yelling, "Get out! Get out! Get out!" She picked herself up and, shaking, managed to unlock the dead bolt, then tumbled out the door right into Mr. Louis Loomis's arms.

"Babygirl, you alright?" he asked. Sheba was trembling uncontrollably. "That boy didn't hurt you, did he?"

"Mr. Louis Loomis," Sheba said with tears running down her face, "he was half-naked and had a movie camera. And he wanted me to drink cheap liquor because he thought I was cheap. He hit me and would've tried to force me if you hadn't been there."

"Why, that low-down scoundrel," said Mr. Louis Loomis.

"That is a sin and a shame, especially for a man calling himself a preacher."

"Y'all got some jive-time preachers up in that church," Sheba said, still crying. Mr. Louis Loomis patted her gently on the shoulder, gave her a handkerchief, and took her hand in his. He said softly, "Babygirl, you having such a hard time coming back to church because of devils like that thang in that house, aren't you?"

Sheba sniffled and nodded.

"I'm gonna give you some advice," Mr. Louis Loomis said, as he unlocked the car and held the door open for her. "Don't let the devil run you away from God."

"Huh?"

"Don't let the devil *run you away* from God."

Sheba stopped talking. The car was so quiet that you could hear every breath. Finally, Viola said, "We know all we need to know. I say we go to our men and tell them what time it is. There ain't no way on God's good earth that those men gone push that man off on me."

"That's right," said Nettie, and the other women agreed. They were so mad, they wanted to hurt somebody. Sylvia started up the car.

"What you doing?" Nettie asked.

"Going over on Melvin Sr.'s job and getting his tail straight before he even has a *chance* to think about going wrong and voting to hire that devil," Sylvia answered. She started backing the car out of the parking space so fast that she almost hit the old drunk man who was sitting on a crate in the lot, collecting half-eaten burgers and fries, and a quarter here and there, to get "som'in' to drank."

"Wait!" Katie Mae said. "Do you think we need to fight with our men right now? Maybe Rev. Clemson won't even want the job after all that trouble with Sheba."

"No," Nettie said firmly. "We are not waiting on anything. We are going straight to our men about this. They need to know exactly what they have done by inviting that devil into our church home."

"But Cleavon . . . ," Katie Mae started to protest. The last thing she wanted to deal with was Cleavon after he found out that Rev. Clemson had been exposed by Sheba Cochran, of all people. The tension in her house would be so awful, she would be afraid to breathe, for fear that he'd hit the roof.

"But Cleavon, nothing," Sylvia said. She put the car in reverse and started backing out again.

This time the drunk man grabbed his crate and ran to the other side of the lot. When he knew he was in a safe spot, he looked at them, pointed a finger to his head, and twirled it around to signify, "Y'all is crazy."

IV

Cleavon banged on the conference table, furious that the committee didn't even want to discuss hiring Rev. David Clemson.

"Man, if you bang on that table just one more time," Melvin Sr. said, "you will leave this meeting missing a hand."

He was through with the subject of David Clemson. Sylvia

had come down to their catering business and given a performance that could have won her an Academy Award. He was just thankful no customers were around when she jumped up in his face and said, "Melvin Earl Vicks, Sr., if you hire David O. Clemson, III, you got to get out of my house."

Cleavon pounded the table again to let Melvin Sr. know that he wouldn't be pushed around. Melvin Sr. got up out of his chair, walked around the conference table, and snatched Cleavon up by his suit collar.

"I told you to stop. And you ain't hiring that trash to run my church."

Cleavon raised his hand to take a swing at Melvin Sr., but Bert grabbed his arm and stopped him cold. "Why can't you ever quit while you're ahead?" he said. "We not hiring David Clemson, Cleavon, and that is that."

"Y'all a bunch of punks," Cleavon spat out, and his cousin Rufus started to rise.

"Sit your butt down, Rufus," Bert said. "Melvin Sr. will mop up this floor with the both of you. And especially you, Rufus."

Rufus Johnson sat down and scowled. Bert Green, Melvin Vicks, Sr., and Wendell Cates got on his last nerve. Sometimes he wished he had not let Cleavon pay off some of his bills, because he hated being on this committee.

"Oh, so you and your boys gone let a perfectly good preacher slip right through your fingers on account of that trollop Sheba Cochran?" Cleavon pressed. "I talked to Clemson about her, and he told me Sheba begged him to meet her at that house and practically waylaid him on the porch she was so eager to get next to him. Said she'd never experienced a preacher before, and—"

Mr. Louis Loomis had remained above the fray, chewing on a fat bologna sandwich with lettuce, tomatoes, cheddar cheese, mustard, pickle, and red onions on it. Now he set it down and took a sip of iced tea.

"Boy," he said, wiping his mouth and hands, "how you have formed your mouth to say that mess is beyond my comprehension. Remember, I was there. And if the Lord had not put a temperance on my spirit, I would have gone in that house and pistol-whipped that Negro, *after* I gave him a good pimp-slapping."

Cleavon opened his mouth to argue, but couldn't—Mr Louis Loomis was a pretty irrefutable witness. All he could do was sneer, "Pistol-whipping? Pimp-slapping? I would have sold my mama's mink stole to have seen that, old man."

"I hope Vernine can survive without that doggone stole, 'cause you just might get to see that, son," Mr. Louis Loomis said matter-of-factly.

"That's enough," said Bert. "I motion that this committee vote NOT to hire Rev. David O. Clemson, III, as our pastor. Does anyone second?"

"I second the motion," said Melvin Sr., his ears still smarting from Sylvia's blessing-out.

"It has been moved and properly seconded that we will not hire Rev. Clemson," Bert said. "All in favor say aye."

Everyone on the committee but Cleavon and his cousin Rufus raised their hands.

"Nays?"

Cleavon and Rufus raised their hands defiantly.

"The ayes have it," Bert said. "We are not hiring David Clemson."

"But who are we going to hire?" Wendell asked.

"I don't know about hiring," Mr. Louis Loomis said, "but I do know that we need to interview this man."

He pushed a resume across the table to Wendell, who read it over quickly, nodded, and passed it back to Mr. Louis Loomis.

"Who is it?" Bert asked.

"Rev. George Wilson from Memphis, Tennessee," Mr. Louis Loomis answered. "Seems like his first letter of application got lost, so he sent us another one."

"Good thing he wrote again," Bert said, trying not to look accusingly at Cleavon. He was so glad that he had stopped Cleavon from going through the church's mail and assigned the job to Mr. Louis Loomis. He read over the resume and letter, then started grinning.

"Looks like we have a winner here. Rev. Wilson has been a pastor for eleven years. He has held mortgage-burning ceremonies for two of the churches he pastored, and he has a glowing letter of recommendation from Rev. Theophilus Simmons."

"When he coming?" Melvin Sr. asked. "Rev. Simmons is *the man* among preachers in St. Louis. And if he's recommended Rev. Wilson, the only thing I want to know is, when he coming."

"Let me see that," Cleavon said, sucking on his teeth. Bert handed him the resume and recommendation, which Cleavon studied, frowning. He didn't like Rev. Simmons because Rev. Forbes never liked Rev. Simmons. Theophilus Simmons always blocked Forbes's power plays when the black ministers in St. Louis decided to sponsor a political candidate or participate in a citywide project.

Cleavon turned down his lips and sucked on his teeth some more. "I'm not impressed. So, he paid off two little country churches down in Tennessee. Anybody can do that."

"Both churches were the same size as our church. And anybody *can't* do that—or, let's say, none of our other pastoral candidates could do it," Bert replied.

"Well, that's still not enough to warrant an interview. He's a small-town country boy. We need a man who's sophisticated enough to be a big-city pastor, like my other candidate, Rev. Earl Hamilton."

"Rev. Wilson already has an interview date set," Mr. Louis Loomis said evenly. "Mr. Chair," he addressed Bert formally, "the Lord led me to invite Rev. Wilson for the interview. I apologize for not following protocol and asking you to issue the invite. But there are times when I, as a child of the King, am compelled to do as He wills."

"Well, Mr. Louis Loomis," Bert said, trying not to laugh, "the Lord just laid it on my heart to honor your actions."

"Since you didn't follow protocol, we need to *un*invite this country bumpkin," Cleavon said.

"Can't do that, Cleavon," Mr. Louis Loomis said. "The man has already made arrangements to come all the way to St. Louis, and we can't very well take back the invite now. It would make the church look bad."

Bert, Wendell, and Melvin Sr. started laughing. Memphis, like Pine Bluff, Arkansas, was a hop, skip, and a jump from St. Louis.

"Yeah, Cleavon," Melvin Sr. said. "If we couldn't run the

risk of insulting Bozo the Clown—I mean, Rev. Patterson—then we certainly can't risk insulting a preacher with a recommendation from Rev. Theophilus Simmons."

"So, when he coming?" Wendell said again.

Rev. George Wilson eased his silver and white Cutlass Supreme into the parking space marked "Pastor," then got out and leaned back against the car to survey the church. Gethsemane was nearly a hundred years old, and it looked venerable, with its sturdy old red brick, well-maintained stained-glass windows, and heavy walnut wood doors. Its solidity hinted at a formidable history and a favorable future, despite its turbulent present.

Bert Green, as head of the Deacon Board, greeted him at the door with a firm handshake and a warm smile. He took him upstairs to meet the search committee members, most of whom were immediately impressed with Rev. Wilson. They found him to be personable and down-to-earth, with a whole lot of horse sense. He also had a good sense of humor and was a well-read biblical scholar. When he was introduced to the congregation, the ladies were struck by what a fine-looking man he was. He was forty-three and nicely built, and had light, tobacco brown skin and deep golden brown eyes that sparkled when he smiled.

The search committee had agreed that each candidate should be allowed to conduct the Sunday service according to his personal taste, so that the congregation could decide whether or not they liked his style. One way that Rev. Wilson distinguished himself from the other candidates was by the African stole he wore, which he told everyone was made of Kente cloth from Ghana. And then he got the church fired up when, at the end of the first of the senior choir's A and B selections, he came out of the pulpit, kissed the hand of the lead soloist, Sister Hershey Jones, and said, "Sister, your voice is a blend of Aretha Franklin and Sister Willie Mae Ford Smith, with some extra spice the Lord bestowed solely upon you. I want you to pick another song and let the anointing of the Holy Ghost bless this congregation through your elegant voice. Praise God!"

Hershey Jones sang Andre Crouch's "Through It All," and service got so charged up that Viola whispered to Nettie, "Good thing Hershey is saved and don't touch alcohol. 'Cause she so hot, if she drank, she'd light right up."

Nettie laughed and thought that Rev. Wilson looked awfully natural sitting in the pastor's chair.

After the service, everybody was talking about his sermon, "Black Folks and the Twenty-third Psalm." When they were downstairs at the dinner, Katie Mae's grandmother walked up to Cleavon and said, "Didn't you just love the way the Reverend broke it down on Psalm Twenty-three? I just wanted to throw my purse up at that young man and shout out, 'PREACH, PREACH' when he said, 'Walking through the valley of the shadow of death sometimes means that you walking in the midst of folks who are intent on courting evil, and at your expense. But you don't have to fear that 'cause God is always right with you when you walking that valley."

The last thing Cleavon wanted to hear was an excerpt from George Wilson's sermon. He gave Katie Mae's grandmother a tight smile and tried to ease away before she could say any more.

Rev. Wilson, who had been standing nearby, overheard Katie Mae's grandmother and walked up to them. He put an arm around her shoulder and said, "Now, you are my kind of member—quoting from my sermon. Not *talking* about it—you up in here *quoting* it. Sister, I'm scared of you."

"I don't mind scarin' a man, long as I don't scare him off," the eighty-year-old replied sassily.

George leaned down and kissed her, which made her grin and say, "Oh, Reverend, you know you need to quit."

"Naw, Sister, you know *you* need to quit. 'Cause you something else, I can see that right now," he said, reaching out his hand to Cleavon for a palm slap.

Cleavon left George's hand hanging in midair, unslapped. He turned away and started talking to a woman in a dress that was way too tight and short for church, *or* the club, for that matter.

When George looked hurt and confused, Katie Mae's grandmother said, "Look out for that there Cleavon. That boy ain't right. And he'll do a whole lot of dirt at your expense."

With the words of his own sermon ringing in his ears, George offered a silent prayer. He knew that Cleavon was the kind of enemy who cast such a deathly shadow that he would need the Lord by his side whenever he came upon this man.

V

Ever since Rev. Forbes's death, Sunday mornings at Gethsemane had been missing something. Not that Forbes was an ideal pastor—far from it—but he could preach a good sermon, and the members were used to his ways. Over the previous few Sundays the members had felt like they'd been invited to a fancy dinner at which the host hadn't prepared enough even to nip their hunger, let alone fill them up.

Rev. George Wilson's service had been out of the ordinary, giving them spiritual food so down-home and good, it stuck to the ribs of their soul. As far as most of the members were concerned, this man belonged in their pulpit. Yet, despite this seemingly good fit, Nettie and her group were cautious and wanted to make sure that George was all that he seemed, not just a clever and smooth game player like Rev. Clemson.

Sheba agreed with them wholeheartedly. But for her the most troublesome thing about Rev. Wilson was that she couldn't find a way to get next to him after the service or at the dinner. By the third time Sheba sashayed past Rev. Wilson at the dinner without any results, she gave that up and started praying for a little help.

The Lord delivered the answer to Sheba's prayer in record time, and He even threw in a bonus by making a way out of no-way that led straight to Pompey's Rib Joint #Two on Monday afternoon. Sheba spotted George Wilson as soon as she stepped up in Pompey's. He was alone and sitting at a table by the window, reading a thick book. She took a deep breath, then walked into the restaurant and right over to him, making sure there was a big sexy smile on her face.

"Aren't you Rev. Wilson, the guest preacher over at Gethsemane Missionary Baptist Church?" Sheba asked, with a little swing of her hips and sassy tilt of her head.

George looked up at Sheba, reading glasses falling down

on his nose, and smiled. He was trying to remember why she was so familiar, when it occurred to him that she was the woman who kept trying to come on to him yesterday at church. He stood up and shook her hand.

"Yes, I'm George Wilson. And you are?"

Sheba smiled some more and ran her tongue across her top lip. She said, "My name is Sheba Cochran. I was a guest of Bert and Nettie Green at church yesterday. They are my neighbors."

"As in Bert Green, the head of the Deacon Board?"

"Umm-hmm," she answered with a soft purr.

George couldn't help but wonder how Deacon Green fared living next door to a Sheba Cochran.

Sheba stood there watching him a few seconds and then decided to move her hips about just a little. George caught the movement but didn't respond to it.

"Would you like to sit down, Miss Cochran?"

"I sure would," she replied, and slunk into her chair like a temptress would sit down with a man in a movie.

Rev. Wilson ignored that maneuver and signaled for the waitress to come to their table. He looked back at Sheba and said, "I take it you haven't ordered yet, right?"

"No, I haven't, Reverend."

"Neither have I. I was told by my good buddy, Rev. Theophilus Simmons, not to leave St. Louis without coming up in Pormpey's Rib Joint #Two. I'm hoping the food is as good as he says it is."

"It is," Sheba said in a sweet, relaxed voice that sounded more like her real self than she had since she'd met him.

He liked this change in her. All that sashaying, lip-licking, fake purring, and putting-on got on his nerves. He said, "What should I order?"

"I recommend the rib tip sandwich if you real hungry. And the ham sandwich with lettuce and tomatoes is good if you just want a quick bite to eat."

"What are you having?" he asked.

"I like the fried turkey sandwiches."

"Pompey's has fried turkey sandwiches? Hrnmm, been a while since I've had one of those. Most folks don't like to fool with frying a turkey."

"Yeah," Sheba said, "but Mr. Pompey know he can fry some turkey. He seasons that bad boy to perfection, drop it in that big ole barrel outside, and let it fry until it is brown, crispy, and juicy."

"You making me awfully hungry there, girl," George said, grinning.

Sheba liked that grin, though it had so much "mannish" in it, she wasn't sure of how to proceed. She was supposed to be checking him out.

In an attempt to regain some control over this situation, Sheba picked up the book Rev. Wilson had been reading and said, "You like W. E. B. Du Bois?"

"Yeah," George answered. "I just started this one."

"I've read several of Dr. Du Bois's books, but not *Black Reconstruction*."

"What books of his have you read?" he asked, becoming more and more curious about a woman who sashayed and purred and read W. E. B. Du Bois all in one heaving breath.

"*The Philadelphia Negro,* his book on the slave trade, his autobiography, and of course, *The Souls of Black Folk*."

"Of course," he answered with a taste of surprise in his voice.

"Rev. Wilson, don't be too shocked that a woman who looks like me reads Du Bois. I've read Ralph Ellison, Langston Hughes, Anne Petry, and Zora Neale Hurston, too."

"I've never read any books by Zora Neale Hurston," he said. "Are they good?"

"Her books are very good. I've always loved the way she writes about people like me. You know it's near to impossible for me to find myself in a book, 'less it's about me cutting up my old man or being on welfare or something like that."

George smiled again. He was beginning to like this woman despite all of that sex-kitten foolishness she had thrown his way. She gave him the impression that her feet were planted firmly on the ground, and she had what he always called "the genius of the folk." George couldn't help but wonder why this delightful woman had been working so hard to get next to him. The way she'd acted at church and when she'd first come into Pompey's didn't fit with the way she was right now.

"Tell me, girl," he said in a smooth and mellow voice. "Why are you so intent on *pre-tending* like you want to get next to me?"

"Well," Sheba thought, "this man is smart and perceptive." Neither Rev. Patterson nor Rev. Clemson had caught on to her, and they were very worldly men.

"Miss Lady," he said. "don't try and play me for a fool. You're up to something. And I'd appreciate your respecting me enough not to keep up this game, now that you know I'm on to you."

Sheba was in a tight space on this one. She couldn't break the women's confidence, but she didn't want this man to think she was one of those women who shamelessly chased after preachers. She took in a deep breath and blurted out words that had quietly and surprisingly settled in her heart.

"I want to come back to church, and the only thing holding me back is finding a church home with the right kind of pastor."

"I see," George said. "So, you have been checking out all the pastors coming through Gethsemane, huh?"

She nodded.

"And, uh, what kind of competition am I up against for this job?"

"None," Sheba said flatly.

"None?" he asked.

"None," she repeated. "The two men they interviewed before you weren't nothing but trouble. The first one was a jive-time jackleg preacher. And I don't know what possessed that man to wear his hair like he did."

George raised one eyebrow.

"He was bald at the top—had a great big clean circle in the middle of his head—and then had an Afro that wrapped around the bottom part. That half-moon Afro had to be about this big."

Sheba held her hands four inches away from her head.

"Sounds to me," George said, trying not to laugh, "that you all got clowned."

"Big time," Sheba answered, smiling back at him, and then frowned.

"You okay?" he asked.

"Yeah, I was thinking about the second man. He could preach real good but when you got close up on him, he was just like Christmas tree lights hung in a dirty window with raggedy drapes." She suppressed a shiver, recalling just how dirty and raggedy Clemson turned out to be.

"Finding a good man to pastor your church has been hard on you, huh?"

"Finding a good man to pastor this church is like trying to find a lot of money laying around in a greasy paper bag in an old parking lot."

"That's pretty bad," George said, thinking about what Theophilus Simmons had told him about Gethsemane and its internal politics. Then he added, "Man, that's a good church. But right now, it reminds me of a fine woman at a party full of thugs. Like that fine woman, Gethsemane needs a righteous brother to come in and let everybody know he looking after her."

They sat quietly for a few seconds, until George said, "What's your impression of me?"

"You seem like a decent man," Sheba answered.

"Seem?"

"That's what I said, *seem.* But to be fair to you, Rev. Wilson, I do get a good feeling from you. So I'm going to trust my feelings and give you some advice. You will not become the pastor of this church if you do not meet with the women this week. I know the men think they can hire a pastor without the women's approval. But I can tell you that will not happen."

"So how do I get a meeting with the women, Sheba?"

"Call Bert Green and he'll work it out for you."

"Sounds good to me," he said. "Will you be at the meeting?"

"You can count on it, Reverend. I want to make sure that what you walking around dressed as is real and not sheep's clothing tailored to camouflage a wolf."

Sheba stood up and looked around for the waitress, who was so slow that the expression "slow as molasses" was way too fast for her.

"I was hoping you'd eat lunch with me," George said. "Figured you might want to check me out a bit more."

"I wish I could," Sheba said. "But I'll have to take my sandwich with me, because my lunch hour's almost over."

"Where do you work?" George asked.

"Down on Market Street at the Main Post Office. I work in the back, sorting out the mail. Not a fancy job, but I'm happy with it. The pay and benefits ain't bad, either."

"I hear you," George replied. Good, steady jobs were hard to come by.

"I'll see you at the meeting, Rev. Wilson," Sheba said as she gave the waitress her money for the sandwich. She held out her hand and gave him the sweetest smile.

George held her hand a moment. "I'm looking forward to it," he answered in a voice that was so sexy Sheba had whispered "Oh my" before she could shut her mouth. She pulled her hand out of his and hurried from the restaurant, hoping she hadn't made a fool of herself.

Once George was certain that Sheba wouldn't catch him checking her out, he watched her walk out of Pompey's and on down the street. He thought she had a nice round behind sitting up on her little thin-shaped self. George smiled inside of himself, thinking it had been a long time since a woman inspired a sparkle like that inside of him.

Sheba attended every one of the meetings Rev. Wilson held with the women at the church. And the more she saw of him, and heard what he had to say, the more she found herself liking this man. First and foremost, George Wilson was just a plain old nice guy. But more important, he clearly had given his life over to Christ. He was, as Nettie's mother, MamaLouise Williams, said, "not ashamed to let folks know that he had the Holy Ghost." And that, all of the women agreed, was an essential credential for a preacher trying to become the pastor of your church.

Furthermore, the ladies were relieved that Rev. Wilson believed they deserved a more visible role in the running of the church, and that they even had a right to be ordained if they were called into the ministry. For the most part, they were ready to hire him, but Nettie, Viola, and Sylvia wanted to get Sheba's final report on him first.

This time they were at Sheba's house and gathered around her kitchen table, their mouths watering when she served a piping-hot peach cobbler that filled the whole room with the smell of peaches, cinnamon, and brown sugar. And there was vanilla ice cream to top it off.

"Is Katie Mae gone make this meeting, Nettie?" Sheba

asked as she poured everybody some coffee and then put fresh cinnamon sticks in each cup.

Viola leaned forward and inhaled the aroma of her coffee. "Ummmm, this smells heavenly."

Nettie got some peach cobbler and put a scoop of ice cream on top before answering, "She's not coming because we're meeting at your house."

Sheba frowned. "I thought she and I had gotten past all of that."

"It's not Katie Mae this time," Nettie said. "It's Cleavon. He's mad about the way things are going with hiring a pastor. And when that jackass is upset about something, he gives Katie Mae a hard time."

"Yeah," Viola added, "that man would die a thousand deaths if she came over to your house."

"Well, I for one am glad the girl stayed home," Sylvia said between bites. "Cleavon would just butter her up to get information he don't need to have. And that man know how to put it on Katie Mae when he want something."

Sheba secretly wondered how Cleavon Johnson managed to do all of that. He was too mean and selfish to "put it on" a woman good enough to turn her head.

"So," Nettie said, watching her ice cream melt over the cobbler, "what y'all thinking on Rev. Wilson?"

"He the one," Viola said. "We don't need to interview anybody else. Rev. Wilson is the pastor we need. I know it in my heart."

"I agree," Sylvia said. "What about you, Sheba, since you've had the most contact with the man."

Sheba smiled kind of dreamy-like and "I think Rev. Wilson is absolutely perfect."

"Huh?" Nettie said.

"I mean, I think he'll make a very good pastor—good enough to make me think about coming to church on Thanksgiving and Palm Sunday."

"That good?" Viola stated. "Umph, he really have it going on, for you to add some extra days to your worship schedule."

"Yeah, Rev. Wilson got a whole lot going on for him," Sheba responded with a soft sigh.

"I'll talk to Bert," Nettie said. "He likes Rev. Wilson a lot and wants to hire him."

As soon as the search committee sat down to discuss hiring Rev. Wilson, Cleavon jumped in with his objections.

"You all practically had heart attacks over hiring Rev. Clemson because he wasn't trustworthy with a street woman. And now y'all just chompin' at the bit to hire a man who ain't even married. Now, if a married man couldn't be trusted to behave, what do you think will happen with a man who ain't got a wife warming his bed on a nightly basis?" Cleavon demanded, and then answered his own question, "I'll tell you what'll happen. The Negro will go runnin' through the women in this church like he runnin' through a puddle of water."

"And Pastor Clydell Forbes, the biggest two-timing dog on two feet, was more trustworthy than Rev. Wilson, right?" asked Mr. Louis Loomis. "Next thing I know, you'll be trying to tell me that those two women who climbed up in his coffin hollering and screaming 'Please, Big Daddy, don't leave me' were his cousins."

"What does the late Clydell Forbes have to do with all of this?" Cleavon said defensively.

"Everything," Mr. Louis Loomis answered. "Because if that Negro would have left all those women alone, took better care of himself, and avoided that heart attack, we wouldn't be sitting up in this room without a pastor before our anniversary. And there ain't nothing wrong with Rev. Wilson, Cleavon, other than you can't run over him and run this church through him."

"He could be one of those men who don't like women," Cleavon countered. "What would you say about that?"

Turning away from Cleavon, Mr. Louis Loomis addressed Bert. "Hire George Wilson. He's the right man for the job, and you and most everybody with some sense on this committee knows it."

"Over my dead body," Cleavon jumped up shouting.

"That *can* be arranged, you know," Melvin Sr. said.

"Talk 'bout a blessing in disguise," Wendell half-mumbled.

"Cleavon," Bert said, "Rev. Wilson is my choice, plus the women want us to hire him."

"That's because that pansy promised he would do stupid, idiotic things like appointing a woman to our Finance Committee. He even had the audacity to say that he would ordain some woman who got a crazy notion that she been called to preach. Come on now . . ."

"Are you through?" Bert asked.

When Cleavon didn't answer, he said, "Let's go ahead and

vote on hiring Rev. George Robert Wilson as our new pastor. All in favor?"

Four hands shot up, representing half of the committee.

"All opposed?" Bert went on. Cleavon and his cousin Rufus raised their hands.

"Any abstentions?"

Two members of the committee abstained.

"Why y'all tripping?" Bert demanded, tired of looking for a pastor.

"Well, for one thing," Cleavon said, "we have one more candidate to interview before we decide on anything about anybody. Earl Hamilton knows the value of a dollar and has strong ties to the business community. Yet you-all are being pigheaded about even scheduling an interview week with him."

"Because he's a dead fish," Mr. Louis Loomis said. "Rev. Earl Hamilton is tight and boring, and he has far too many 'strong ties' for my comfort to not-so-nice white preachers, like Ray Lyles out in St. Charles."

Cleavon was so mad that he could spit tacks. He leaped up out of his chair and walked up on Mr. Louis Loomis, who was sitting down. Mr. Louis Loomis barely blinked as he said, "Watch yourself, Cleavon," in a deadly voice, with one hand placed firmly on his belt.

Cleavon threw up his hands but backed off and addressed the rest of the committee. "We are not discussing hiring George Wilson until this committee sees my next candidate, Rev. Earl Hamilton."

Bert was out of patience. But if bringing in Earl Hamilton would help keep the peace in his church, then it was a worthwhile move.

"Call Rev. Hamilton, Cleavon," he said, and then abruptly stood up. "Meeting adjourned."

When Bert went home and told Nettie that they could not hire Rev. Wilson until after they interviewed Rev. Earl Hamilton, she lost all faith in those men. The very next day, she rounded up all the missionaries' and women's auxiliary groups for an emergency session. The moment the last woman walked into the Ladies' Parlor, Nettie signaled for the doors to be locked. Only then did she cut loose.

"Y'all, we are in some serious trouble. The closer we get to our anniversary date, seems like the farther away we are from having a pastor. We need a pastor bad, but we need a good pastor. The church keeps suffering from all this foolishness that these men been putting us through, and I for one can't stand another breath of it."

"Amen," Viola called out.

"Now we have found the perfect pastor, and the men are still not satisfied. Instead of offering the job to Rev. George Wilson, they rounding up Rev. Earl Hamilton, who don't know what kind of church he wants to be up in, black or white."

"That's right," Sylvia said. She had gone to high school with Earl Hamilton, and even back then, his philosophy was "White is right; black get back."

"So—," Nettie started in.

"Before you do any more rabble-rousing, Nettie Green," Cleavon's mother, Vernine Johnson, interrupted, "you need to think about Earl Hamilton's credentials. No sense in being rash and foolish and hiring one man before we have a chance to examine another's qualifications for the job."

"Why in the world would we think that tired Uncle Tom Earl Hamilton is a qualified candidate for our church?" Viola asked. She couldn't stand Cleavon's mother. Vernine was always posturing and acting like she was so much better than everybody else, when half the time she didn't even know where Cleavon's daddy was.

"*Be-cause,*" Vernine stated, straightening out her ranch mink stole, "Rev. Hamilton is a graduate of the Yale Divinity School, he holds several honorary doctoral degrees, and he comes from a long line of preachers, doctors, lawyers—"

"—and Indian chiefs," MamaLouise, Nettie's mother, said. "He's all that and more, but he not a bit more saved than your son, Vernine. That is why we all up here arguing like cats stuck outside in a thunderstorm."

"Let's not bring our children into this, Louise Williams," Vernine said haughtily, "because if we do, we have to discuss your children and why they are so fond of that hoochie mama/welfare queen over there." She gestured toward Sheba, her diamond rings and bracelets sparkling with every movement of her hands.

"Heifer!" MamaLouise said loudly. She really wanted a piece of Vernine Johnson and hoped this dispute would goad her into a confrontation.

"Ignore her, Mama," Viola grumbled.

Vernine snatched up her purse, strutted to the door, and flipped the end of her ranch mink back over her shoulder.

"Ignoring me will be difficult. You see, this very room was remodeled *and* decorated by *me*."

"So, what's your point?" Sheba asked, thinking that Cleavon Johnson couldn't help but be a jive-time poot-butt with a mama like that.

Vernine didn't open her mouth, just stormed out the door and slammed it shut as hard as she could.

At that point, Katie Mae's grandmother stood up and said, "The devil is so busy in church right now. Y'all get up out of those chairs, grab somebody's hand, and bow your heads."

When everybody was up and holding hands, she started praying, "Father, as You can see, we got something on our hands. Now You have sent a blessing our way in the form of Rev. George Robert Wilson. Father, let that blessing become manifest in our midst by making a way out of no-way for him to become our pastor. Guide us, dear Lord; show us what to do and how to do it. In Jesus' name we pray and claim the victory. Amen."

They all stood with heads bowed, hands held, and hearts united in complete silence for a long moment, letting the Holy Spirit wash over them, getting rid of all of the devilment that had plagued the meeting moments before. Finally, Katie Mae's grandmother said, "Y'all, I know what we can do. We gone follow Queen Esther's example. You ladies with husbands who have a say-so in who is hired to pastor our church, please ask the Lord to guide you on how to petition your man and let him know what time it is."

VI

The first woman to make a Queen Esther move on her man was Sylvia, who fixed Melvin Sr. some chitlins, spaghetti, collard greens, coleslaw, corn bread, and fresh-squeezed lemonade on a Wednesday night. She took off work that day to get it all done by the time Melvin Sr. got home. When he sat down to the delicious-looking meal, he took several mouthfuls and said over and over again, "Baby, this a real treat. Chitlins in the middle of the week—a meal fit for a king!"

"And fixed by *the queen* who's about to get you straight," Sylvia thought as she watched Melvin Sr. smack his lips and pile some more chitlins and greens on his plate.

Viola believed that a Queen Esther move required something your man always wanted but secretly felt he didn't get nearly enough of. When she read over the Book of Esther in the Old Testament, what struck her most was that Esther was kind of sexy-like and knew how to make the king feel like he was "the man." So she decided that the most effective thing she could do would be to get all perfumed and fixed up at 3:30 A.M., then awaken Wendell for a "fast romp," one of his favorite things to do in the wee hours of the morning.

As Viola later told Nettie, she turned that man every which way but loose, talking some good love talk, and in earnest telling her husband, "You know you my daddy, boy." When Nettie got up off the floor from laughing at her crazy sister, she asked what Wendell thought of all of this. Viola said, "Girl, all that boy could do was grin, talkin' 'bout, 'Baby,

baby, baby, you put the exclamation point on the end of the word *good!*' right before his wore-out tail fell off to sleep.

"Then, when we finally woke up later that morning," Viola continued, "girl, I was so tired, I almost forgot why I was doing all that fast-tailed mess. Had to drink a sixteen-ounce RC Cola to wake up and straighten Wendell out on hiring Rev. Wilson. But, Nettie, girl, it show was good. I pray that I have some more work to do for the church real soon. 'Cause you know, the Lord's working in this kind of mysterious way is right up my alley."

Katie Mae, who had not been at the meeting with the other women, had gotten an earful about the "ghetto heifers trying to run her church" from her mother-in-law. The entire Johnson clan, including Cleavon's cousin Rufus, who was on the search committee, was very upset over this Rev. Wilson–versus–Rev. Hamilton thing. She knew she would have to tread carefully with Cleavon because he was bound and determined to hire Earl Hamilton.

So she decided to try a "tough-love" approach. Saturday morning she got up real early, dressed, and then nudged Cleavon, who was very sleepy, and told him, "I have to go and see about my grandmother. She's been complaining about her arthritis and needs some help today. You will have to watch the kids until I get back."

"Huhhh," said Cleavon, barely awake.

"The kids shouldn't be any trouble," Katie Mae lied, knowing full well that she and Cleavon had the baddest-acting children in church. Then she ran out of the house, hopped in her car, and drove off, not in the least bit worried that Cleavon would try to track her down—he hated talking to her grandmother.

Katie Mae did go over to her grandmother's house, but not to help, since her grandmother was in perfect health. Instead she went over there to eat, hang out with her cousins, watch TV, and sit around the table talking about how much Cleavon's family got on everybody's nerves. When she came home, it was late and the kids were acting crazy—fighting, shrieking, and running wild in the house. She got them settled down, then went looking for Cleavon and found him stretched out on their bed with a damp towel draped across his forehead.

Katie Mae sat down on the edge of the bed. "You alright, Cleavon?" she said soothingly, knowing full well that he wasn't.

"I'm tired," he said softly, which let her know he was exhausted. Normally, Cleavon would have torn the roof off the house over her leaving him with the kids like that. But when he was this tired, with his defenses down, she had a chance of reasoning with him.

"You worried about this business of hiring the new pastor, huh?"

"No Katie Mae, I am just tired from dealing with your bad-tailed children all day," he replied.

"Well, Cleavon," she said, "you know you probably won't feel so tired once this pastor business is over with. I know that you can't back out of interviewing Rev. Hamilton at this late date, but you are not obligated to hire him, either."

Cleavon wanted to jump up and hit the ceiling but couldn't muster the energy to act out. He just glowered at

Katie Mae from under the towel. She was nervous, he could tell, which meant those bossy women's-libber friends of hers had put her up to trying to sway him to hire George Wilson. He opened his mouth to get her straight but quickly realized that force might drive her into their camp. So he shifted tactics, taking her hand and patting it gently.

"Baby, let's let the church business rest for now," he said. "I missed you today and need a little *tendin'* to. Go put those children to bed and come on back up in here and take care of your man."

"Okay, Cleavon," Katie Mae said brightly, thrilled at such an unexpected show of affection from her husband. Maybe it didn't really matter all that much who became their pastor, she began to think. After all, Earl Hamilton did have some impressive credentials.

After she hopped up to get the kids, Cleavon got undressed, slipped under the cool crisp cotton sheets, and slapped his palms together with a smug grin. No doubt about it—he was *the man* in his house. He had been running Katie Mae since they were dating, and he would continue to run her until one of them went to meet their Maker.

Nettie, meanwhile, was having trouble deciding on a Queen Esther move to try with Bert. She read the Book of Esther twice and prayed on the matter for three days. Then, just when she was feeling discouraged, Viola called to report that she'd put a second Queen Esther move on Wendell for good measure, and Nettie suddenly got the inspiration for her own.

She figured the best time to get Bert's attention was late at night, since he loved midnight treats. So while Bert was watching the sports report on the ten o'clock news, Nettie filled the tub for him, adding Epsom salts and bubble bath to make it extra nice. When he eased into the water, oohing and aahing at how great it felt, Nettie went and changed into her one real femme fatale nightgown—a sheer white negligee, held together only with flimsy pink ribbons at the sides. She even put on the fancy pink high-heeled house shoes that she and Viola had bought from the Frederick's of Hollywood store at the Northwest Plaza shopping center.

She sprayed herself with Bert's favorite perfume, Chanel No. 5, and then went to get the special snack she had hidden in the back of the refrigerator. It was his favorite, fresh Mississippi-made hogshead cheese on saltine crackers, perfectly arranged on a fancy china plate. She pulled a frosted glass out of the freezer and filled it with ice-cold Pepsi-Cola. Then, holding the Pepsi in one hand and the plate of hogshead cheese in the other, Nettie sashayed her way into the bathroom, trying to look sexy.

Bert was lying in the bathtub with his head resting on a thick towel, happy and relaxed. As soon as he saw Nettie, his whole face lit up. She was so cute standing there, looking like one of those women in the movies, and making him think of what it must be like to be Sidney Poitier. And he could smell that hogshead cheese all the way across the bathroom. He sat up in the tub, reached out his hand to take the plate from her, and popped a hogshead cheese–covered saltine into his mouth.

Nettie laid a folded towel on the tub to make a cushion for herself, so she could sit with Bert. She held the Pepsi while he ate his hogshead cheese, closing his eyes and smacking his lips every time he popped a cracker into his mouth.

"Baby, you sure do know how to treat your man right, don't you?"

Nettie just gave Bert her special *smile* and said, "Ummm-hmmm."

He handed her the empty plate, took his Pepsi, sipped it, and said, "Ahhh," because it was so good and icy cold.

"I tell you, don't know what I did to have my baby come all up in here looking like she Nancy Wilson or Diana Sands or somebody like that."

As he sipped his Pepsi, Bert ran his eyes over Nettie, still sitting on the side of the tub, with her nightgown revealing a shapely little chocolate brown hip.

"But I don't think none of those Hollywood women got a thing on you, baby. Just look at you. And *umph,* that show was some good hogshead cheese you fixed up for me, girl."

Nettie smiled sweetly and said, "Anything for you, Bert, honey."

Suddenly Bert stopped sipping on his Pepsi and sat up straighter in the tub, narrowing his eyes. Nettie was up to something. He should have known it as soon as she stepped up in the bathroom in that nightgown. He loved that gown on her, but she always complained about its being too "exposing" and falling all away from her body. And those shoes—Bert looked down at her feet, wondering where Nettie had found those pink satin slippers, exposing her pretty feet and pink painted toes. And here she was, sitting there all smiles, with the gown lying open and those shoes swinging on her feet.

"This got something to do with hiring Rev. Wilson, don't it, Nettie Green?"

Nettie didn't say a word, just stared at the bathroom wall like she was seeing it for the very first time.

"I should've known," Bert said, making agitated swirls in the water with his hands.

Nettie coughed and said, "Now Bert, honey, don't get yourself all flustered and run your pressure up when you just got relaxed. The evening ain't over with, you know."

"You don't have to point that out to me, woman. I know how to use the sense God gave me."

Nettie blew air out of her mouth. She'd thought that putting on this old "floozy woman" nightgown would make Bert easier to talk to. But since he was not acting like King Xerxes did when Esther approached him, she decided to just let him have it. If Bert K. Green wanted to fight and let this old nightgown go to waste, so be it.

"Bert, ain't nobody been *up* to anything. We are trying to stop this so-called search committee from making a terrible mistake and losing a wonderful pastor, by taking too much time to hire him. You know, a pastor and congregation kind of like a husband-and-wife situation. You can up and marry just about anybody who willing to marry you back. But if you don't marry the right person, your life will be nothing but drama and heartache.

"We—and many of the other ladies who are dues-paying and tithing members at our church—are fed up with all of this foolishness y'all letting Cleavon and his people get away with. We have been through a clown and a nasty-movie star. Now you gone put us through more torture with an Uncle

Tom, when the Lord has laid a blessing right in our laps. And y'all 'bout to stand up and drop that blessing right on the floor."

"Baby, half the search committee ready to hire Rev. Wilson, but two members don't know which way they want to go. And of course, Cleavon and that idiot Rufus gone try and push us into hiring Rev. Earl Hamilton."

"Why they want to hire that man?" Nettie asked.

"Baby, for the same reason the Johnson clan ganged up on the church six years ago and forced Pastor Forbes on the church. I wasn't the head deacon back then, and I didn't have enough say-so to fight it. But I do now.

"Nettie, I agreed to let Rev. Hamilton come for an interview, hoping that he'd live up to his reputation and put something on the minds of the undecided committee members. You know the Johnsons are big supporters of the church. And I don't want to create more mess on this committee than there already is, by pulling rank, overriding the vote, and taking it to the congregation to put Rev. Wilson in the pulpit."

"So, just to keep the committee together, you gone see the church torn to shreds. 'Cause that is exactly what Cleavon and his band of no-good, triflin' fools will do, if y'all sit back and give them the chance. And I don't care how much money Cleavon's stuck-up family gives the church. No amount of money can justify hiring the wrong pastor."

Bert started running some more hot water to avoid dealing with Nettie, but she wasn't through. "Bert, you and Wendell and Melvin Sr. and even Mr. Louis Loomis, for that matter, can twiddle your thumbs with Cleavon all you want to. But as for me and my girls, we ain't playing with that joker."

Bert stepped out of the tub and Nettie handed him a fluffy blue towel. He began to dry his body vigorously in frustration, as if that towel could rub out all of his problems at church.

"You gone rub all the skin off yourself," Nettie told him. "I keep telling you to pat yourself dry and protect your skin."

He handed her the towel and said, "You do it then, since you the self-proclaimed skin care expert in this house."

Nettie took the towel and began to pat him dry. Bert stood there a few seconds, lost in the sensation of the warm, soft towel being pressed gently against his body by his wife.

"Baby?"

"Yeah, Bert, honey."

"Hang in there with me on this, okay? I believe that when the undecided committee members get a whiff of Rev. Earl Hamilton, they'll come around. You know he'll put on a good show. But in my opinion, he just like boiling water with some onions dropped down in it. It smells like you cooking meat, but all it is, is onions in boiling water."

Bert walked into the bedroom, with Nettie right behind him. He put on his favorite boxer shorts and sat down in his favorite green velvet chair, then pulled on his favorite girl's hand, urging her to come over to where he was sitting.

"Baby, you sure do smell good."

"I know, Bert. But if your plan don't work, what you gone do then? Honey, you know good and well that Cleavon and his crew not gone give up that easy."

Bert played around with one of the ribbons on the night-gown.

"Baby, Rev. Hamilton is not going to pastor my church. But we do have to get around those Johnsons."

"Well, Bert, honey, I hope you do get around those Johnsons. Because Bert, if y'all don't stop Cleavon, we women gone make our presence *known,* big time. See, we got it all figured out. First thing, not a one of us putting another dime in the collection plates until y'all hire Rev. Wilson. Then, we not cooking no more dinners, and we not gone clean up that church, either. I'll say it again—we ain't playin', Bert."

"Baby, I know y'all ain't playin'," he said, as he pulled the ribbon loose. Nettie's talking to him about church and fighting, with a hand on the bare hip peeking through that little nightgown, was getting right up under his skin.

"You feeling better?" he asked, with a sly grin tugging at the corner of his mouth.

"I'm feeling a little bit better," Nettie answered, as she gave him her special *smile* and pulled at the other ribbon.

Bert felt her smile travel all the way down into his soft, light blue boxer shorts. He said, "Baby, you sure do know how to take care of your man right. Don't you, girl?"

Nettie put her arms around his neck and whispered, "How right you want me to treat you, Bert honey?"

He slipped out of his boxer shorts and said, "You tell me, baby," in a low husky whisper that sent such warm shivers through Nettie, the toes on her right foot started to curl.

The next Sunday morning, Cleavon gave the morning prayer and introduced the guest pastor, Rev. Earl Hamilton, with great pride. MamaLouise leaned over and whispered to Mr. Louis Loomis, "You'd think he was introducing Dr. Andrew Young instead of that boy."

After the choir sang, Rev. Hamilton stepped up to the pulpit podium and said, "Good morning, God's children. Is it not the most stupendously spectacular wonder that we are all gathered together in this house of worship?"

"Y'all," Sheba whispered, "*how* did he manage to rub out all the black in his voice?"

"Yeah," Sylvia whispered back, "he sound like Richard Pryor when he talking 'white' in one of his jokes."

"Please," Rev. Hamilton continued, "bow your heads, so that we can grace this service with a prayer."

He then lifted his hands up in a gesture that made Sheba think of one of those back-in-the-Bible-days portraits and said, "God, our Father, I beseech Thee to shower this congregation with the sparks of understanding, so that they will partake of the teachings You have given me to translate from You to these sheep."

Bert closed his eyes tight and massaged the space between his eyebrows like he had a terrible headache.

Nettie placed her hand on his knee. "You alright, Bert honey?"

"Yeah, baby," he answered, sounding like he was in pain.

"You sure?"

"Yes, Nettie. Just that this joker's voice is so whiny, I can hardly stand it."

After the opening prayer, Rev. Hamilton launched into a very dry sermon about the evils of the new black music the children were listening to, called "funk." He had even gone so far as to say, "And as this music infiltrates our community, oozing out of the radio, infecting our ears and beating us down with the depravity of its pulsating rhythms, we find that we cannot escape it. It comes out the tavern door, shakes the dance floor of blue-light-in-the-basement parties, corrupts our backyard barbecues, our school marching bands, and even our churches, masquerading as good music in the form of awful songs like 'Oh Happy Day.'"

At that point, the church grew so quiet that you could hear the sleeping babies breathing. "Oh Happy Day" was the song the choir had sung right before the sermon, and it had had everybody, with the sole exception of Rev. Hamilton, on their feet clapping and swaying and singing along with the choir. Even Cleavon had been out of his seat, swinging and enjoying the song.

Bert leaned over and whispered to Nettie, "Why don't I go home, get my pistol, and load it up, then give it to that fool, so he can shoot himself in the foot."

"I wouldn't want you to do that, Bert, honey."

"And why is that, Nettie Green?"

"Because *I* want to be the one who shoots him with your pistol."

Bert laughed and gave Nettie's shoulder an affectionate nudge.

But Sheba, who was sitting with Bert and Nettie, couldn't laugh. She was deeply disturbed by Rev. Hamilton. What he'd said about the choir was just plain rude, and showed what little regard he had for the people of Gethsemane. She watched him closely for the rest of the service. When the offering was brought down to the altar to be blessed, she saw him scoop up a handful of the money and ogle it with pure lust in his eyes.

By the end of the service, Bert's faction of the search committee was more determined than ever not to hire Earl Hamilton. Cleavon knew that his candidate hadn't made a good impression, but he was nowhere close to giving up. His dumb cousin Rufus, who owed him a bundle of money, would go along with whatever he told him. The two undecided committee members posed more of a challenge, but then Cleavon thrived on challenge. Finding a way to get them into his corner would be fun.

And Cleavon did just that, managing to pull those other two votes his way and splitting the committee right down the middle—four in favor of Rev. George Wilson, four in favor of Rev. Earl Hamilton.

"Why don't we take a recess, then come back and straighten this out," Bert said, his eyes leveled on Cleavon's two new converts.

One of the men patted his breast pocket, which held tickets to the upcoming Stevie Wonder concert and an engraved invitation to a black-tie reception for the artist. Bert Green was right, of course—but right hadn't gotten the man these tickets.

The other man studied his feet, regretting that he couldn't afford to vote his conscience, not with Cleavon paying two back car notes for him so he could keep his new white Lincoln Continental.

When they came back to the table after the break, Bert took one more vote, and the tie remained.

"You have the power to override this vote, Mr. Chairman," Cleavon stated. "But I have the power to influence the pastor's salary and benefits. If you vote for George Wilson, I will keep his salary so low, he won't be able to afford cheap, imitation Kool-Aid."

"And you oughta know how cheap that is," Mr. Louis Loomis grumbled, "as much as you sell of that nasty stuff at your stores."

"I've had just about enough of you, old man. You say one more thing to me and I'll—"

"—And you'll what, Cleavon Johnson?" Mr. Louis Loomis demanded. "I ain't scared of you, your daddy, your tight-lipped snobby mama, or your old senile grandpappy, who did all that dirt all of those years and now don't have to remember a thing."

"Did you just bring my mother into this?" Cleavon yelled. "You don't talk about my mama."

"Well, I just did," Mr. Louis Loomis replied evenly.

"Sit down, Mr. Louis Loomis," Bert said. "And Cleavon, you shut up. I'm tired of both of y'all—fussing and arguing all of the time. Cleavon, you know you not acting right on this. And Mr. Louis Loomis, you know you wasting precious breath on Cleavon—don't know why you have such a hard time ignoring him and his craziness."

"I might be crazy, Bert K. Green. But you're still not hiring Rev. Wilson."

Bert started to argue but checked his words as a vision formed in his mind. He remembered what Nettie told him would happen if the committee didn't vote to hire George Wilson. He said, "Okay, Cleavon, you win. This Sunday you can tell the church that the committee is hiring Rev. Earl Hamilton."

"Bert?" Wendell asked.

"We are letting Cleavon make the announcement and that's final."

"But . . ."

"Wendell, I am the chair of this committee and I've made my decision. *Let* Cleavon tell the church, and then let the Lord handle the rest."

Perplexed as they were, the pro–George Wilson faction on the committee relaxed. They trusted Bert—but even more, they trusted the Lord to "handle the rest."

VII

The next Sunday Cleavon walked up into the pulpit after the morning devotional, pulled a handkerchief out of his breast pocket, wiped his face like he was a preacher, and announced, "The search committee has chosen a pastor. As soon as we can straighten out our differences, we will be hiring and installing Rev. Earl Hamilton as the new leader of Gethsemane Missionary Baptist Church."

Nearly every woman in church sat up in shock. Cleavon Johnson must have had a lobotomy, they thought, to remove what little bit of his mind he had left.

"We'll just see about that," Katie Mae's grandmother said, and wrote a note on her program instructing her church sisters to keep their money in their purses at collection time. The secret message spread like wildfire through the sanctuary. The women ushers took the note up to the balcony, where they passed it from pew to pew; and to make sure nobody was missed, they took it down to the basement, the kitchen, the ladies parlor, and even the bathroom.

All of the offerings that Sunday—regular morning offerings, tithes, sick-and-shut-in and benevolent funds—were pitiful. Because a lot of the women gave the money for themselves *and* their husbands, the church's earnings for the week dropped 73.5 percent.

But Cleavon Johnson was unmoved. The next Sunday he took to the pulpit again to proclaim, "Many of you have been calling the members of the search committee, worrying us about our decision. You need to know that the decision has been made, and it will not be changed."

At that point, the women pushed the matter further, by not only withholding their money but also shutting down the after-church dinner. They went right downstairs when service was over, divided up the meats and other dishes among themselves, and wrapped them all up in packages to take home. The guest minister—one of a string who had been filling in during the pastoral search—had to go away unfed, and was so appalled that he put out the "bad-mouth" on the church.

The next Sunday was Communion Sunday, and still the women's boycott continued. None of the men knew where to buy the crackers and grape juice for the service, but Cleavon claimed that he had it under control. He went to one of his stores and got some loaves of a white bread from the day-old section—instead of his more expensive crackers—along with some cheap imitation grape Kool-Aid. The bread was hard, dry, and stale, and the grape drink was terrible—weak, chemical-tasting, and bitter, even though the package was clearly marked, "No added sugar necessary."

As soon as Mr. Louis Loomis chewed on that bread, he winced and reached for the juice, which puckered up his face.

"You alright, Mr. Louis Loomis?" Bert whispered.

"What's in that juice?" Mr. Louis Loomis asked, through watery eyes. "It's the nastiest stuff I've ever tasted." He coughed and then said, "Forgive me, Lord, for saying that at the Lord's Supper."

Bert swallowed his juice fast, trying not to breathe. As he did, he heard Nettie's mother, MamaLouise, praying, "Father, forgive us our misdeed this morning. We are trying so hard to do Your will, and we need some heavenly help to get this nasty stuff down and keep it down. Amen."

The service itself was equally dispiriting. Now that word was out on the strife in the church, their expected guest preacher had bowed out. On such short notice, all they could do was ask the one ordained minister in the church to lead them in worship. He was an elderly man, long retired, who had grown tongue-tied and hard to understand. He was also prone to sleeping in church, and an usher had to wake him up when it was time to preach.

Collecting himself, he rose creakily to deliver the sermon. Lifting up his hands, he proclaimed, *"Leh uz aw tand up in gi fro awergifs ufdu udnez ufdu yaw,"* to the puzzled stares of church members. One of the schoolteachers in the congregation decoded the sentence phonetically and wrote it out to be passed down her pew. Her note read: "Let us all stand up and give from our gifts of the goodness of the Lord."

The entire congregation, men and women alike, was getting fed up. Many decided that as long as the search committee remained silent, allowing Cleavon to continue to maintain that he was hiring Earl Hamilton, they would forgo attending church on Sunday and meet privately for prayer and Bible study in members' homes. They made it clear to Bert, Wendell, Melvin Sr., and Mr. Louis Loomis that they were not coming back to church until the committee got sense enough to hire Rev. George Wilson.

With no offerings coming in, the church coffers grew so depleted that Cleavon had to pay for gas, electricity, phone, and water out of his own pocket. He had never conceived of the possibility that the women in his church would turn on him and the search committee with such a vengeance. Finally he had to acknowledge that he couldn't win this battle—at least not right now.

So Cleavon temporarily threw in the towel, conceding to the hiring of Rev. George Wilson, using the split vote to his advantage to only hire him as the interim pastor. According to the dusty church bylaw Cleavon invoked, interim pastor was a temporary, six-month position. Once the six months were up, the church could install the interim pastor as the permanent one, or hire somebody else. It was the "hire somebody else" part that Cleavon liked so much.

Bert sat back at that meeting and let Cleavon put on a floor show. As much as he wanted to see George Wilson installed as the permanent pastor, he had peace to let the Lord work it all out. He knew in his heart that if they put George

Wilson in that pulpit as the interim pastor, he would win such a following that it would be virtually impossible to remove him in six months. And Bert felt that, for some reason, Cleavon just hadn't been able to figure that out.

Rev. George Robert Wilson was installed as the interim pastor of Gethsemane Missionary Baptist Church on Christmas Day. It was a beautiful morning—sunny, crisp, and cold, with soft falling snowflakes cleansing the air. The church looked magnificent, for the women were so happy with their victory that they had gone all out with their Christmas decorations.

The entire sanctuary was trimmed with fresh-scented evergreen boughs laced with red and gold ribbons and bows. There were vibrant poinsettia plants on all the windowsills, and two large bouquets of rich red roses stood at the foot of the altar leading to the pulpit. The dark walnut pews with their red velvet cushions and the deep red carpeting on the floor looked more warm and welcoming than ever against the background of green branches and red and gold satin. The men had found a lush, perfect cone of a Christmas tree, which everybody at church, young and old, had decorated with homemade ornaments, strings of popcorn, and candy canes. And on top of the tree, Rev. Wilson had placed a beautiful black angel wearing a white, gold-trimmed African robe—his gift to his new parishioners.

Ushers were posted at each door of the church, holding large red baskets tied with white ribbons. As members filed in, they got a hearty "Merry Christmas," along with an orange, a candy cane, and a small bag of pecans—a reminder of times when these were the only gifts many people were able to give.

The first person George Wilson saw that morning, when he took his place in the pulpit, was Sheba Cochran, with her four children. He smiled when he caught her eye, not missing the blush that spread across her cheeks. George thought that Sheba looked awfully pretty in a red velvet suit that matched her children's, over a white lace blouse with ruffled cuffs that flopped out from under her jacket sleeves, and shiny black patent-leather boots with slick-looking red heels. Her face was made up right nice too—not too much makeup but just enough to look good to a man—and her hair was fluffed out in a new, very becoming Afro puff.

Watching Sheba Cochran and her four children, George was struck by the thought that he had definitely done the right thing in accepting the interim pastorship of Gethsemane and that he had very good reasons to fight to stay on—at least five that he could think of right offhand.

When Sheba saw Rev. Wilson smiling so warmly at her and her children, she felt a little wheel a-turning in her heart. But that moment of connection was just one small ripple in the wave of fellowship that was sweeping the church that morning. Most of the members were feeling good and very blessed. The perfect sweetness of the Holy Spirit was so strong in the church, it was almost as if they could stick out their tongues and taste it.

Rev. Wilson wasn't one to suppress the Holy Ghost when it was running like a current through a congregation. He told the members, "I guess my first day here gone be kinda hot and sweaty. Because y'all looking like you ready to cut loose and have what a bishop's wife once described as 'crazy church' on me."

"Now you talking, Pastor," Mr. Louis Loomis said, as the pianist, who could barely keep his fingers still on the piano keys, signaled to the rest of the musicians to start playing. Sister Hershey Jones broke out singing, further fanning those sweet, hot, Holy Ghost flames. Then Sister Hershey, a very substantial, well-built sister, picked up the hem of her choir robe and started in on the dance she was so famous for. As she claimed a spot at the front of the church and started moving her feet—which were tiny in comparison to the rest of her—at the speed of light, the whole church was set on fire.

Sister Hershey danced with her arms extended in front of her, feet moving and head bobbing in sync with the movement of her arms. Just watching Sister Hershey made folks want to jump out of their seats. As the music got hotter, they started hopping up to dance, as if the flames of the Holy Ghost had landed on them the way they had on the folks at Antioch in the New Testament.

At first, Sheba just sat there and watched. But then the Holy Ghost hit her so hard, it felt like she had been smacked right in the back. She got up out of her seat and pushed her way past her startled children into the aisle. There she placed her hand on the small of her back as if it ached and started dancing so, she dropped her purse on the floor and would have come out of her shoes if she hadn't been wearing boots. Nettie, Viola, and Sylvia rushed to her side in case the girl fell out. But Sheba simply slowed down to begin walking in a small circle, calling out, "Thank You! Thank you, Jesus!

Thank you, Lord. You brought me and my babies here to put our feet on the rock of Jesus. Thank You, Thank you, Lord. You a good God. You a *good* God!"

The entire time Sheba was shouting, George was watching her from the pastor's chair, with pure joy lighting up his face. It didn't occur to him that he should go to her until he saw one of the deacons, Mr. Louis Loomis, leading Sheba's children down to meet her at the altar. "Rev. Wilson," Mr. Louis Loomis said, "I know this is not protocol and that I really don't have a right to do this. But I believe that this young woman standing before us done got the Holy Ghost, and she really want to be saved. You understanding me, Rev.?"

George immediately left the pulpit and joined them. He took both of Sheba's hands in his and asked, "How long have you been without a church home?"

"Since I got pregnant with my oldest, Gerald here, when I was seventeen and my mama threw me out on the street."

"You sure you want to make Gethsemane your church home and your children's church home?"

"Yes."

"Then, we gone oblige your certainty this morning," George said. "Do we have any deaconesses in the congregation who I can assign this fine family to?"

Louise Williams, Nettie and Viola's mother, stood up and said, "Reverend, I'll take this family."

"Thank you, Sister . . ."

"Louise Williams."

"Thank you, Sister Williams."

"It's MamaLouise, Rev. Wilson," Phoebe Cates, Viola

and Wendell's daughter, hollered out from her seat in the balcony. "Don't nobody call my grandmother Sister nothing. She MamaLouise."

Everybody was laughing now.

"Thank you," George told Phoebe, chuckling himself. "Well, Sister MamaLouise Williams, I will assign this fine family to you."

George squeezed Sheba's hands. They were rough from hard work but had a sweet strength that touched his heart. He smiled into her eyes, thinking they were beautiful, simply because they revealed the true nature of her character. After meeting her at Pompey's, George had picked up on some gossip about Sheba Cochran, but he didn't care whether or not the talk was true. Before him stood a good black woman whose heart was open to the Lord. And she wanted to dedicate her life and her children's lives to the Lord. What more could anyone ask of a person?

"State your name and all of your babies' names for the church," he said.

"Pastor, my name is Sheba Loretta Cochran. This baby standing next to me is my oldest son, Gerald. He is eighteen. Then, this girl right here is Lucille Renee, and she is seventeen. Next to Lucille is Carl Lee, twelve. And next to him is my baby, baby girl, La Sheba Loretta, eight."

"Are you are all candidates for baptism?"

They all said yes, as "Amens" rang out around the sanctuary.

Then Rev. Wilson asked, "Would some deacons come forth to stand behind Sister Sheba and each of her children?"

Bert, Wendell, and Melvin Sr. volunteered and took their places with Mr. Louis Loomis and MamaLouise behind the Cochran family. At that point, George placed his hands on either side of Sheba's head, and began to pray. "Thank you, Lord, for bringing this woman and her beautiful children to our church this morning. Thank you for shining Your light of salvation on them so brightly that it carved out a path straight to You. Now, I ask in Jesus' name that You anoint this entire family, beginning with the mama, making them one with You, so that they will all be saved and sanctified and filled with the Holy Ghost. Let this very moment signal a new life in Christ Jesus for them all. Forgive them their sins and heal all of their hurts and sorrows. Make them new in You. In Jesus' name I pray, amen."

The reverent hush in the church deepened as George whispered to Sheba, "Do you accept Jesus Christ as your Lord and Savior now?"

"Yes," she said softly.

George lifted his hands off Sheba's head and gave her forehead a featherweight touch. With that, the Spirit rose up so strong in her that Sheba was knocked back, with her arms thrown over her head, as she fell out, slain in the Spirit. Bert and Wendell, who were standing behind Carl Lee and La Sheba, moved to catch her before she hit the floor.

Everyone in the congregation was still and quiet. They all knew about getting slain in the Spirit and had seen it at some revivals held at Gethsemane, but it had been years since a pastor did this at a morning service. Rev. Wilson went on to ask each of Sheba's four children if they wanted the Holy Ghost. When they said yes, he touched their heads, and one by one, just like their mama, they all fell out. There they were, the whole family lying on the floor, side by side, slain in the Spirit.

Melvin Jr. was sitting next to Phoebe and wondering, like Bert, where her cousin Bertha Kaye was. He whispered, "My mama always said that Miss Sheba's children love themselves some of 'they mama.' And she's right. Even Gerald, with his almost-grown self, falling out 'cause of his mama."

"Well," Phoebe whispered back, "Miss Sheba never did do anything all plain-and-boring like. Stands to reason she would be the first one to fall all out in church under the new pastor."

Melvin Jr. chuckled and then got serious as he studied his new pastor. On the surface, Rev. Wilson was low-key and unassuming. But underneath, there was power in that man—the power that comes with an anointing from the Lord.

Why had there been so much fighting, Melvin Jr. wondered, to keep a pastor like Rev. Wilson out of this church? To put him in as interim pastor didn't make much sense, especially after this morning's service. "But when," Melvin Jr. thought, "did Mr. Cleavon Johnson or any other member of his family put anything, including the church, ahead of themselves?" It took a women's revolution in the church to get even this far toward hiring a good pastor. Melvin Jr. closed his eyes in prayer. It was going to take a whole lot of prayer and effort to keep Rev. Wilson in that pulpit.

Part 2

The Devil Is Very Busy in Church

I

The New Year, 1976, rolled right in, giving Gethsemane less than six months to get the anniversary celebration going. With George spearheading the planning, committees began to form, including the History & Archive Committee, selected to document the rich heritage of the church; the Flowers Committee to handle both the landscaping and the interior decoration; and the Food Team who claimed it would create the most lavish spread ever served in church, along with a special cake big enough for the entire congregation to share. After all the conflict over choosing a pastor, folks seemed happy that they could finally settle down and work together in peace. But as Katie Mae's grandmother always warned, "When the saints are caught up in the business of the Lord, the devil gets mad and gets busy in church."

Gethsemane was a special church, Bert Green thought as he drove past it while running a Sunday morning errand for Nettie. Its deep red brick, if a little shabby and cracked now, still had a warm glow, and its stained-glass windows, with their simple scenes depicting stories in the Four Gospels, were beautifully vibrant. Later that morning, a hot new choir, the Holy Rollers, was going to rattle those windows. Even the scent of the church was beautiful, thanks to the spicy potpourris the women's auxiliaries sprinkled over the soil of the potted plants in the sanctuary.

Gethsemane was such a warm and loving church that you felt good just being there. That's why it troubled Bert so much that Bertha Kaye, his only child and namesake, had been missing for so many Sunday mornings. The girl had stopped coming to church on a regular basis shortly after Rev. Forbes's death. She didn't even show up for services Christmas Day—just brought herself by the house to eat and collect her presents. And when Bert got on her about it, the girl had the nerve to burst into tears, run to her old bedroom, slam and lock the door, and then, from the sounds of it, throw her spoiled self on the bed like some petulant rich girl in the movies.

That crying and acting out on Christmas Day was the last straw as far as Bert was concerned. Even as a little girl, Bertha didn't fool her daddy, and she wasn't getting by him now. Neither was Nettie, who Bert suspected knew something, if not all, that was up. Bert resolved to start the New Year off by remedying whatever was wrong with his baby—and he was going to find out just what that was today.

It was the second Sunday of the month, when Nettie always cooked a big breakfast for their family and friends before the eleven o'clock service. When Bert arrived with the milk Nettie sent him out to get, everybody was already there: MamaLouise; Mr. Louis Loomis; their neighbor

Sheba Cochran; Melvin and Sylvia Vicks, with their son Melvin Jr.; and Viola and Wendell Cates, with their daughter Phoebe. Bertha's seat remained empty, one more stark reminder to Bert that something was up with his baby.

Nettie had set the table with her favorite gold-rimmed china and used her cream lace tablecloth, fancy gold satin napkins, and the brass napkin rings with "Bert and Nettie Forever" engraved on them. The cream and gold complemented the soft neutral tones of the dining room: walls with ivory moire draperies, a pale beige area rug on the golden hardwood floors, and a soft sand, ivory, and off-white abstract oil painting on the wall facing the large picture window. Nettie had a special color scheme for each room in the house: sunny yellow for the kitchen, sage green for the living room, pale blue for the master bedroom, lavender for the guest room, and pink for Bertha's old bedroom.

As soon as Nettie finished putting out all the food, Bert had everybody gather and join hands to bless the table. "Father," he prayed, "we thank You for this gathering of family and friends to partake of the bounties of Your love in the form of this wonderfully prepared meal. Bless the sweet brown hands that made it. And bless the food to nourish and keep us all healthy and strong. In the name of Jesus Christ our precious Lord and Savior we pray. Amen."

"Amen," everybody said, and dug into the delicious-smelling breakfast of homemade blackberry pancakes, crispy bacon, sausage patties, fluffy scrambled eggs, fresh-sliced pears, fresh-squeezed orange juice, and Nettie's wonderful coffee.

When Bert was satisfied that everybody had been served,

he took a spoon and tapped the side of his crystal water glass.

"As always," he began," I am glad that we are all here to enjoy this good meal together. But even though I'm glad to see y'all, I am not happy about my baby not being here. Now, the girl has been missing church, she is not here with us this morning, and I want to know what is up with her." He looked straight at Nettie as he asked, "Does anybody have any idea what is going on with Bertha Kaye?"

At that point, Nettie hopped up to get Bert some more coffee, taking extra care as she sweetened it with honey, added a touch of cinnamon, and made sure it had the perfect amount of cream for Bert. He liked his coffee the color of rich caramel—said that color tasted good.

Bert thanked Nettie for the coffee but didn't let her off the hook: "Well, baby, what you got to say for yourself and that daughter of yours?"

"Not much, Bert honey," Nettie answered, starting to return to her seat. But Bert tugged on her hand and pulled her right back over to his chair.

"What you know that I don't know, girl?" he asked gruffly.

Nettie didn't answer right away. This wasn't the first time Bert had put her on the spot at a family breakfast. Viola always thought that her sister would be better off just telling the man what he wanted and often needed to know when nobody was around. But Nettie hated to give Bert bad news and would always keep it from him as long as she could, until the man got tired of it and called her out in front of everybody. And it always worked.

But Nettie wasn't ready to cave in yet. "Now Bert, honey,"

she said, "no need in us disrupting a perfectly lovely breakfast talking about troublesome things. Why don't you sip on your coffee before it gets cold and get some more pancakes."

"Bad move," Phoebe thought, having witnessed enough scenes between Bert and Nettie to know the script. She slurped on her coffee, unintentionally drawing attention to herself.

At that, Bert let go of Nettie's hand and zeroed in on the other person in the room who usually had the scoop on Bertha Kaye. Phoebe and Bertha, both only children of sisters, were just like sisters themselves and knew almost all of each other's secrets. Close as they were, the two women were different as night and day. Bertha was flighty, comical, prissy, and spoiled rotten with her big, pretty, full-figured self. Phoebe was more serious—a lawyer—very athletic, no-nonsense, long and tall, with an incredibly beautiful head of hair that hung way down her back.

"So, Phoebe Josephine," Bert said, knowing that the use of Phoebe's full name would put her on notice that he wasn't playing. "What can *you* tell me about Bertha and her whereabouts?"

Phoebe took as big a gulp of coffee as she dared, to buy some time. She really didn't know what to tell her uncle.

"Baby, stop slurping on your coffee," MamaLouise admonished. "Now, if you have something to tell your uncle, you better tell it, because he really needs your help."

Phoebe almost huffed air out of her mouth. Why did she have to be the one to spell it out? She sipped some more coffee, being extra careful not to slurp it. If she did, all of them would swear she did it on purpose. Everybody knew Phoebe could have "her habits" on her, and her habits included being irritable and then deliberate in her refusal to cooperate.

Bert was watching his niece expectantly, drumming the table with thick heavy brown fingers. Phoebe could see that she had no hope of escape.

"Uncle Bert," Phoebe began, "Bertha has been going to another church out in St. Charles."

"St. Charles?" Bert asked. "The only church that I am familiar with out in St. Charles is that . . ." He snapped his fingers and turned to Nettie. "Baby, what's the name of the church that's always on TV? You know the one. It's called . . ."

"The American Worship Center," Nettie answered, hoping he wouldn't keep pushing.

"The American Worship Center," Bert repeated. "That's it, but—"

"Nettie," MamaLouise said impatiently, "is Bertha going to the American Worship Center?"

"Yeah, Mama. She is."

"Why?" MamaLouise demanded, astonished that anybody, let alone her own granddaughter, would want to go to that church. The televised services didn't look that inviting, and she had never seen any black people at them.

"Don't know, Mama," Nettie answered truthfully.

"Well, it must be something," Bert interjected. "And I aim to find out. How long you been knowing this, woman?"

"Two and a half weeks."

"Two and one half weeks?" he yelled, jumping up from the table so fast, he knocked over his chair. Everybody in the room grew quiet. Bert hardly ever lost his temper, but when he did, it was like standing in the middle of a tornado.

"Now Bert, honey, don't go getting all upset, running your pressure up. I—"

"I, nothing!" he snapped, and snatched the chair up, flinging it back in place. "You kept quiet on this, *Nettie Cordelia Williams Green,* because you knew I would get all up in that silly girl's business. And I don't care if Bertha Kaye *is* supposed to be grown, she is silly sometimes. Don't know where she got it from. You got good sense, Viola got good sense, MamaLouise got good sense, and I got good sense."

Bert pulled his car keys from his pocket and went to get his hat and coat.

"Where do you think you're off to?" Nettie asked, pulling on his arm.

Bert pried her hand away. "I'm going to get my baby. She ain't got no business out there."

"Maybe not," Nettie insisted. "But you're not the person to go out there and get her. All you'll do is fuss at Bertha and she'll dig in her heels, just to make sure you know she grown so you can't tell her what to do."

"She might do something even more foolish, like joining that church," Sheba said, wondering if that was exactly what Bertha was planning to do. Recently she had asked Sheba for a copy of her tax forms for some "application" process.

"Why don't you go, Phoebe," Bert said. "She'll probably listen to you."

Phoebe sighed heavily. "But it's Second Sunday," she reminded Bert. Second Sunday at a black Baptist church was the very *best* Sunday, commemorating the days when poor churches could hire itinerant preachers only twice a month—on the second and fourth Sundays. But it was on the second Sundays that those congregations really had "chutch."

For his first Second Sunday as pastor, Rev. Wilson had installed the new choir, the Holy Rollers, who promised to tear up the service with their high-powered, on-fire singing. Phoebe couldn't wait to get to church.

"Your uncle Bert just asked you to do something, Phoebe Josephine," her father, Wendell, stated in a no-nonsense voice. "Now you do right and go see to your cousin."

Meanwhile, Sheba had been keeping an eye on Melvin Jr. Lately she had noticed that he and Bertha spent a lot of time together for people who couldn't "stand" each other. He had almost jumped when Bert started questioning Phoebe and had kept his eyes glued to the table during their exchange. So she asked, "Why don't you go with her, Melvin Jr."

"Don't you think I would add insult to injury, Miss Sheba, if I showed up with Phoebe? You know how much I get on Bertha's nerves over the simplest of things."

"No, as a matter of fact, I don't," Sheba answered him evenly.

Melvin Jr. sighed out loud, not caring who heard him, and got up to get his coat and car keys. "I might as well drive."

Mr. Louis Loomis locked eyes with Sheba, acknowledging that she was on to something. "You know, Sheba," he said, "I think you and I need to accompany these young folk. They don't need to tangle with the American Worship Center, or Bertha Kaye, without a little seasoned backup."

"I know that's right," Bert said. He got up and walked

them to the door, just to make sure they left right at that moment, before anybody had a chance to back out.

II

The American Worship Center was way out in the boondocks, far enough away from St. Louis that no black people could stumble up on it by accident. It was so far out that when Phoebe tried to locate the KATZ soul radio station, all she got was fuzz and static.

"Shoot," she spat out. "Can't get nothing out here but country-western music. It's bad enough I can't go to my own church today but at least I could get to hear Evangelist Elroy Thorn, Rev. Cleotis Robinson, Martha Bass, or the O'Neal Twins. Heck, I'd be happy listening to somebody testifying on one of Rev. Ike's red prayer cloths about now."

"Maybe you'll get lucky and somebody at this church will sing one of those singers' songs," Melvin, Jr. said dryly as he pulled off 70 West and found the street leading to the church. "And if you would let my boy Jackson put an eight-track player in this car, we'd be listening to a tape instead of the static that is supposed to be KATZ. But you and Bertha Kaye show kinfolk—you both hardheaded and don't listen right when a man try to tell you something for your own good. I knew I should have driven my own car."

"And you could've done just that, Melvin Jr.," Phoebe retorted, "if you had more than a half of a fourth of a tank of gas in your car."

"Women," Melvin Jr. grumbled, and made a left turn,

hoping it wouldn't take much longer to find this place. He didn't like driving around St. Charles looking lost and maybe drawing attention from some white folks nervous that they were out here to start some trouble.

"Melvin Jr.," Sheba said, "when did you get so grown and mannish that you know all about women being hardheaded with men?"

"What you mean, Miss Sheba?" he asked, trying to play dumb.

Sheba sat up and poked her face up forward, so Melvin Jr. could see it in the rearview mirror. Reaching up, he shifted the mirror to escape her expression, which clearly said, "Oh, you know exactly what I mean."

Melvin Jr. wished he did not have to come out here to deal with Bertha. He had a sinking feeling that he was connected to her running away. Melvin Jr. was in love with Bertha Green. He didn't even remember when it happened—falling in love with the girl he had fought with all of his life. Maybe he'd always loved Bertha and was just too pigheaded to admit it to her or to himself.

Mr. Louis Loomis once tried to talk to him about love. He told him, "Boy, a good woman without a man in her life is just like prime real estate that's been overlooked. Sometimes real good property can be on the market for what look likes forever and a day. You think it'll always be there, then somebody comes along and sees he has found a treasure and takes it right from up under your feet."

"Why didn't I listen to Mr. Louis Loomis and tell Bertha that I loved her and couldn't live without her?" Melvin Jr.

thought. "Why didn't I use the sense God gave me to grab a hold of the best thing that ever happened to me?"

They finally found the church, and it took them fifteen more minutes to find a parking space. The parking lot stretched out across several acres of land and was so full that cars were parked in made-up spaces. Melvin Jr. saw a spot on the grass and made himself a parking space too.

"It sure is crowded," Mr. Louis Loomis said as he took off his hat and scratched at his head. "You know, I never would have thought so many people would come here. The preaching is so boring that it puts my TV to sleep."

"You ain't never lied on that," Sheba said, watching the steady flow of people moving toward the church. "And I show don't see any black folks up in here."

"There are some brown dots over there," Phoebe said, pointing to a lone black family leaving their car a few rows away. She gave them an enthusiastic wave.

"Humph, that's a shame before God," Mr. Louis Loomis snorted in disgust, as the father steered his family away from them, walking all stiff and tight to hide that dipping-strut sway that would have made him look like a bona fide *black* man. "Some folks just hate it that the Lord made them black."

Sheba watched the man trying to walk all upright and pinched and thought, "Such a waste."

As soon as they reached the church door, Phoebe got to scowling.

"What is wrong with you?" Melvin Jr. asked.

"I don't like the way this church looks."

Sheba backed up a few steps and studied the building for a moment. It had a long, square, industrial shape and was made of pale gray concrete blocks, softened a bit with stained-glass windows in gold, blue, and gray. "It looks more like an office building than a church," she said.

Phoebe agreed. "It sure is different from Gethsemane. There aren't even any trees out here. It's just standing in the middle of a big, empty field."

The spacious vestibule they entered made their own look tiny by comparison. Though rather cold and uninviting, it had clearly benefited from a very high-priced decorator. It had white, textured walls with pewter gray trim on the windows, and a black marble floor with white and silver veins, topped by a black rug in a pattern of soft gray flowers and tiny white doves.

"Well," said Mr. Louis Loomis, "it may not look like a church, but it show do look like a whole lot of money."

A group of members arrived, stopping dead in their tracks as they caught sight of the brown huddle in the vestibule. Not one person said good morning or even nodded in greeting. The rudest among them just stared, with shock on their faces and mouths struggling to form the question: "And just what are *you* doing here?"

"At least we look good," Sheba thought. She was decked out in a cream-colored sequined dress, and was sporting her hot pink ostrich feather hat like a crown, along with hot pink stretch-satin elbow-length gloves, hot pink shoes, and a matching shoulder bag. Conscious of how she stood out, Sheba moved to the wall to check her reflection in a large, oval mirror set in an opulent antique silver frame. Adjusting the hot pink veil on her hat, she had just taken out her lipstick for a touch-up when a condescending voice cut through the silence.

"You are in the house of the Lord. Act like it."

Staring in the mirror, Sheba locked eyes with a flushed-face "Big Missy," a starched and poofed-out dark blond hairdo sitting high on her head. Knowing that Big Missy wanted to intimidate her, Sheba decided to act like she wasn't even there. She put her lipstick on slowly and deliberately, enjoying every second of the woman's agitation over being ignored. Then, to add more fuel to the fire, she made a big to-do of blotting and puckering her lips, before twisting the lipstick back into the tube.

"Jezebel," said Big Missy, loud and clear.

Dropping her lipstick into her purse, Sheba turned to face the woman. In a low, threatening voice, she said, "I guess you ought to know, since your *mama* is a Jezebel. And if you say just one more thing to me, *Big Missy,* you'll need Peter, James, and John to help you escape the flames of my wrath."

"Miss Sheba!" Bertha exclaimed, suddenly materializing out of thin air. Putting her hands on her generous hips, she demanded, "What are y'all doing here?"

Phoebe stared her cousin up and down and felt relief when she saw what she was wearing. Bertha was "clean" in a creamy yellow silk suit with mother-of-pearl buttons and a matching hat, purse, and shoes. She whispered a prayer of thanks to the Lord that the girl, with her pretty, sexy, cocoa brown, size-eighteen, five-foot-eight, silly self, didn't let this old dry-tail church take away her taste in clothes. Bertha still had that classic, fully accessorized look that black women considered essential for church.

Melvin Jr. lit up at the sight of Bertha and started toward her with wide-open arms, but her stern look knocked the wind out of him. Backing off, he wiped the hurt from his face as best he could, while holding up his hands as if to say, "Have it your way."

"I *said* what are y'all doing here? Don't y'all have a church of your own to go to this morning? Don't know why you-all are out here all up in my business—and uninvited, I might add."

"Well, Bertha Kaye," Phoebe said, "we certainly do have our own church. But the question is, do you have a church of your own to go to? 'Cause this place certainly don't look like anywhere I'd go looking for someone like you, Cuz. So we came to find out why you're here."

"And because my daddy sent you."

"Well," Phoebe said, "what did you expect when he found out that you sashayed your big, wide butt out of a perfectly good church to come here?"

Bertha didn't want to deal with the biting truth of Phoebe's words. Trying to ignore the conviction in her heart, she lifted her hands up in praise mode and said, "Our church is one of acceptance and love. We give to You, O majestic Lord, the misguided sheep of the world."

"You trippin', Bertha Kaye," Phoebe huffed, not caring one bit about Big Missy and the others studying them like monkeys in a zoo.

Mr. Louis Loomis, who was growing tired of the stares,

turned to the crowd and said, "This is an A and B conversation—so C your way out of it."

Most of the onlookers started drifting away, but Big Missy and another woman decided to stand their ground. Big Missy said, "You people have no respect for anything, let alone God's own house."

Mr. Louis Loomis could see straight through this woman. He knew her type, black or white, red or green. She reminded him of Cleavon Johnson's mother, Vernine—all wrapped up in religion and just as mean and rude, nasty and ungodly-acting as can be. He said, "What would you know about how to act in God's house, holding on to the devil's hand like he your date?"

Big Missy turned on her heel and marched off, indignant over that old man's practically calling *her* a heathen.

Bertha herself kind of wished that her fellow members would just go away. She knew that her people didn't like this church, and she also knew that all four of them—Mr. Louis Loomis, Miss Sheba, Phoebe, and Melvin Jr.—loved a good fight. What better place for fight-loving people to be than here, where it would be easy to provoke a confrontation?

So she tried another, more peacemaking reproach. Smiling broadly, she said, "As much as I love you all, my sisters and brothers in the Lord—"

"Help her, Jesus," Mr. Louis Loomis prayed, hoping to cut off having to listen to nonsense. But Bertha was persistent. "I have to speak the truth. And the truth is that my old church, *your* church, has not transcended the muck and mire of wanting to keep the Body of the Lord segregated and separate. Gethsemane is a *black* church. And my church simply wants to be called 'church.' "

Sheba had to catch herself from popping "Girl, please" out of her mouth. Instead, she said, "Bertha Kaye, I think I speak for us all when I say that I like being a member of a black church. If a black church was good enough for Dr. Martin Luther King, Jr., it's show 'nough good enough for me."

Bertha knew she couldn't counter that, but she wasn't giving up without a try. Giving Sheba a dry-toast smile, she said, "Despite our obvious style differences, we shouldn't fight with each other."

When no one replied, she smiled a bit more brightly and added, "Come on, let me show you-all our bookstore—something few *all-black* churches have."

Phoebe sniffed in disgust, thinking that cut was a very low blow.

As Bertha led them down the corridor to the bookstore, Phoebe pointed to a large oil painting on the wall and asked, "Who is that?"

"Pastor Lyles. I think the portrait does him more justice than the TV."

"It does?" Phoebe said, studying the image of a bland-looking man with hard gray eyes.

"Yes," Bertha replied.

"Pity," Phoebe murmured. Rev. Lyles would have blended right into the background of the picture had he not been wearing a rich black silk robe, trimmed with the most beautiful silver material she had ever seen.

"Well," Bertha said, "Pastor Lyles may not have the look

that you-all like, but he certainly can preach like no one I've ever heard preach the word. He is so intellectual in his delivery—no emotionalism, no hollering and screaming. And when he speaks, he's so still, you hardly know he's moving."

"Makes you wonder if he's kinda dead, huh?" Melvin Jr. scoffed.

Deciding not to let Melvin Jr. get to her, Bertha explained with obvious patience, "Pastor Lyles preaches like he does because he prepared himself for the ministry in the wilderness."

"Humph," Mr. Louis Loomis said under his breath, "I need to sell you an acre of the Mississippi River, Bertha Kaye, if you really believe that craziness."

Melvin Jr. chuckled. "Fool," he said, "you got to know that chump ain't been training about nothing other than taking your money."

"What would you know, Melvin Jr.?" Bertha shot back. "You don't go to this church."

"Then tell me, Bertha. What wilderness he been out to? Ain't no wilderness to speak of out here."

"Well, Mr. Know-It-All Melvin Earl Vicks, Jr., *my* pastor trained in Montana. I know they got some wilderness out there."

Melvin Jr. laughed out loud. "Girl, ain't nothing in Montana but a bunch of cowboys hoping black folks can't find their way out there and come set up some rib shacks on their streets."

"Forget you, Melvin Jr. Didn't nobody invite you here to tell me about my church."

"You're right, Bertha Kaye," he answered in a mean, tight voice, "didn't *no-body worth mentioning* invite me here."

"Boy, you getting on my *very* last nerve," Bertha hissed at him.

"Ditto, baby," Melvin Jr. snarled. He curled his lip like he had a toothpick sticking out of his mouth and shot Bertha a cocky glance—the kind brothers give sisters when they're standing on the corner with their boys, acting cool and checking out "the scenery."

Bertha was furious and thoroughly embarrassed. Seeing the ruby tint on her cheeks, Melvin Jr. smirked, then flashed her a searching look that made Bertha turn away, all fidgety and breathless. Fists clenched, she started walking off with fast, prissy steps.

When she reached the Abundant Grace Bookstore, Bertha snatched open the door and stood there fuming as they all piled in. Now, for the first time—which was surprising, since Bertha always paid attention to people's clothes—she took a good look at what her visitors were wearing. That fact alone let her know just how bad those four had been acting all morning.

Mr. Louis Loomis' had on a suit with "Sears" written all over it. If he didn't love himself some Sears, Bertha didn't know who did. Miss Sheba's outfit was so loud you needed some shades to block out the glare. And Melvin Jr., much to her chagrin, was as sharp as ever. His three-inch Afro was groomed to perfection, his sideburns and mustache trimmed neatly, and the mint green leisure suit he was wearing fit him like a glove, highlighting every muscle in his arms and thighs. To take her mind off the man's thighs, Bertha dropped her eyes down to his forest green leather platform shoes. Melvin Jr. was just too fine for his own good.

Then she cast an eye over Phoebe, who was wearing a classy red knit dress.

"Why you staring me down like that, Bertha? Something wrong with the way I look?"

"No, I like your outfit," she told her cousin. "But why did you pick that color?"

"Red is my favorite color. You know that."

"It may be your favorite color but red is a color black women do not need to wear," Bertha said, knowing full well that she was only picking a fight with Phoebe to get her mind off Melvin Jr.

"And why is that?" Phoebe demanded.

"Well," Bertha said, with great care in her voice, "Pastor Lyles once told me that red is too alluring on black women—especially real brown ones like us. Red on brown women can raise illicit passions in some men, even in this church—men who would otherwise remain chaste and brotherly in their thoughts."

"Well, I don't know about all that, Cuz, since the men at *my* church don't think like that. Your pastor must be kind of freaky-deaky to even think up that kind of junk. Any man who think like that up in this warehouse y'all call a church ain't nothing but a nasty coyote, who wouldn't know the Lord if He smacked him upside the head so hard it gave him an Afro."

"Lower your voice," Bertha told Phoebe. "This is my church and these men are my brothers in the Lord."

"Brothers, huh? What brothers you see up in here, other

than Melvin Jr. and Mr. Louis Loomis? Show me these *brothers* you so worried about, Bertha Kaye."

"Well, there is one family . . ."

"You mean that Oreo with his wife and kids?" Sheba said. "The one who prancing around here with his butt so tight, he need Ex-Lax just to take a step?"

"Why don't y'all have any black men at this church, Bertha Kaye?" Mr. Louis Loomis asked with some concern.

Bertha sighed with just a tad bit more drama than necessary. "I don't know, Mr. Louis Loomis. Perhaps this church isn't right for them." She tried to force a cheery smile onto her face. "But then, I do keep praying that the Lord will send a brother to this church who has what it takes to become a full-fledged member. I am hoping to find a good Christian man here."

At those words, Melvin Jr. looked very hurt, then mad, and stormed off to another section of the store.

"Now look at what you just did," Phoebe scolded. "You out here in Mayberry looking for a good brother and you just ran off one with your foolishness. Bertha, you must have faith like Abraham, when God sent him a ram in the bush, to believe you gone find a brother worth having up in here."

Bertha's eyes followed Melvin Jr. across the store until he disappeared behind a shelf of Bibles. She was teary for a second, and then said with a cheerfulness that sounded forced at best, "Let's take a look around the store—it has everything imaginable."

Ironically, the store did have everything. It just didn't have everything imaginable, because nobody imagined anything black to put on the shelves. Leading them to the music section, Bertha started pulling out albums and eight-track tapes she wanted them to look at. She handed Mr. Louis Loomis, who only liked old-time bluesy-sounding gospel, an album of hymns by Hubert Westerlake, a St. Louis baritone who thought he could sing like Tennessee Ernie Ford. Mr. Louis Loomis couldn't even bear to take it from her hand, so he just let the album fall to the floor.

Sheba picked up an eight-track tape by the American Worship Center Quintet. "Lawd, I know this is one messed-up store if they trying to sell this," she said. "Listen to the names of these songs: 'On a Hayride with God,' 'No Milk in My Coffee or Tea, Just Jesus the Lamb for Me,' and a Christian remake of the Bee Gees' 'Stayin' Alive.' "

Sheba was laughing so hard, she had to wipe her eyes. Bertha frowned at her and glanced around.

"Girl, quit worrying about those people," Sheba said. "You know that anybody, black or white, would think those songs sound stupid."

Melvin Jr. reappeared, frowning, and said, "It's almost ten forty-five. Does your church start at eleven, or are you all on a different and better schedule than the rest of us?"

"What do you think, Mr. Vicks Jr," Bertha snapped, "since you think you different and better than everybody?"

By now the hallway was filled with worshipers, all moving in the direction of the arrows marked "Sanctuary." Melvin Jr. started toward the bookstore door to join them but, glancing back, saw that Bertha had not moved. "You are planning on going to church, aren't you, Bertha Kaye?" he asked.

Bertha stood still, with both hands on her hips, for a long moment, as if to say, "You make me, Melvin Jr."

Melvin Jr. unbuttoned his suit jacket and hung his hands on the waistline of his pants, with his feet wide apart. All of a sudden, Bertha started moving toward the door real fast, as if she knew exactly what Melvin Jr. had just said.

"Those two are always fussing and fighting," Phoebe thought. "Why can't they see that they are crazy about each other?"

The one time she'd asked Bertha if she ever thought about Melvin Jr. as a boyfriend, all Bertha said was, "Phoebe, how I'm gone go with Melvin Jr.? Everybody at church know that we been fighting and talking about how much we can't stand each other since we were four years old. Now, how are we supposed to get around all of that and then step up in church with the nerve to be in love?"

III

"You sure the Holy Ghost can get in here this morning?" Mr. Louis Loomis asked, staring at the pictures of the deacons and assistant pastors on the wall. "Some of these people look like they would stand right at this door to the sanctuary and tell the Lord Himself, 'I dare You to come in.' "

Bertha pulled one of the heavy doors open and a stern-faced usher handed each of them a program.

"Isn't he going to lead us to our seats?" Phoebe whispered.

"No!" Bertha said, irritably. "Will you-all be quiet and just sit down? Good Lawd, don't take all of this drama to walk in church and sit down."

"Speaking of drama, missy," Mr. Louis Loomis said quietly, letting her know he wasn't happy with that little outburst.

Ignoring him, Bertha asked, "But first does anyone have to go to the bathroom? If so, do it now. Pastor Lyles has the doors locked after service starts, to stop folks from running in and out distracting others."

"I just wish your pastor would try to stop me from going to the bathroom," Sheba said.

"Come on," Phoebe urged. "Let's just go sit down before my cousin here busts a gasket."

She started walking down the wide aisle, thinking that the inside of this church looked like a cross between a fancy movie theater and a convention center. The sanctuary had the same decorating scheme as the vestibule and the bookstore: white textured paint, pewter gray trim, and lush wall-to-wall black carpeting. The pulpit was a large stage, which Bertha proudly informed them revolved and had an orchestra pit that held up to a hundred musicians. Melvin Jr. looked at the orchestra pit, pointing out to Mr. Louis Loomis that it would be nice to have a big band to play for the men's chorus they were putting together, called the "KMs," short for the "King's Men."

There were no pews in the church, just black velvet chairs with impressive chrome trimming, which were very comfortable when Phoebe sank down in one.

"Don't sit there, Phoebe," Bertha said, pulling her cousin to her feet.

"Why not? I like this seat."

"We are sitting down closer because I am joining this church this morning."

"Say what?" Melvin Jr. asked, horrified, as Phoebe scowled in disbelief.

Mr. Louis Loomis and Sheba didn't say a word. They simply made eye contact, thinking, "We'll see about that, Miss Lady."

Bertha turned away and led them down to the front, past row upon row of white faces. "Lawd, girl," Mr. Louis Loomis told Sheba, "I show do hope this place don't catch-a-fire. 'Cause if all these white folks get to running out of this building, we dead."

Sheba laughed. "Yeah, it'll be just like a horror movie, when all the black people have to die before the movie music stops playing good."

Bertha sighed loudly and murmured, "Lord, give me strength."

They got settled in their seats, and then suddenly the lights in the pulpit became blazing bright, the orchestra pit rose up, and the two TV cameramen took their places. The stage floor rotated, and a huge choir that looked to be a hundred strong appeared, all draped in fancy black robes with silver brocade stoles and silver brocade edging their sleeves. Behind the choir was a large mirrored cross that reflected the changing colors of the blue, yellow, and red lights hanging over the stage.

As the orchestra struck up the first chords of the song, Phoebe strained her ears, thinking that the tune sounded familiar. When the choir started in on the first verse, it hit her that they were trying to sing Elroy Thorn and the Gospel Songbirds' newest song, "Faith Is Something Else."

But this rendition didn't sound *anything* like the original.

The choir had eradicated the beat so completely that Melvin Jr.'s mouth fell open as he leaned toward Phoebe saying, "How . . ."

"Lord knows, I don't know how they managed to do that one, son," Mr. Louis Loomis answered. "You gone have to consult the Lord on that. Although I fear even He gone be hard pressed to give you an answer."

The soloist took the microphone, and Bertha whispered, "That is Mrs. Lyles, the pastor's wife."

Four notes into Mrs. Lyles's solo, Mr. Louis Loomis whispered in a very loud voice, "That woman 'bout to run my pressure up so high, I'm gone have a stroke."

"Mr. Louis Loomis," Bertha said, hoping to quiet him. "Mrs. Lyles may not have the strongest voice but she does sing from her heart."

Just then Mrs. Lyles hit a high note that made her sound like she was choking on water going down the wrong way. Melvin Jr. sat straight up and exclaimed, "Oh no!"

Sheba, who had been studying on a way to make Bertha see that she did not need to be at this church, suddenly found it. When Mrs. Lyles strangled out another note, she stood up and started waving her arms around, hollering out, "Sing, girl, sing that song! Jesus!"

Pushing past the people in her row, she moved out into the side aisle, where she started doing the foot version of the Holy Ghost dance—hunching her shoulders up and down, with her arms tucked in at her sides and her feet moving real fast. Though it looked like she was doing an Irish jig—*Soul Train* style—her movements perfectly highlighted the faintest beats of the song.

Sheba's dancing so upset one church member that she put a handkerchief up to her mouth, as if she were trying to quell her nausea. Her husband stroked her back, saying, "Put your head down between your knees and try not to look at her until your stomach settles."

When Phoebe and Mr. Louis Loomis saw how disturbing Sheba's performance was to these people, they stood up and started clapping and shouting out, "Praise the Lord, everybody. Thank you, Jesus!"

Sheba sneaked a peek at all those mad folks staring at her, at Bertha's horrified face, and at one lone elderly husband and wife who looked positively inspired by her dancing. Seeing that old couple grinning and clapping, unmindful of their fellow members pulling them to sit down, convinced Sheba that what they all needed now was "Showtime at the Apollo."

She busted out and started doing the Four Corners, with her knees bent and her hips and legs rocking up and down, while shouting out, "Yes!" She then broke into the Camel Walk, pumping her body up and down the aisle, stepping like a camel on hot desert and calling out, "Jesus!"

Melvin Jr. was on his feet now, rocking to the beat to egg Sheba on. That infuriated Bertha, who started pushing out of the row, looking as fierce as her grandmother MamaLouise. So Sheba decided to wind up the show, signaling to Mr. Louis Loomis and Melvin Jr. that she was getting ready to "fall out." As they rushed to her side, she hissed, "Hat!" so they'd cradle her just right and keep her hat on her head, before she collapsed into their arms and was lowered gently to the floor.

As she lay there motionless, the church members muttered nervously among themselves, not sure if they should help that woman or leave her be. Finally one of the ushers tapped Mr. Louis Loomis on the shoulder and asked, "Do you think it would be safe to move her to the church infirmary, or should I call a doctor to examine her right here?"

"Jesus keep me near the cross," Mr. Louis Loomis thought, but told the man, "Son, she'll wake up and be just fine when the Holy Ghost gets finished running His course."

Thoroughly perplexed, the usher eased away, fearful of setting off another dangerous fit.

Bertha had returned to her seat, where she sat staring straight ahead with her lips pressed together, trying to act like what was happening not only *wasn't* happening but had absolutely nothing to do with her. It worried Phoebe to see the stubborn set of Bertha's jaw and the look of resolve on her face. To provoke a reaction from her cousin, she raised her arms up and said, "Jesus, let me get in that aisle! I need some of that Holy Ghost to rub off on me."

Climbing over Bertha, she reached down and touched Sheba's hand to "get herself some." Then she jerked her whole body back, waving her "touched" hand in the air, as if a jolt of electricity had hit her. "Awww, glory," Phoebe called out. "God is up in here this morning!"

Eyes still closed, Sheba flashed Phoebe a faint smile as she offered a silent prayer: "Father, be patient and have mercy on us. We mean no disrespect to Your house. But we had to create a flame where there was no flame, to set fire to this dry grassland and smoke the snakes clear out."

At that point, Sheba felt a current running through her

that was so powerful she had to pray to hold down a real shout.

After what felt like an eternity to Bertha, the song mercifully came to an end. Through it all, she had kept her eyes trained on the altar, unwilling to give her people the satisfaction of a single glance. To steady herself, she'd kept whispering, "Our church is one of acceptance and love" in a voice that was so weak and full of doubt, even she couldn't make herself buy into that nonsense.

IV

As the last chords of the song faded away, the orchestra pit sank back into the floor and the stage shifted, taking the choir with it. When it revolved back around, Pastor Ray Lyles was standing center stage with his arms stretched out toward the audience. The TV crew, who had turned off the cameras during Sheba's "show," now uncapped them and trained them on their pastor. Throughout the church, there were ripples of disappointment that Sheba's dancing and dramatic collapse hadn't been caught on tape for all their friends to see.

Ray Lyles wanted no such record of the disruption. As it was, those four blacks out in the aisle were such a sore sight that they made his head hurt. From the moment they'd arrived at his church, the deacons had been running in and out of his office with complaints, very upset that Bertha Green knew these people. One deacon had even whispered that he seriously hoped "Miss Green will not exercise her right to join this church at this time." His wife Priscilla (aka Big Missy) was still seething after her run-in with that hot-pink-wearing, overly plumed creature lying on the floor in some kind of black-church-related trance.

If Bertha Green had been anyone else, Ray Lyles would have publicly rebuked her and then told the ushers to show her and her crazy people to the back door. But he couldn't do that just yet. He needed a black like Bertha Green—badly—as a link between the American Worship Center and the fertile black church community in North St. Louis. Even the poorest blacks supported their churches, and Ray Lyles planned on getting himself a heaping helping of that sweet potato pie—building the American Worship Center into a national religious conglomerate with himself, a "po' white boy" from an impoverished white neighborhood in South St. Louis, as the CEO.

Ray Lyles had barely thought about black folk and North St. Louis until he'd made a surprising discovery. He had stumbled on a document in his wife Betsy's papers, making her heir to a plot of land in North St. Louis that would be eligible for repossession later this year. The land, which was located smack dab in the middle of black St. Louis, had an old church on it and was worth much more than he would have thought possible for that area. And then, amazingly, Bertha Green turned up. She not only came from the church resting on his wife's land, but her father was its head deacon, with considerable influence over what happened in and to that church.

The more Ray thought about it, the more it intrigued him to try to expand his empire into the least likely place, North

St. Louis. And when Bertha Green showed up, he recognized that she could be his front door key into a black North St. Louis church. But like any good thief in the night, he had the back door covered too—with the document restoring Betsy's right to the land when the grant of use expired—just in case the locks on the front door were changed.

And now, on the very morning Bertha Green had finally agreed to join the church, her people were here raising Cain, stroking his members' fears about blacks joining their congregation. He knew about people being slain in the Spirit, but this display seemed a bit extreme and ostentatious to him, even for blacks. He stared straight into the TV cameras, summoning an act of God to force a tight smile on his face, as he opened with his customary greeting: "Good morning, God's rightful children."

"Good morning, Pastor Lyles," his congregation answered politely.

"Saints, guests of the saints, and of course, prodigal children," he began, looking at his wife sitting in the choir section and drawing strength from her encouraging smile. Betsy Ashton Lyles was his right hand, and had helped him build this church from the ground up. Without her love and constant support, he knew he would still be clerking at a supermarket in Cahokia, Illinois.

Pastor Lyles smiled back at his wife and said, "I welcome you all to this Sunday morning service. I know that you are eager to hear what message God has laid on my heart. But before the Word of God comes to you from me, we have some important housekeeping business to attend to.

"In keeping with the tradition established when our

church was founded seven years ago, today is a special Sunday. It is Second Sunday, when anyone possessing a certificate from our esteemed Board of Deacons, confirming successful completion of the new member's training program, can be granted full membership, with all the rights thereof, in the American Worship Center.

"Now, I know that there are several of you sitting out there in the congregation with these certificates. And if the Lord has laid it upon your heart to join church today, I implore you to come forward and take your rightful place as a Child of the King in our beloved church.

"One young lady in particular," Lyles continued, smiling at Bertha, "has worked so diligently to earn what we at the center call our 'members' stripes' that I would like to call her forth to become one of our saints this morning."

All of a sudden, Pastor Lyles started coughing uncontrollably, and an usher hurried to get him a glass of water. Watching her soon-to-be pastor, Bertha was possessed by the uncanny feeling that the man was literally choking on his own words. She drew in a deep breath and gritted her teeth. Her folks, coming up in here and showing out, had to be the reason. Miss Sheba had been out, slain in the Spirit, so long that she could have had an in-depth conversation with each of the four-and-twenty elders in heaven.

"Bertha Kaye Green," Lyles said, gaining control of his cough, "represents an important step in the American Worship Center's mission. As you know, I have been working hard to bridge the gap between our church and the blacks' churches in St. Louis. This has been a difficult task, due to a poor response on their part. Our Father in heaven knows that it is long past the time when white Christians and blacks should attend separate churches. The fact that eleven A.M. on Sunday is the most segregated hour in America is a travesty. I don't know why the blacks are so resistant to worshiping with us."

At that point, a gurgle came from Sheba on the floor, which sounded almost like a muffled laugh. Then she suddenly came back from "being with the Lord," muttering, "Yes, Jesus. I hear you. I'll do just that. Thank You, Jesus. It was nice talking to You, too."

"But with prayer and faith," Pastor Lyles was saying, "and the help of good blacks like Bertha Green, we can all come together, unmindful of our differences, blind to color, and march forward with the banner of the American Worship Center raised high for the Lord."

"That boy is blind to any and everything that he has not set his sights on, like your pocketbook," Mr. Louis Loomis grumbled. "And about the only thing he marches forward to do is beg, beg, and beg some more on that TV show of his."

He gave Bertha a long, hard stare. "Babygirl, are you sure you want to be a part of this church?"

Phoebe placed a hand on her arm and said, "You are too hardheaded for your own good, Bertha Kaye. Mr. Louis Loomis is right—you don't need to be in this place."

Bertha was sick and tired of her folks trying to pressure her, but she was also nursing a deeper, secret anger. Because not a one of them, as much as they all claimed to love her—her daddy included—had an inkling of how heavy and burdened her heart was when she first left their church. It was a shame that Pastor Ray Lyles had picked up on her heartache before her own folks had a clue that something was wrong. Bertha started to rise from her seat to make the American Worship Center her new church home.

"Stand up, Bertha Kaye Green," Ray Lyles was saying. "Stand up and come to become right at the altar of the Lord."

As Bertha moved to step into the aisle, her folks got up to gather around her. But they were stopped short by a burly usher, who said loudly, "You people have been a problem since you walked into the Lord's house. That"—he gestured toward the stage—"is sacred ground. Don't incur the Lord's wrath or offend our members more than you already have. Now, *sit down.*"

A smattering of applause greeted his speech, which he acknowledged with a slight courtly bow. Then he extended his arm to a shamefaced Bertha to escort her onto the stage.

"Bertha Kaye," Mr. Louis Loomis declared loudly. "Don't you walk up on that stage with this devil. He's like that fool who threw Shadrach, Meshach, and Abednego into the fiery furnace."

Bertha hesitated, resisting the usher's hand on her elbow for a second. But when he tried again to propel her forward, she yielded with a very heavy heart. Joining church was supposed to be a joyous occasion. But Bertha felt worse now than when she'd first decided to run off from Gethsemane.

Tears came to her eyes as she prepared to walk up to the stage. And when Sheba saw them, she tugged at Mr. Louis Loomis's sleeve, insisting, "We can't let her go up there alone." Mr. Louis Loomis stood, and locking arms with

Sheba, he moved in close behind Bertha, with Melvin Jr. and Phoebe right on his heels.

As soon as Bertha was within arm's length, Pastor Lyles grabbed her hands to pull her forward, away from her people. But when he drew her to the right, they followed. When he yanked her to the left, they shifted too, mirroring his movements, close at her back. Finally, he gave it up, let go of Bertha's hands, and held out his own. An usher presented his Bible, which he accepted as, while opening it, he motioned for the congregation to stand.

"Saints, friends of saints, and"—looking directly at Bertha's entourage—"prodigal children. Our sister in the Lord stands here before us with a desire to be admitted into this great church."

Pastor Lyles turned toward Bertha. "Do you, Bertha Kaye Green, wish to become a full-fledged member of the American Worship Center?"

Bertha smiled feebly and mumbled yes in such a pitiful-sounding voice that Phoebe whispered, "Thank you, Lord." She knew that voice, which said, "I don't know how to get out of the corner I just backed my self into" loud and clear.

"Now, Bertha, you have worked harder than most to earn the right to become a member of this church—"

"I am sure she has," Sheba said out loud.

Pastor Lyles tried to ignore Sheba, but found it hard to stop staring at the plume on her hot pink hat. Then it struck him that her performance had been a blessing in disguise, a chance to offer the congregation a lesson. He continued, "Bertha, you came to us in need of salvation. And everyone in this sanctuary"—his eyes strayed to Bertha's people—"*al-*

most everyone here knows that you could not find God at your former church."

"What—," Mr Louis Loomis began.

"As children of God, we come to know Him through our minds, by studying His teachings, not through inflammatory sermons and sensual music that whips up the lowest passions. We have seen the effects of that kind of worship right here this morning in our church. A woman"—a touch of scorn crept into his voice—"with a crazy notion she was touched by God passed out here, just like a drunk. That is why Bertha Kaye Green has chosen to renounce her former church and join us in the light of truth."

Sheba was forming her mouth to get Ray Lyles straight when Bertha's voice rang out. "I ain't renouncin' nothin'. And you best quit shooting off at the mouth about Miss Sheba and my church." She put her hands on her hips and got up in his face.

Ray Lyles studied Bertha for a moment. He had never seen her sound or act so *black*.

"Thank you, Lord!" Phoebe called out, and slapped palms with Sheba.

Suddenly Bertha looked queasy. Tears streamed from her eyes and her shoulders began to heave. But then she managed to regain control.

"Bertha, are you feeling okay?" Lyles asked, concerned about her wave of nausea and momentarily forgetting her reversion to ghetto talk.

"Except for this morning sickness, I feel pretty good right now, thanks to you, Pastor Lyles."

"Morning sickness?" Ray Lyles repeated in dismay. The

last thing he wanted among his flock was an unmarried pregnant black woman. If word got out that women like that were welcome here, he might as well go outside and staple a great big welfare check right on the front door of the church.

"Yeah," Bertha answered with plenty of attitude in her voice. "You heard me as right as I heard you when you disrespected my church. *Morning sickness,* as in pregnant. And this *bro-tha* standing right here is my baby's daddy."

"I knew it," Sheba exclaimed. "Remember when I kept telling you about all those dreams about fish? I knew it, I knew it, I knew it."

"You sure did, babygirl," Mr. Louis Loomis said, shaking his head, wondering why Bertha hadn't told Melvin Jr., or even her own mama and daddy. Sometimes Bertha Kaye acted like she had rocks in her head, crowding up her brain so bad that she couldn't think straight.

For a moment Melvin Jr. looked relieved that Bertha had run off for a fathomable reason. But then he got mad. "Have you lost your mind?" he said. "Running off from me and your church to these wouldn't-know-Jesus-if-He-smacked-them-down-to-the-ground folks, talking 'bout how you looking for a good brother, with *my* baby in you."

Melvin Jr. ran his hand over his Afro and shook his head. "Girl, if you wasn't in a delicate condition, I'd sit down in a chair, turn you over my knee, and give you the spanking your daddy should have given your spoiled self years ago. Always did go off and do a bunch of foolishness. Used to make me mad when we was little, and you done made me spittin' mad now that we grown."

Bertha started crying. "Melvin Jr., I—"

Melvin held up his hand and, backing away, said, "I don't want to hear it, Bertha Kaye."

"But . . . ," Bertha sobbed. "Melvin Jr., wait!"

He stopped.

"How could I stay at Gethsemane, pregnant, alone, and Daddy the head deacon at church?"

Melvin Jr. walked over to Bertha and grabbed her by the shoulders. If she hadn't been pregnant, he would have shaken her until her teeth rattled. His heart ached as he asked her, "How could you think you would be alone? How could you think I didn't love you, girl?"

Bertha shook him off. "You never told me you loved me, Melvin. How was I supposed to know? If you didn't love me, how could I burden you with my baby?"

"*Our* baby, Bertha," Melvin Jr. said, opening his arms to her.

Crying hard, Bertha fell into his arms, reveling in the comfort of his embrace.

"I've always loved you," Melvin Jr. said. "Even when we were children, I loved you so much, baby, I thought you could see it in me."

"Well, Melvin," Bertha sniffled, "no matter what you might think I could see, I needed to hear it from you."

"Yeah, Melvin Jr.," Phoebe and Sheba said together, practically in tears themselves, "a woman needs to hear that from a man."

Ray Lyles stood there simply aghast at this drama, straight out of Catfish Row in *Porgy and Bess*, playing out in front of all of his parishioners.

"It's a good thing you are leaving, Miss Green," he said

coldly, "or else I would have had to put you out of my church. You deceived us, calling yourself a godly Christian woman when you were nothing but a promiscuous, pregnant, unmarried, black *girl.*"

"Now, just a minute," Melvin Jr. said, walking up in Ray Lyles's face. "You better apologize to Bertha now, or I will knock you clean across this stage."

"Are you threatening me in my church?" Lyles demanded. "Ushers!"

Twelve men in dark gray suits rushed toward the stage, one of them waving a baseball bat.

"Aww-naww," Mr. Louis Loomis said, taking off his suit coat and handing it to Phoebe. "Get Bertha Kaye out of here with that baby. She can't get hurt when we get to whipping tail."

Phoebe grabbed Bertha's arm and dragged her over to where Sheba was shedding her gloves and unpinning her hat to duke it out alongside the men.

A couple of the ushers were taking off their coats. The one with the bat stood next to his pastor, hitting it in the palm of his hand.

Mr. Louis Loomis reached for his belt and Melvin Jr. got down in a boxing position that would have intimidated Leon Spinks himself.

"That's enough," Ray Lyles said suddenly, disturbed by a vision of headlines about a racial assault in a white church. He knew how much blacks loved to capitalize on that kind of sensationalism.

Motioning for the ushers to back off, he approached Mr. Louis Loomis and Melvin Jr., fixing them with his preacher's glare. "It is because of people like you," he declared, "that the Body of Christ remains so separate."

Mr. Louis Loomis narrowed his eyes in anger and said, "Boy, do you really know why black folks keep the Body of Christ separate? It's because we know in our hearts that far too many of you cannot, will not, and don't want to welcome us in your churches. Today we've been stared at, scolded, insulted, and treated like we were heathens simply because the good Lord saw fit to make us black. Is that what you folks call being Christian enough to unite the Body of Christ?"

Melvin Jr. said, "Don't waste your breath on that man, Mr. Louis Loomis. Let's get out of here."

"You are not going anywhere until you apologize to Pastor Lyles and the members of this church," said the usher holding the bat in his hand, as he tried to block them from leaving.

Mr. Louis Loomis didn't even blink. He got still for a moment and then said, "I am going to ask you only once, devil, to get out of my way. And if you need any further instructions, I will take that bat right out of your hand and play ball with your head like I'm one of the St. Louis Cardinals."

The man turned red, put the bat down to his side, and moved aside.

Melvin Jr. made a point of dramatically shaking the dust from his feet in front of the congregation and then led his folks off the stage and out of a side door. Once they were outside, he grabbed Bertha's hand, laced his fingers through hers, and said, "Welcome home, Mrs. Vicks."

Ray Lyles watched the door close on Bertha Green. He could barely hear the murmurs, whispers, and "Oh dears" above his own thoughts. Never in a million years would he have imagined blacks traipsing up in his domain, challenging him, and trying to make him look like a fool.

"Well, as the saying goes," Ray thought, "he who laughs last, laughs best. And I am going to get my best last laugh if it's the last thing I do."

V

One month later, Phoebe sat at Bertha's kitchen table eating breakfast and feeling thankful. She was so happy that her cousin, whom she loved like a sister, had gotten back in her right mind, had rededicated her life to the Lord, and was marrying one of the nicest men Phoebe knew.

Bertha put her hands on her round tummy. "Phoebe, you think it's okay for me to have a big wedding being this pregnant?"

"What did Rev. Wilson say?"

"He said that I could have any kind of wedding I wanted, as long as it was in church, that I married Melvin Jr., and that I hurried up and got married before the baby came. Miss Sheba said the same thing."

"Miss Sheba?" Phoebe asked.

"Miss Sheba was in Rev. Wilson's office the first time I went to talk to him about the wedding."

"You know something?" Phoebe said, raising her eyebrows. "Miss Sheba sure does spend a lot of time talking to Rev. Wilson. At first you couldn't get her out of the club long enough to drive past church on her way home. But now that she's saved, you can't get her out of church *or* Rev. Wilson's office."

"I know," Bertha said. "I bet she got a thing for him. But I don't think that's so bad. Rev. Wilson *is* single, and I ain't never seen him with no girlfriend. And as weird as this is going to sound, he look like he something else behind closed doors. There's some kinda smoke in his eyes and his voice and his smile when he not acting preacherly."

Phoebe started laughing. "Girl, I thought it was just me. He does seem kinda hot underneath all that preacher stuff. And you're right about his voice. When he's out of that pulpit, he comes across real smooth."

"You know what I think?" Bertha said. "I think it would be the funniest thing if Miss Sheba and the pastor got hooked up and she wound up being our First Lady."

"You need to hush on that one, Bertha Kaye Green. Miss Sheba married to a preacher and the First Lady at our church?"

"It would be kind of fun to have Miss Sheba as the First Lady. Wouldn't you just love to see her get Mr. Cleavon straight?"

"Yeah," Phoebe answered. "That jive Negro is flat-out wrong—ain't worth nothing and think he the man. But I don't think he all that much a man. He run around but when he leave a woman, he don't seem to leave her all that sad."

"That's 'cause he ain't doing much o' nothing to those women," Bertha said. "Because when a man lay something on you, you can't keep away from him, and it'll make you act all crazy-like, especially if he leaves you. Remember when Granddaddy died?"

"Of course I do," Phoebe answered, remembering how MamaLouise lay down on the floor next to the casket, crying and talking about, "Kill me, God. Put me out of my misery. Lord, I cain't go on without my man." She grinned at Bertha. "You would act more tore up than MamaLouise if, heaven forbid, something happened to Melvin Jr."

"You sho' talkin' right on that one, Cuz. Because Melvin Jr. got what it takes to keep me running after him when we're supposed to be too old to run. I could be a hundred ten and I'd still be trying to trot over to that man."

She started trotting around the kitchen like she was an old woman chasing Melvin Jr., lifting her leg up in the air every time she pretended to catch him.

Phoebe broke out laughing, watching Bertha cut the fool, saying, "You crazy, girl. You know your pregnant self is crazy."

Bertha chuckled and kept trotting around the kitchen, calling in a fake old-lady voice, "Come on, baby. Come on, Big Daddy."

Phoebe shook her head. Even when they were little girls, Bertha would always do something crazy to make her laugh. Seeing her cousin act so silly and so content, Phoebe wondered why she would run off to the American Worship Center, when it was so obvious Gethsemane was where she was meant to be.

"Why did you leave us, Bertha? You said it was because you were pregnant. But you had to know that we all would have understood and prayed for you and Melvin Jr."

Bertha stopped clowning as the impact of Phoebe's words hit her. She got quiet and her eyes filled with tears. Picking up a paper towel, she dabbed at them and said, "Phoebe, I've been wondering that myself, for the longest time. I think it was because I felt so unworthy to stay at Gethsemane. I knew better, but I went over to Melvin Jr.'s home and lost my little mind. I am a woman of God. I was supposed to help set an example for Melvin Jr., not go and do everything I was grown enough to do."

Phoebe kind of leaned back in her chair and looked at Bertha as if to say, "Just how 'grown' were you?"

"*GROWN*," said Bertha, reading her mind.

"I see, I see," Phoebe said, thinking that Bertha and Melvin Jr. needed to hurry up and get married. Melvin Jr. was mannish and Bertha, prissy as can be, was secretly a red-hot mama.

"So it was like a punishment," Bertha went on. "It's like I had to give up something I loved to pay for what I had done."

Phoebe studied her cousin a moment and said evenly, "Bertha, what right did you have to take matters into your own hands? I wasn't aware that God had turned in His resignation letter. He still on the throne, I believe."

Bertha couldn't say anything, because Phoebe was right. She should have gotten on her knees and prayed or gone straight to Rev. Wilson. Bertha had known she was headed for trouble with Melvin Jr. the very first time he stopped one of their fights with a kiss.

"Bertha," Phoebe said, breaking the silence. "Tell me something. When did you and Melvin Jr. ever stop fighting long enough to get *grown*?"

"We were fussing when it happened," Bertha whispered, embarrassed.

Phoebe started cracking up. "You and Melvin Jr. are the only people I know who would get *that mad* at each other."

"Well," Bertha said, stroking her chin like she was a brother on the corner. "What can I say? Some folks get mad, and *some* folks get *mad.*"

Part 3

Mr. Oscar

1

Learning a new church—its history, its business, and the needs of its congregation—was a difficult task under the best of circumstances. But when a pastor was faced with the demands of an anniversary *and* constant conflict and opposition from a fierce opponent like Cleavon Johnson, the job could be near to impossible.

George Wilson had grown weary of Cleavon and his bulldog determination to control Gethsemane and run him out of the pulpit. About the only consolation George had was his faith that somehow, some way, the Lord was going to see him through this raging storm.

Cleavon Johnson had launched his line of attacks on George almost as soon as the man put his key in the church office door. And the assaults had been both creative and nonstop. The utilities were cut off just when George was scheduled to move in, forcing him to spend several days getting his lights, water, and heat turned back on. Then he had to scramble again when Cleavon's Finance Board let the pastor's health and car insurance lapse.

But petty warfare was only part of Cleavon's game. Late one Wednesday night, after prayer meeting, Cleavon sat in his car down the block from the church nibbling on one of Pompey's fat pig ear sandwiches and sipping on some Seagram's. When the last light in the church went out and Rev. Wilson had gone, Cleavon wrapped up what was left of his sandwich, drained his liquor flask, and slipped inside the pastor's office with the spare key no one knew he had.

With his flashlight propped on the desk, Cleavon quickly opened the pastor's safe and found exactly what he was looking for. Reading the papers under the light, he grinned from ear to ear.

"Umph, umph, umph. Whoo, baby!" he said breathlessly, sucking on his teeth like he was sampling something awfully good. With the papers safely stowed in his breast pocket, he closed the safe, finished his pig ear sandwich, tossed its greasy wrapper into the trash can, and left, chuckling to himself with pure, unadulterated satisfaction.

But the next morning, all George had to do was follow the stale smell of the pig ear sandwich remains to the trash can, where he discovered some wax paper with "Pompey's Rib Joint #Two" stamped on it. After examining the paper, George called Mr. Pompey Hawkins to ask if he had any idea who might have ordered a pig ear sandwich with lettuce and tomatoes.

"Lawd, Reverend," Pompey Hawkins said, "the only one of my customers who mess up a pig ear sandwich with lettuce and tomato is your church member, Cleavon Johnson. And he got that sandwich last night."

George's first inclination was to call Cleavon and jack him

up. But after thinking and praying on the matter, he called Phoebe Cates to take her up on her offer to serve as legal counsel for the church. Phoebe, who was itching for a fight with a member of the Johnson clan, immediately set out to issue Cleavon a court order for the contents of the safe.

But her grandmother MamaLouise pooh-poohed that tactic, saying, "Baby, this situation calls for a Negro law maneuver and not that fancy Perry Mason stuff. Phoebe, you have to get low-down and funky with Cleavon to get what you want from him. Because that's about all someone on his curbstone level understands."

Phoebe took her grandmother's advice to heart. She retrieved the pig ear sandwich wrapper from Rev. Wilson and stapled it to a note: "If you don't bring back whatever you took, I'm gone haul you off to court for breaking and entering, right after I crack that safe upside your big fat head."

When Cleavon discovered that greasy note tacked on his fancy and very expensive white front door, he had what Nettie called a "hissy fit." He snatched the note off the door and drove over to George's office, walked in without knocking, and threw the note, along with a brown envelope, right onto George's lap.

As interim pastor, George had never had the combination to the safe, so he had no idea what was in it. But his gut told him that if something was worth breaking into it to get, Cleavon would never return it without a fight. He opened the envelope and sifted through the contents twice, unable to shake the feeling that something was missing. He looked up at Cleavon and said, "Is this all of it?"

"And what if it isn't, George? How would you ever know?

And what could you do—get your babygirl lawyer to haul my butt to court?"

"Well, I just might, Cleavon," George said, never taking his eyes off of him.

"Is that right?" Cleavon said, thumbing his nose like he was getting ready for a fight.

"You the man," George answered calmly, then steered Cleavon to the door, shutting it in his face. Sighing heavily, he said, "I *really* need you, Lord," and then dialed up Bert Green to get the name of a good locksmith.

II

George had his hands so full, between Cleavon and the anniversary, that it took him a while to get fully up to speed on the needs of his congregation. Fortunately, there were other dutiful stewards of the Lord in the church who kept an eye on their fellow members and stood ready to step in with prayer and help if necessary.

One of those praying stewards was MamaLouise. And MamaLouise was led to take her friend and sister in the Lord, Mozelle Thomas, under her watch-care the day that Oscar, Mozelle's husband, retired from his job as a janitor at the Federal Building.

On his last day of work, Oscar cleaned out his locker and then went home to do what he had always done over the last forty years—pick on Mozelle. Sitting at the kitchen table with his hands folded, he watched her down on her hands and knees, cleaning out the bottom cabinets he had complained that morning were too messy. Mozelle hadn't expected him back so soon. It had barely been three hours since she had sent him off with a hearty "congratulations" breakfast. But when Mozelle didn't immediately stop what she was doing to attend to him, Oscar scraped his chair noisily on the floor and said nastily, "I been sitting here for six minutes now and you have yet to stop that nonsense."

Mozelle ignored her husband for one more minute, to give herself time to rein in her temper. The last thing she wanted or needed today was a fight with Oscar because she got angry and gave him "too much lip." She stood up and turned around to face him, bristling inside at the harsh expression she found.

"You hungry?" she managed to ask softly, hoping to soothe his irritation.

"What do you think?" he demanded, smacking his hand on the tabletop. "What do you think I been sitting here for? I could have starved to death while you were down there digging in that cabinet. You have to be the stupidest woman I have ever laid eyes on." He shook his head and raised his hands up in complete frustration. "I don't know why you don't know how to take care of me after all these years—"

"But, Oscar," Mozelle protested, "you just—"

"Shut up, Mozelle, and just forget it. I'll go and get myself something to eat with Christmas Jefferson."

"But Oscar . . ."

He stormed out of the house, slamming the door as hard as he could, leaving her with tears streaming down her cheeks. Mozelle had hoped that Oscar would be so happy about retiring from a job he hated that he would finally be able to celebrate life and enjoy her company. But here he was acting like he had just been told he would have to work all of his natural-born days, plus a couple hours more after he was dead.

As the weeks went by, not only did Oscar remain mean and sullen, he decided that the best way to spend his new-found spare time was to run around St. Louis posing as a big-shot player with his friend Christmas Jefferson. But being a bona fide St. Louis player required a lot more style and flash than what Oscar had. So the first thing Oscar did, with the encouragement of Christmas, was buy a brand-new, burnt orange Cadillac with white leather interior, shiny whitewall tires, and silver belt buckles running down the back of the trunk. Oscar even had a fancy eight-track tape recorder installed, along with top-of-the-line speakers, plus a shiny fake antenna on one of the windows, so that everybody would think he had a TV in his car.

The car itself put anything ever owned by Shaft, the Mack, or Superfly to shame. But when coupled with that outstanding sound system, it qualified as a genuine, super-bad "diggin' the scene with a gangsta lean" automobile. You could hear Bobby Blue Bland moaning and snorting about two blocks before you even saw Oscar in his new car. And to make sure everyone got a good look at him in that big smooth vehicle, he took to driving real slow, leaning down so low you could barely see the colored toothpicks he sported to match his shirts.

At first Mozelle tried to ignore what behind Oscar's back she called "his old-man shenanigans." Even though he was making a fool of himself, she felt that maybe he did deserve some time to be silly after all those years of hard work. So for a while Mozelle acted as if nothing had changed, and she rode around with Oscar in that loud orange car, never so much as blinking when folks honked and cussed them out because he was driving slow enough to block traffic.

Unfortunately, the burnt orange Cadillac was only a dark cloud heralding a breaking storm. Shortly after Oscar bought the car, he decided that he needed a new wardrobe. His good clothes—expensive and exquisitely tailored suits—just didn't look right with his new car. He ordered Mozelle to pack up all of those "old-timey" clothes in the cedar chest. And the next day, he and Christmas Jefferson went over to Londell's Men's Shop and picked out some pink, red, and lemon-lime polyester three-piece suits and coordinating brightly printed silk shirts with big collars; a turquoise leisure suit; and two fur-trimmed Superfly outfits, one in purple and one in powder blue.

Oscar inaugurated his new look on the Second Sunday in February, when everybody came to church to hear the Holy Rollers Choir. He timed his entrance carefully, waiting till the pastor and the choir were positioned at the back of the church, with the service about to begin. Poor Mozelle tried to hang back and ease into the church, but Oscar wasn't having that. He signaled for her to take her place slightly behind him. Then he ambled slowly down the center of the aisle, feet akimbo, cane in his right hand, a toothpick as purple as his suit hanging out of the left side of his mouth and his matching suede hat, trimmed with rabbit fur, tilted forward. The sanctuary was so quiet you could hear a pin before it dropped, when it was still tumbling through the air.

"Oscar Lee," Mozelle whispered nervously, her voice cutting through the silence, "our pastor needs for us to move so the service can start."

"Shut up," he hissed through his teeth, and then proceeded slowly to his seat.

Rev. Wilson stood at the back of the church, trying to decide whether to see how far this fool would go or to order him to sit down. "See how far this fool would go" won out, and George let the show roll. George was glad that he did, too, because he would have kicked himself if he had stopped Mr. Oscar Thomas in his tracks and cut off the second half of this performance.

Oscar strutted down the aisle and stopped at the pew where MamaLouise and Mr. Louis Loomis were sitting. He nodded for Mozelle to take her seat, while he stood straightening the wide lapels of his coat and correcting the angle of his hat. Then he pulled a lime green silk handkerchief out of his breast pocket and, bending over, dusted off his shoes. Finally he balled up the handkerchief and tossed it in Mozelle's lap, gave an usher the "Black Power" sign, and sat down.

"About time," Phoebe whispered to Bertha. "And check out those clothes."

"Yeah, about only thing missing on Mr. Oscar's outfit," Bertha offered, "is a mouthful of gold 'teefuses.'"

"I heard that," Melvin Jr. said, laughing out loud and not caring who heard him. "You know something, y'all," he said, staring at Mr. Oscar, "I never noticed it before, but Mr. Oscar looks a whole lot like a ghetto version of Sammy Davis, Jr."

With one exception, the whole balcony crew—Phoebe, Bertha, Melvin Jr., Jackson Williams, and Melvin's sister, Rosie Johnson—started cracking up. Latham Johnson, Rosie's husband and Cleavon's nephew, sat with his arms folded across his chest, mouth all tight, wondering what was so funny about that old man in that tacky getup. He glanced over at his wife, still laughing with her brother, and scowled, thinking, "She is so ghetto."

George pulled out his handkerchief and wiped his face. All he really needed to do was wipe his eyes, but he didn't want his parishioners to figure out that he was laughing. He nodded at the organist and pianist to start playing, so tickled he could barely say, "I was glad when they said unto me, let us go into the house of the Lord."

MamaLouise could not believe that Oscar would walk up in church like that. He had cut the fool many a day, but this was a stretch, even for him. She leaned across Mozelle and whispered, "Oscar Lee, you gone remember Whose house you in and rest your hat?"

At first Oscar acted as if he didn't hear Louise. But his head was hot, and he didn't want to start perspiring, marring his own cool composure with a sweaty new suit. So he "rested" the hat on his knee, giving Mozelle cause to slip out a relieved sigh, and even to hope that Oscar had had his day and would behave during the rest of the service.

But that hope was short-lived. At collection time, Oscar hopped up, put his hat back on, grabbed his cane, and did an old-man version of the pimp-daddy walk down the aisle to drop a wad of bills into the basket. On the way back to his seat, he kept glancing to the left and right, hoping that the high rollers in the congregation would greet his new look with a few hand slaps. But nobody played into that nonsense. And in fact, later on, when Oscar "copped" one cool pose too many at the dinner, Katie Mae's grandmother announced, "Oscar Lee, I'm gone pray your strength, 'cause you must be mighty sick to carry on like you been doing all morning."

That made Oscar so mad that he huffed and puffed up, high-stepped himself over to the table where Mozelle was eating peacefully, and gave her a signal that it was time to go home. When she opened her mouth to protest, he whipped out another handkerchief—this one in lavender silk—to mop invisible sweat off his face and neck before he said, "Mozelle, when we get home, I want you to read Paul's Scriptures about how a wife is supposed to act."

Mozelle was about to defend herself, but when she saw Oscar bristling and turning as purple as his suit, she decided to avoid creating a scene. Louise was so outraged that she started to scold Oscar, but Mr. Louis Loomis shook his head no. Whatever she said would just be further provocation, which Oscar would probably take out on Mozelle.

Since no one at church had the sense enough to appreciate him or his new look, Oscar decided that he needed more sophisticated company. So, the very next morning, he called Christmas Jefferson to accept his offer to join that happening social organization for "senior and ultracool black men in St. Louis," the Mellow Slick Cougars Club. The club had a serious reputation, because a number of its elderly male members were known throughout the North Side as supersmooth ladies' men. And for Oscar, who had never been viewed as smooth or sexy, being invited to join this group of retired players was a dream come true.

As soon as Mozelle found out, she called Louise, hardly able to talk for crying so hard. "Girl, Oscar Lee done gone and lost his mind, joining that old good-timing Christmas Jefferson's Mellow Slick Cougars Club."

"Now, Mozelle, you know that is some country St. Louis mess," Louise said, just shaking her head at the phone. "The Mellow Slick Cougars Club? I sure wish I could have seen the old fool who made that one up. I bet he stayed up all night until he got just the right name with the right amount of chitlin flavor in it."

"Louise," Mozelle said, sniffling, but now with a chuckle in her voice, "you know your self ain't right."

"Well, if it smell like chitlins, then it is chitlins—or something worse. That club ain't about nothing, plain and simple. There's nothing wrong with our menfolk having a place of their own. But this Cougar Club mess they done concocted don't offer nobody nothing but a bad excuse to do wrong.

"And Mozelle, how in the world did Oscar Lee get into that club? Even with Christmas Jefferson sponsoring him, he ain't cool enough to be a Mellow Slick Cougar. Look at Christmas—*The World* newspaper is always reporting that he was seen here or there, at this dance, that club, this tavern opening, and at every thinkable celebration and sale over at Londell's Men's Shop. Oscar Lee ain't never had and never will have the kind of man-about-town exposure of a playboy like Christmas Jefferson."

"I was kind of thinking the same thing," Mozelle said. "Oscar's just too dry and stiff to be a successful player. He don't even know how to have a good time. But what I do think got him in the club was paying cash for a whole year's dues, and that car—a lot of them liked the car, especially the color. At least, that is what I overheard Old Daddy, the founder of the club, saying when he came by the house to tell Oscar he was in. When they saw his car, they felt that he really did have enough cool and style to be a Mellow Slick Cougar."

"Old Daddy?" Louise said. "Girl, *what* is his real name?"

"I don't think I ever heard. He been Old Daddy for as long as I've known him. And girl, how old is Old Daddy, anyway?"

"Old," Louise answered her. "Louis Loomis almost seventy-six and he said Old Daddy is a good fifteen years older than him."

"You lying, Louise. That man past ninety?"

"Umm-hmm. But he show don't look it. And Lord knows he show don't act it, the way he keep some little fifty-year-old hanging on his arm."

"Girl, you saying something. 'Cause come to tell it, I ain't never seen Old Daddy with a woman old enough to have gone through the complete change. She might be playing with it but she ain't changed nothing yet. Just like that mean Warlene girl he rumored to be fooling around with."

Louise snickered. "You know, last thing I want to do is talk down in Old Daddy's pants," she said. "But he like Lazarus or something. 'Cause if he got them little chickies all up on him, child, *something* getting called back from the dead."

"Ooh, Louise Williams! You ought to be ashamed of yourself."

"Well, I ain't."

Mozelle was giggling so hard, she almost forgot about her troubles with Oscar.

Louise got a bit more serious and said, "You know something, girl. We need to figure ourselves a way to get up in that club. I want to see with my own eyes what is so *mel-low* about the Mellow Slick Cougars Club."

"You and me both. But you know that is the last place Oscar Lee Thomas would ever want me to be."

"Well, that is just too bad. 'Cause we gone get into that club, and Oscar Lee Thomas won't be able to do a thing about it."

III

Soon after joining the Mellow Slick Cougars Club, Oscar started acting like Mozelle was to blame for every unhappiness he ever suffered in his life. Just to be mean, he refused to take her anywhere—not to church, not to the grocery store, not to the doctor, and definitely not to visit her friends. The one time Mozelle, who couldn't drive, confronted him, he picked up his car keys, dangled them up under her nose, and said, "If you think I'm your chauffeur, you thinking like Caesar. And everybody know what happened to him."

So Louise, fed up and thoroughly disgusted with Oscar, started driving Mozelle wherever she needed to go. For as she told her friend, "Girl, there ain't no way I'm leaving you at home buried in all of Oscar Lee's garbage."

Louise's intervention came right on time, too, for it got Mozelle to church one Sunday when Rev. Wilson happened to preach the very sermon she needed to hear.

The morning's service was hot from the start that morning, with the Holy Rollers and Sister Hershey Jones performing "His Eye Is on the Sparrow." Hershey's singing had folks up and running around that sanctuary with such fervor that Mr. Louis Loomis whispered to MamaLouise, "Lawd, these people acting like they at the Twelve Tribes of Israel Holiness Church down the street."

Louise nodded. The Twelve Tribes didn't play. Sometimes they came out the church doors still shouting after service was over, and this morning, Gethsemane was in the same mood. Bertha got the Holy Ghost, fell out, and almost gave poor Melvin Jr. a heart attack. When she came to, he helped her up off the floor, just fussing. "Baby, next time you go in your prayer closet, you need to consult the Lord about the effect of falling out like that on the baby."

The singing and shouting comforted and strengthened Mozelle, filling her with the kind of peace that can be an anchor in a raging storm. And then George began to speak. "Church," he said, "we need to grow in the Lord, to expand in our stewardship and ministries, especially in the neighborhood we have been called upon to serve. But before we can do all of that, we must get right with God. And y'all know that Gethsemane has some serious work to do in that area."

Where there had been plenty of noise and shouting just

minutes before, silence fell, as the congregation tried to digest those words. Clearly Rev. Wilson had struck a nerve, highlighting the political dissension in the church. But the rancor he was talking about also described Mozelle's marriage, Louise thought.

"Now, Gethsemane," George was saying, "there's not a person sitting in here who doesn't have a sense of what can happen if the core and foundation of something isn't rock solid. And for a church to embark upon any venture without first being filled with the Holy Ghost and seeking direction from the Lord, both as individuals and as a Christian body, is crazy. You do something like that, you might as well stand up and then go and deliberately fall flat on your own face.

"So, before this church goes anywhere under my leadership, we gone do some good old-fashioned, country spring-cleaning up in here. And y'all know exactly what I'm talkin' 'bout, too. It's the kind of cleaning your grandmothers made you do. Taking rugs outside to be beat and purified in the sunshine. Cleaning down in every nook and cranny, getting rid of clutter and junk and anything else you don't need. You have to do that first, before you can put your house in order.

"What we need, Gethsemane, is a rejuvenation of the very soul of this church. We all, myself included, got to get rededicated to the Lord."

As Louise listened, she kept envisioning Mozelle doing a spring-cleaning of her marriage and her life. Sometimes trials came to you not to make life bad but to get you moving to the next level. After the service, as she pulled the car out of the parking space that her two sons-in-law, Bert and Wendell, always made sure was waiting for her on Sunday morning, Louise formed her mouth to speak the words that had come into her heart.

"Mozelle, we've been friends since the fifth grade down in Falcon, Mississippi, when we beat up that bully Eugene Willie White for taking your biscuit, fried fatback, and molasses sandwich."

Mozelle smiled. How could she forget that fight with Eugene Willie White? He knew she loved fried fatback on a biscuit with molasses all over it, and he went and took it anyway. She and Louise had to "tear that boy up."

"That's a long time for girls our age," Louise was saying. "But lately, you been getting on my nerves, acting like you actin' over Oscar Lee."

At first Mozelle was kind of hurt, then she got mad. "Fine friend you are, Louise Williams," she said, "to talk 'bout how I'm acting. You had a good marriage with Joseph, and now that he's gone, you done found yourself another good man. So what do you know about the kind of sorrow, loneliness, and heartache that cause me to act the way I do?"

Louise almost stopped driving the car right in the middle of Kingshighway Boulevard. She was shocked to learn that Mozelle knew she had a man. She had been so smooth that not even her nosy daughters, Nettie and Viola, or those two busy granddaughters of hers had gotten wind of it. Lord knows her youngest grandbaby, Bertha Kaye, was always trying to get all up in her business, as if her "Miss-I'm-Gone-Get-Me-a-Baby" self didn't have her hands full.

Mozelle seemed to read her thoughts. She said, "How they gone peep you out, Louise, when they ain't never really seen more than a passing glimpse of that side of you?"

"Huh?"

"You wondering how I know about you and Louis Loomis, when your own children don't have a clue—think you walking around all by your lonesome with nothing but a Bible and a prayer to ease your troubled mind. But girl, this me—Mozelle. I know how you act when you smellin' yourself over a man. Remember, I used to help you sneak out the house to be all up on Joseph and kissing him, when we were young."

Louise blushed. She had only recently started dating Louis Loomis. She'd felt kind of bad about not telling Mozelle but thought it best to wait until some of this turmoil with Oscar had blown over.

"I know," Mozelle went on matter-of-factly, "because you actin' frisky, 'cause you called him 'Louis'—something nobody at our church has done since his wife died—and 'cause he looks at you like he a biscuit and you some gravy he want to sop up."

Louise was glad they had reached a stoplight, because she was laughing too hard to drive. Mozelle was always funny. Folks just rarely saw it, especially when Oscar was around. He didn't have much of a sense of humor and didn't seem to appreciate it in her, either. The look on Mozelle's face warmed her heart, because she had what Louise called her "Little Imp" expression.

"Well, I see you on your way back to the land of the living, because you got some mischief bubbling up in you. So I guess now is as good a time as any to ask you—what's up with that husband of yours?"

"Oscar having an affair with some young woman named Queenie Tyler, who he met over at the club."

"No!" Louise said. "He know his old rusty, Cornhusker behind need to quit. Just how young *is* this little heifer, anyway?"

"That heifer ain't hardly 'little' from what I've heard. And she's about forty or so, somewhere close to our oldest daughter Dee Dee's age."

Louise was just plain disgusted with Oscar Lee, having the nerve to be laying up with a woman who probably went to high school with Dee Dee. She said, "Oscar Lee know he wrong as two left shoes."

"I know," Mozelle said miserably.

Louise pulled into a parking space in front of Mozelle's house, relieved that the burnt orange Cadillac was nowhere to be seen. They walked into the house and dropped their purses on the couch, then Louise headed straight for the kitchen while Mozelle went to change her clothes. After a good look around to make absolutely sure Oscar wasn't there, Louise sat down at the table until Mozelle came back, looking comfortable in a soft pink cotton duster. She opened the refrigerator and took out a colander full of chicken waiting to be fried and started making up the batter and seasoning. She put water on to heat for her pole beans, then stuck the macaroni and cheese she had mixed up last night into the oven to bake.

Louise got up and poured herself some of Mozelle's special "dress-up tea," made with top-secret ingredients. Nobody knew what Mozelle put in that tea, but it show did taste good.

"Kids coming over for dinner today?" Louise asked.

"No. Told them I wanted some quiet time. I'm not ready to let them know things not right with me and they daddy."

She sat down across the table from Louise, and started to cry. "Louise, what have I done that is so wrong, to deserve this from Oscar Lee? I don't know what to do."

"Only thing you done wrong is fail to see that the problem doesn't lie with you. It's Oscar and it always has been Oscar. I've tried to tell you this for years, but every time I opened my mouth, you shushed me, 'cause you didn't want to hear a bad word about him. So, I guess the way he's running around now and showing his little narrow behind is a blessing in disguise."

"A blessing?" Mozelle said.

"Yes," Louise answered firmly, "a blessing. Sometimes storms are just making ways out of no-ways, clearing out what you don't need to make room for your true blessings to come pouring into your life. Quit resisting this storm, Mozelle. You trying to fight this battle all by yourself, but the Father is standing right here, ready and willing to help you. You just got to have the faith and courage to let the Lord do His job. Don't you think that the One who made the heavens and the earth and all the firmament knows what to do with a little banty-rooster like Oscar Lee Thomas? Our Father works in mysterious ways. No telling what wonders of mysteries He wants to work out in your life, if you will only let Him.

"And Mozelle, I just know the Lord leading me to help you. He always did like to enlist the help of his children, because He knows that we learn from helping others and doing His will."

All of a sudden Mozelle started laughing. If ever the Lord had a servant able and willing to get involved when somebody did somebody else wrong, it was Louise Williams. She said, "Louise, it's a good thing you wasn't around back in the Bible days. 'Cause you would have knocked that angel down, trying to get to Mary to tell her that she was about to miss her monthly cycle."

Louise tried to act like she didn't know what Mozelle was talking about. But after a moment, she had to laugh. Mozelle was right. If she were back in the Bible days, she would have run herself ragged.

"Well," Louise said, "if you up to working with a servant of the Lord, I'm up to getting you straight."

IV

The first thing Louise did was make an appointment for Mozelle at her hairdresser, instructing her to give Mozelle a snappy new cut, along with a rinse to make the silver in her hair shine and shimmer when she moved her head. She had Mozelle get her nails done and then took her to Essie Lee Clothiers, located on Delmar Avenue, right on the border of a suburb of St. Louis called University City. "Now," Louise said, "we gone get you some smooth Foxy Brown–looking clothes. If Oscar can walk around trying to look like the Mack, you sure as heck can walk around looking like Pam Grier."

As soon as they entered Essie Lee Clothiers, Mozelle's face lit up. It was the nicest and most welcoming store she had ever seen. When you stepped through the door, your feet sunk into a plush, pale purple carpet. The walls were painted a soft lavender, and the large picture window at the front of the store was framed with beautiful gray silk draperies and matching gray velvet cushions in the large window seat. Two purple suede sofas stood in the waiting area, surrounding a coffee table with a vase holding cream-colored roses. There were also beautiful lush plants in large clay pots hand-painted in silver, purple, and black in the corners of the waiting area and throughout the main section of the store.

And the music—a patron would never hurry with her shopping because the music was bad. This store was always filled with sounds that tickled the ears of its customers, music they would never hear in any other store: Evangelist Elroy Thorn and the Gospel Songbirds, the Canton Spirituals out of Mississippi, the Mighty Clouds of Joy, the Dells and Delfonics, Marvin Gaye and Tammy Terrell, the Temptations, Supremes, Four Tops and Impressions, Curtis Mayfield, Freda Payne, Ann Peebles, the "clean-up woman" Betty Wright, Big Johnnie Mae Carter and the Revue, Shirley Caesar, Aretha Franklin, and so many more.

But more than anything, it was the merchandise that distinguished Essie Lee Clothiers from all others. Everything—clothes, lingerie, hats, and accessories—was unique. Essie Simmons, an accomplished seamstress, designed many of the outfits herself, and she was building an impressive entourage of black designers who contributed other incredible clothes and hats to her inventory. She traveled all over the country, the Caribbean, and parts of West Africa, looking for items to stock her store.

The store manager, Precious Powers, came running over to them, grinning. "Miss Louise," she said, giving Mama-Louise a hug. "Is this my patient?"

Mozelle was about to indignantly say *"Patient?"* when Precious raised up a hand and stopped her before she got started.

"Miss Mozelle, this me, Precious."

Mozelle raised an eyebrow at Precious as if to say, "And?"

"Mozelle," Louise said, "Precious is that girl I told you 'bout who can really fix a woman up good when she need to get her man straight."

"Yeah, Miss Mozelle," Precious said. "Ever since I worked that miracle on my play sister, Saphronia James, women been coming to me for help."

"Saphronia James?" Mozelle asked. The name sounded familiar to her but she couldn't put a face with it.

"You know who she is, Mozelle," Louise reminded her. "She's Mother Laticia Harold's grandbaby. She used to be Saphronia McComb before she married Bishop Murcheson James's nephew, Rev. Lakewood James. He that boy who pastors Mount Moriah Gospel United Church, in Atlanta. Big church, with almost two thousand members."

"They have *over* two thousand members now, Miss Louise," Precious told them. "Lakewood is a good preacher and a wonderful man. But like I always tell Saphronia, better her than me with a preacher. Last thing I need is a case of preacheritis."

"I guess you *wouldn't* have preacheritis," Essie Simmons hollered out from her office, "with that husband of yours, Tyrone."

"You need to quit, with your little red self," Precious hollered back at her boss and friend. "You got preacheritis worse than anybody I know."

"Oh really?" Essie said, walking up behind Precious with a swatch of beautiful peach Ghanaian fabric in her hand. She was looking good in one of her own designs—yellow silk hip-hugger pants with large bell-bottoms, a snug-fitting white stretch lace body shirt with ruffled cuffs on the long sleeves, cream-colored wedge shoes with daisies stamped on the edges of platform soles, and a yellow silk ribbon tied around her reddish-brown Afro.

"Hey, Miss Louise," Essie said, embracing her. Then she turned to Miss Mozelle. "This your first time in my store, huh?"

"Sure is. And so far, I like everything I see."

"Well, you just wait till I get through with you," Precious said. "You gone look like a queen, Miss Mozelle."

Louise loved Essie's outfit. She always did think that Rev. Theophilus Simmons's wife was a pretty little country girl, with a lot of sass and style. And how Essie kept that figure after dropping three babies for that big chocolate man was a question on the minds of plenty of St. Louis churchwomen. She asked, "How's the Reverend, Essie?"

"Doing pretty good. The denomination keep him running a lot. Some folks want him to run for bishop at the next Triennial Conference, but he's holding out. Don't know how long that'll last, though."

"Well," Louise said, "we'll just have to keep him lifted in prayer. And you, Precious. How is *your* hubby?"

"Doing fine. He just a big ole sweetie pie," Precious said, grinning at just the thought of her bighearted, easygoing husband.

"He more than that," Essie stated matter-of-factly. "He is what I call a good black man who loves himself some Precious Powers. Miss Louise and Miss Mozelle, look at that girl's hand."

At first, Precious was bashful and hid her hand behind her back. But Essie tugged gently at her left arm and she put it out there for them to see. The ring was stunning, a one-carat diamond surrounded by eight sapphires, set in white gold.

Mozelle whistled and said, "Babygirl, that's what you call a *rang*. Your hubby want to make sure that all of these Negroes drooling over that rumpa-seat you got hanging off the back of you know they ain't got a chance."

"Yeah," Louise added. "I bet Tyrone sneaks and pees in y'all's front yard every morning before he heads out to work."

"What?" Precious and Essie said. They had heard some country stuff in their day, but this was a new one.

"You younguns," Mozelle said, shaking her head.

"It means that the boy marking off his territory. Haven't you ever seen how a boy dog will pee in his territory to run off all the other boy dogs?" Louise explained. "See, when another boy dog who got an inkling to come around his territory smell that pee, it stops him dead in his tracks. Lets him know that if he goes any further, he gone get his butt tore up."

"Sounds like you are talking 'bout *both* of our husbands with that one," Essie said.

"Umm-hmm," Precious agreed. "Because I know the Reverend probably cover every inch of your yard, every single morning."

Essie laughed. "You ain't right, Mrs. Powers. You know you ain't right."

"Now," Louise said, upon hearing Essie's reference to Precious's married name. "Miss Lady, I been wondering for some time how you found a man with the same last name as yours."

"I don't know, Miss Louise. I just did. But it makes life awfully convenient, don't it?" Precious answered. Then, smiling, she swooped up the pile of clothes she had picked out that morning after Louise called to say they were coming and started walking the two of them back to a large dressing room. In it was a lavender brocade love seat and a table for refreshments. Essie and Precious kept the store stocked with good things to eat—cakes, pies, and cookies, tiny finger sandwiches, chips, fruit-and-vegetable trays, juice, soda, tea, and coffee.

Precious arranged the clothes she had selected for Mozelle in color-coordinated piles. When she was satisfied, she went to get her customers some coffee and dessert. While she was gone, Louise held up a few outfits for Mozelle to begin trying on, each one pretty and perfect for her friend.

But all Mozelle could say, in the midst of all of those scrumptious clothes, was "Louise, I don't think these are the kind of outfits that Oscar would necessarily like or approve of."

Louise dropped the dress she was holding right on the floor and directed her eyes down to Mozelle's black old-lady oxford shoes. "Mozelle," she fussed, "do you honestly think his other woman, Queenie Tyler, wears the type of clothes that Oscar likes and approves of for *YOU*?"

Precious came back with a silver tray on which sat cups of coffee and slices of sweet potato pie with homemade whipped cream on top.

"Lord knows you right on that account, Miss Louise," she said. "I know Queenie Tyler. And Miss Mozelle, honey, if your man with Queenie Tyler, you need to pick from every pile of clothing I brought into this room."

Mozelle silently began trying on the clothes. She wound up getting every outfit Precious and Louise said looked good on her.

Once Mozelle's makeover was done to Louise's satisfaction, she enlisted Mr. Louis Loomis's help to teach Mozelle how to drive. Mozelle had a perfectly good Chevy sitting in the driveway, which Oscar no longer drove because he insisted it was for "old folks." Being able to drive would give Mozelle a lot more power and leverage. When Oscar got mad at her, which he was inevitably going to do, he couldn't punish her by refusing to take her anywhere. Plus, Louise reasoned, if Mozelle could get around without Oscar, he wouldn't know all of her business.

But Louise still wasn't through. She was hot and on a roll. Her next job as the "servant of the Lord" was to instruct Mozelle not to always be home waiting on Oscar after he had been out in the streets with Queenie Tyler. She also told her to quit cooking him big, extravagant meals every night.

Mozelle could really cook, and there were few places, other than Pompey's Rib Joint #Two, you could get food that tasted as good as hers. She always had a full meal going—pinto beans and ham hocks, fresh turnip greens, homemade pickled beets, salad with fresh garden tomatoes and green onions, corn bread, and caramel cake, to describe just one of her weeknight dinners. Folks would pull up to the curb in front of Mozelle's house and get hungry before they'd turned off the car engine.

But after too many nights of eating big meals alone and then giving the rest to neighbors so they wouldn't go to waste, Mozelle finally took Louise's advice. When she first started cooking lighter meals (all from scratch, of course), Oscar complained so, he like to have worried the perm out of her hair. His complaining got so bad that Mozelle almost broke down and went back on her promise to Louise. Then she was granted two blessings in disguise in a single night.

The first blessing came the night Oscar sat down to a delicious meal of homemade vegetable beef soup, rolls, tossed salad, and lemon cake with lemon jelly spread between each of the three layers. As soon as he took the first bite, he frowned and said, "Ahh, Mozelle, this here food cold. And this soup taste like horse pee."

At first Mozelle got teary. How could she have possibly cooked food that tasted that nasty? But those tears dried up in record time, when the Lord blessed her with the impetus to look at Oscar's bread. It was so hot, the butter was running down the sides of it and onto the plate. And if the food wasn't cold, it show didn't taste nasty, either.

Then that second blessing rolled right in behind the first. Queenie had taken to calling the house at a certain time each evening. If Mozelle answered the phone, she would hang up, wait five minutes, call back, and let the phone ring twice. When that happened, Oscar would stop whatever he was doing, hop up and run and shower, get dressed in one of his Superfly suits, and put on his most expensive cologne.

That night, when the phone rang, Mozelle looked up at the clock on the wall and then over at Oscar, who sat fidgeting in his seat, expecting her to answer it. Even though Oscar knew good and well that it was Queenie, he was so used to having Mozelle wait on him that he didn't even bother to interrupt his meal to intercept a call from his girlfriend. But the Lord had given Mozelle perfect peace to ignore that ringing phone, fix her plate, sit back down, and eat her dinner.

Grumbling about her laziness, Oscar threw his napkin down on the floor and went to answer the phone himself. After a brief exchange, he ran and got ready to go out, continuing to fuss about Mozelle until he left the house. As Mozelle stood on their front porch and watched him drive off, what Louise said about letting the Lord fight her battles came into her mind.

"Father," she prayed, "my heart is so full of pain, there are times when I can hardly take it. These tears been roaring through me like a raging flood for years and years and years and years. I'm tired, God, tired down to the bone. I'm tired of my husband being so mean to me. I'm tired of no man seeing me for just who I am and what I have to give. It hurts. And I don't want this pain, this man's trashy behavior, that woman calling my house, or anything close to it in my life anymore.

"Lord, You rolled back the Red Sea to let the Children of Israel cross and then sent the waters rushing in to drown their enemies. So, if You did all of that, surely You can help me with my problem and deal with one little black man. My troubles, my burdens, they are in Your hands, and I am trusting You to deliver me. In Jesus' name I pray, Lord. Amen."

It took about a week for the answer to that prayer to arrive on Mozelle's doorstep. Only then would she realize that the Lord had been delivering all along.

First, thanks to the work of His servant Louise, Mozelle was looking good—the makeup, the new hairstyle, and the new clothes showed off how cute she was, with that cute little figure and round butt still sitting up high like she was thirty-five. Even the pastor noticed it. One day after service, he stopped her and said, "Miss Mozelle, I don't know exactly what's going on with you. But I do know this—the Lord been working on you. You been walking up in this church turning many a deacon's head lately. Ain't nothing like a makeover from God."

Mozelle didn't know what to say to Rev. Wilson. She knew she was looking better than she had in a decade. But at that point she couldn't see it as the Lord's work on her behalf, because she was going through one of the most difficult periods of her life.

The change in Mozelle wasn't lost on Oscar, either. Not only did she look different, he was finding it increasingly difficult to waltz up in their house and rule over her. It upset him that Mozelle didn't seem fazed by all of his cutting up—that God was helping her resist breaking down under his tyranny. And each time Oscar threw a fit on Mozelle, she shed one less tear over him.

Oscar's friend Christmas Jefferson also started noticing how good Mozelle was looking lately. He'd always known of her fine character, but now he could see that she was a fine-looking woman too. Nothing like that combination, Christmas always said: a beautiful woman who was good stock. And since his friend Oscar was getting more action than the law allowed from Queenie Tyler, Christmas thought it might be worth hanging around Mozelle a bit more. Maybe she was lonesome and needed the comfort of a real man.

But Mozelle was sad, not crazy. She could see straight through Christmas Jefferson. He was a player down to the bone and would be one until the day he died. She told Louise over the phone, "Girl, why in the world would I want to trade in a mean old tight-butt for a trifling old buzzard? Louise, it's all I can do to hold on to my religion when Christmas around and not cuss him clean out. And as a matter of fact, next time he come creepin' 'round here, he gone get his self told."

Louise wasn't surprised by Christmas Jefferson's foolishness. But she told Mozelle, "I don't think you need to cuss Christmas out right now. Instead, next time he get all up in your face, ask him to take you to the Mellow Slick Cougars Club."

"Oh, Louise, I don't know," Mozelle said. "I don't know if

I want to make much trouble with Oscar. He would lose his mind if I came up in that club."

Louise blew air out of her mouth, right into the phone, as loud as she could. Sometimes Mozelle walked around like she had rocks up in her head.

"Mozelle, don't you want to know what is so special about this club, that it got your household all tore up? I know I would. How you gone get this thing straightened out if you don't know what you dealing with? Right now, all you got is pure speculation. And speculation, without fact, will put you at the losing end when you call Oscar on the carpet."

Mozelle got real quiet. It hadn't actually occurred to her that at some point she would be calling Oscar on the carpet. She couldn't even think of a time when she had confronted him, and wondered if she had it in her to do it. She sighed heavily, tired of all of this, wishing it would just go away. But she said, "I guess you have a point, Louise."

"I have more than a point, I am plain right and you know it. This mess has gone on long enough, and it's time you put a stop to it. Mozelle, you need to get into that club. To do that, you got to have an invitation from a member—a member like Christmas Jefferson."

"And what if he won't take me?"

"Mozelle, you been married to Oscar Lee too long. Don't you know how to butter a man up?"

"Louise! I ain't gone give that man no—"

"Mozelle, please. You know doggone well I ain't telling you to go off actin' like a street woman. Use your head, girl. What you need to do is cook Christmas a big dinner. He a bachelor and don't have nobody cookin' for him on a regular basis. You know how men love for a woman to fix them some food."

"Oh, so is that how you got next to Louis Loomis, Miss Louise?" Mozelle teased.

Louise blushed so hard, Mozelle could practically see it coming through the telephone. "Uh-huh. Thought so," Mozelle said. "You been cookin' for that boy. Ain't you been doin' that, girl?"

Louise giggled a little. "Well, I did whip up a little something for Louis, you know."

"Yeah, I know. He been looking better lately—like a man who got a woman taking care of him."

"Because he does have a woman looking after him. He got me."

V

Mozelle did as Louise suggested and cooked Christmas Jefferson a good old traditional chitlin dinner. The menu would have made any respectable black St. Louisan's mouth water: chitlins with a few hog maws mixed in, mustard and collard greens, a mustard-based potato salad, spaghetti, corn bread, and dessert. In this case, dessert was two lemon icebox pies—one for Christmas and another one for Oscar.

Having a fancy St. Louis chitlin dinner in the middle of the week put Oscar in such a good mood that he didn't pick at Miss Mozelle while he was eating. And the dinner was so good, he asked her if she would fix him an extra plate to take to the club, making Miss Mozelle wonder if he was taking those psychedelic drugs that so many people were concerned about. He had to be half out of his mind to believe it was okay or even safe to ask your wife to fix a plate for your woman.

But since she had some plans of her own, she cheerfully fixed the plate, making it look extra pretty and even including little packets of salt, pepper, and hot sauce, fancy paper napkins, and a plastic fork and knife. As she wrapped the food in wax paper, she also wondered about Queenie Tyler. She didn't know of too many women who would eat food a man brought to her piping hot from his wife's kitchen.

When Oscar had been gone a good hour, Christmas Jefferson pulled up in his shiny black Lincoln Continental and strutted up to the front door. He was dressed up extra special in a hot pink silk, Superfly maxi coat with matching pants, dark purple silk shirt with a matching tie, and a black hat with a pink and purple silk ribbon around the crown.

"Evenin', Mozelle darling," Christmas greeted her, in that smooth voice that blended the Mississippi Delta and North St. Louis street. "Mighty sweet of you to fix me a meal on a weeknight."

"Well, Christmas," Mozelle said carefully, "Sometimes you led to do something nice, and I was led to cook you dinner."

"I see," Christmas replied, and followed her into the kitchen.

When he took a seat at the table in the kitchen, Mozelle had to be careful not to stare too hard at his socks and shoes. They were so snazzy, they were kind of sexy-looking. He was wearing some sheer silk men's hosiery in hot pink with dark purple specks, and his shoes were made out of the softest, shiniest patent leather she had ever seen.

"No wonder Christmas has so many women," Mozelle thought. "I'd bet some money at the racetrack that boy starches his draws."

Mozelle watched Christmas carefully while she was fixing up his plate. When she knew he couldn't see her face clearly, she caught him looking at her bosom, hips, and thighs like he was thirsty and wanted a drink. When she faced him, Christmas checked himself and sat back in the chair, leaning on his elbow and gazing into her eyes. Unnerved, she quickly glanced down at the floor.

"Mozelle, darling, what made you invite me into your kitchen?" Christmas asked. "You ain't never fixed me a whole dinner before, and I don't know why you're changing up on me now."

He reached out and took her hand in his, letting his fingers slip through hers, down to her fingertips, caressing them just long enough to get away with it. Mozelle was surprised at how soft and strong Christmas Jefferson's fingers were. She had always thought that when a skirt-chasin' man like Christmas touched you, the mere idea that he had Bible knowledge of all those women would make you cringe. She felt just the opposite from his touch.

She jumped back from him so fast, he almost laughed, but he knew better. Mozelle Thomas was one of those good true-blue women. Any mockery or teasing about her lack of knowledge of men would scare her off.

Christmas couldn't help but think that Oscar Lee was a fool. How could the man have been married to this girl all these years and never seen the fire and passion in her? But then he remembered how Oscar kept his wife underfoot, making it impossible for him to even glimpse the real Mozelle. Christmas had seen her more deeply in these last few minutes, he figured, than Oscar had seen in over forty years of marriage.

He was tempted to call Mozelle's bluff about cooking him dinner. Christmas was a player from way back in the day, and he could always tell when a woman was up to something even when he didn't know what the something was. But he decided to play along with the girl. A St. Louis chitlin dinner on a weeknight, *plus* the chance to watch Mozelle work in her kitchen, got his nature going big time. When he'd been messing with her hand, he'd been glad his coat was folded over his lap and hid the physical changes she had caused in him. The girl had him feeling like he did when he was a young blood of forty.

"Mozelle, darling, this food smelling mighty good. You so sweet to pack it all nice and fancy for me. I don't get my food fixed up like this often. If there is anything that I can do for you to repay the favor, let me know."

"Well, I'm okay, Christmas."

"Naw, girl, I mean it. You need anything—*anything*—just tell me. I'm a gentleman and can't take advantage of your hard work with all of this good food."

He watched her fidget a bit, trying to figure out a way to ask him for what she really wanted. Mozelle was so cute and funny as she tried to work her way around him that Christmas was sorry when the truth came out.

"Well, Christmas, things not going well with me and

Oscar," Mozelle said. "And I was thinking that if I went to y'all's men's club, I would be able to figure out what's wrong."

Christmas had to fight to keep his eyes from narrowing into hard slits. Oscar, always that doggone Oscar Lee. What he wanted to tell her was that there wasn't nothing wrong with Oscar Lee Thomas, other than he was a selfish, narrow-minded fool who had been coochie-whipped by Queenie Tyler. But he held his peace and said as nicely as he could, "You wanna go tomorrow night, Mozelle?"

Actually, Christmas could have taken her tonight, but he decided that Friday would be better. If there was one night of the week when Oscar would show up with Queenie Tyler on his arm, it would be Friday. And if Mozelle wanted to see what was going on with Oscar Lee, he was going to give her an eyeful.

Mozelle thanked him, handed him the food, and walked Christmas to the front door. He slowed down his pace, deliberately trailing Mozelle so he could get himself a good eyeful of her behind. Christmas couldn't help but wonder if Oscar ever had sense enough to grab himself a good handful of that high little booty, with the girlish bounce still left in it. Then he thought, "Probably not."

VI

"Mozelle, Christmas gone be here in a little bit, and you still standing there, worrying and not getting dressed. Put on that new pantsuit you bought at Essie Lee Clothiers."

Mozelle held it up in front of her, just staring at herself and the suit in the long mirror in her bedroom. "Oh, I don't know about this, Louise. The suit fits real snug, and it's such a loud pink. I don't want to step up in that club looking like I'm some kind of floozy."

"And Queenie is just what a woman ought to be, right?"

Mozelle wanted to cry. She hated hearing about that Queenie.

"Get dressed," Louise insisted. "Ain't gone solve nothing standing there looking like Sad Sack. You know I want to help you get at Oscar awfully bad to spend more than a thought of my time with that triflin' old coot Christmas Jefferson. Don't know what all those women see in him. He whorish down to the bone, and I just cain't stand no whorish man, especially an old one. Run all around on a woman and when *her* nature get going, he through, and you cain't even pray him straight."

"Well," Mozelle said, "I think he got all those women because he smooth, got debonair in him, and can back up all he throw your way."

Now it was Louise's turn to stare, wondering how Mozelle knew so much about Christmas Jefferson.

"Close your mouth before a fly land in it," Mozelle told her. "I didn't do nothing. But last night when Christmas came by here to get his dinner, he made a smooth pass at me. Do you here me? *Smoooooth.* And if my old-lady eyes were serving me right, I don't think you'd have to pray up a thing. More like, wear yourself out trying to pray it back down."

Louise started laughing and said, "You wrong. This time you know you wrong, Mozelle Thomas."

"I may be wrong, but I show is *righttttt* on what I saw."

"Girl, what did the boy do, to make you so righttttt?"

"Not a whole lot on the surface. He just touched my fingertips and slipped his fingers through mine. Now, I ain't never been a bit more interested in Christmas Jefferson than I am in the man in the moon. But I will tell you this much—whatever he did with his fingers had so much heat and suggestin' in it, I almost jumped out of my house shoes when he did it. So, he know things that some men just don't know."

Louise started fanning herself and said, "Oooh, chile. Good thing I'm coming with you. He know I'm coming?"

"No," Mozelle said, finally starting to put on the suit.

Louise watched her acting so self-conscious, thinking that Mozelle didn't even have an inkling of how pretty she was, with her pale brown complexion, gray eyes, and shiny silver hair, cut in the cutest style to frame her pixie face. She was sure to draw attention from more men than Christmas Jefferson at the Mellow Slick Cougars Club, which is exactly what Louise was hoping for. Much as the truth might hurt, it was high time that Mozelle realized she could do better than that nasty, womanizing piece of work, Oscar Lee Thomas.

Louise sprayed Mozelle with some Estée Lauder perfume and fluffed her hair, examining her face to make sure she had on that reddish-pink lipstick she had told her to wear. Then, just when Mozelle started looking like she might chicken out of the plan, the doorbell rang. Louise answered it, tickled at the expression on Christmas Jefferson's face when he looked right into hers.

"Evenin', Christmas."

"Evenin' to you too, Louise," he said dryly, and followed her into the house.

"I really appreciate you taking me and Mozelle to the club tonight."

Christmas took his hat off and held it carefully by the brim. It was off-white with a gold ribbon around the crown, matching his white silk suit and the gold pinstripes running through it. Louise had to admit that Christmas was looking good tonight. Very few men would have had the sense to match up a gold and white pinstriped suit with a navy blue and white pinstriped shirt.

Christmas fingered his hat gingerly for a few seconds, then sucked on his side tooth and said, "Frankly, Louise, I wasn't aware that I had ex-ten-ded *you* an invitation to anywhere."

"Oh," Louise answered, "that's funny. *Mozelle* told me that you wouldn't mind if I came along. She thought we would have a nice evening going to the club together. Not like you and she were going on a date, seeing that she a married woman and all."

Christmas was furious, and the expression on his face betrayed it. But he reined himself in and said, with the slightest taste of "nice-nasty" in his voice, "Well, you know Mozelle, Louise. The girl always was too sweet for her own good."

"Yeah, she is that," Louise answered, thinking, "Old dog, you won't be sniffin' up on nothing tonight."

Louise and Christmas stood there facing off like boxers in the ring, waiting for the starting bell, until Mozelle walked into the living room. Car keys dangling from her hand, she asked, "Y'all ready to go?"

Christmas quickly ran his eyes over her, thinking how good she looked in that pink suit. He always knew Mozelle was cute, but dressed like this she was a fine little handful of woman. Moving quickly to the door, he held it open for her, then made a point of letting the screen door slam in Louise's face.

Taking Mozelle by the elbow, Christmas began to lead her to his car, hoping to make Louise feel so uncomfortable that she would change her mind about coming. But Mozelle pulled away from him gently and said, "I'm driving myself and Louise, Christmas. We'll follow you."

Christmas stopped dead in his tracks and glared at Louise, thinking, "I know you behind all of this." But Louise didn't blink an eye, smirk, or give any other little self-satisfied sign to let him know she had "one up on him." In that instant, Christmas realized that this arrangement was Mozelle's own doing, making him wonder what else Miss Lady had up her sleeve.

"How long you been driving, Mozelle?" he asked her.

"Long enough."

"Oscar know?"

"What do you think?"

Christmas knew full well that Oscar didn't have an inkling that his wife could drive. For the first time since he'd arrived at the house and found out Louise Williams was coming with them, he felt excited. The evening was turning out alright. Mozelle was looking good and sexy, she was coming to the club at his invitation, and she could drive. He couldn't even begin, by a long stretch of the imagination, to think about what Oscar would do when he discovered what was brewing right up under his nose. But he sure couldn't wait to get to the Mellow Slick Cougars Club to find out.

VII

Christmas pulled into the homemade gravel parking lot, which used to be a backyard, of the Mellow Slick Cougars Club. The club was located in a neat two-family flat over on Natural Bridge Avenue, not too far from Kingshighway. Old Daddy, the club's founder, lived in the upstairs apartment and used the first floor, along with a finished basement, for the club. There was nothing special about the building, which was exactly what the members liked about it. The club was exclusive, and they didn't want any folks not invited to come dropping in and getting on everybody's nerves.

Christmas got out to show Mozelle and Louise where to park and told them to wait for him while he parked his own car. But Louise was so eager to see the club, she walked right on in without him, dragging Mozelle with her. She spotted a table in a corner and pushed at Mozelle to sit down. Christmas came in looking for the two of them just as the bartender, who was also the bouncer, started to walk over to their table to ask them if they were with a club member.

After reassuring the bartender, Christmas sighed in exasperation and said, "Why didn't y'all wait on me like I told you to? You not even supposed to be up in here, Mozelle. If Oscar Lee finds out I'm the one who brought you here, he gone have a major fit."

"But won't Oscar be here tonight? It's Friday. Don't he come up in here most Fridays?" Louise asked, looking almost eager to see what Oscar would do when he saw Mozelle.

Christmas tried to look uncomfortable, as if he was about to reveal something that he just wished he didn't have to share. But he wasn't doing all that a good a job with his acting. Louise caught the little grin on his face as he opened his mouth to say, "Well, he do. But lately, seems like he been elsewhere some Fridays."

"And where's that?" Louise demanded.

Christmas removed his hat, scratched at his head, and said, "Now, y'all know I'm too much a gentleman to go 'round putting my buddy's business in the street."

"Even when the main person you talking to is the buddy's own wife?" Louise asked, with a frown.

Christmas cut his eyes at her. He never could *stand* that Louise Williams. She was bossy and thought she had rights women weren't supposed to have. She had messed up everything tonight, butting in on his date with Mozelle. He had wanted Oscar to see Mozelle, knowing he would act a complete fool over her coming to the club without his permission. And when Mozelle got all distraught, Christmas was going to be right at her side, ready to give her all the comfort she needed, throughout the night.

Rather than answer Louise, Christmas got up to tip the bartender, who was also the DJ, five dollars to play his favorite getting-next-to-a-woman song. As soon as the first notes of Jerry Butler's velvety voice came on, Christmas took Mozelle's hand and pulled her up for a dance. She looked back at Louise as if to say, "Now what do I do?" But all Louise did was wave her hand, indicating that a dance wouldn't hurt nobody.

Mozelle followed Christmas reluctantly, wondering, as she walked to the tiny dance floor, how long it took the men who'd laid the flooring to get the linoleum tiles in that perfect order of red, black, and gold squares. Everything in the club was red, black, and gold—even the napkins, paper plates, and stirrers for the drinks. She doubted that the members were so meticulous about order and color in their own homes. She'd have even bet some money that most of them acted like Oscar at home and didn't do a doggone thing.

As soon as they got onto the dance floor, Christmas pulled Mozelle close to him and started trying to do the slow drag dance, moving his hips up against her and rubbing his palms across the middle of her back. Mozelle stepped back, looking at him as if he was crazy, and said, "If you don't start dancing right, I'm sitting down."

Christmas wanted to get mad at her for breaking up his smooth moves, but he had waited so long to hold Mozelle Thomas that he wasn't going to allow a little setback to stop him. Besides, it was nearly time for the real show to begin—when Oscar walked in and saw his wife in another man's arms.

Finally the record ended, but not soon enough for Mozelle, who had been scanning the room anxiously to see if Oscar arrived. But he hadn't and she felt a stab of pain in her heart, thinking about where he was, who he was with, and what he was doing. Maybe coming to the club hadn't been a good idea. Maybe the truth was more than she could bear.

Christmas didn't notice Mozelle's sadness as he walked her back to their table. He was looking around to see if the club's lone waitress, Warlene, was on duty tonight. He didn't know who hired that girl, who had to be the surliest waitress in North St. Louis, with her high-yellow, dark-blue-eyed, and wavy-red-haired self. He would never forget the time she got mad at one of the members she dated for a while and as revenge refused to bring the rest of them so much as a chip of ice, because, as she said, "Y'all old Negroes workin' what's left of my last nerve. And I don't *feel* like gettin' none of y'all a doggone thang."

But Warlene could do no wrong in the eyes of the club's president, Old Daddy, who told all of them to leave her alone. And now that Oscar was hot and heavy with Warlene's best friend, Queenie Tyler, he, too, had become her defender.

Christmas waved at Warlene to come over and take their drink orders. Rolling her eyes, she moved as slowly as possible in their direction, stopping to talk to some folks along the way. Then, just as she finally reached their table, Oscar and Queenie Tyler walked in. Tossing her order pad and pencil down in front of Christmas, she ran over to talk to Queenie.

Christmas would have been furious if Warlene had run over to anyone except Oscar and Queenie. But this was the moment he had been waiting for all evening. He sneaked a glance over at Mozelle to gauge her reaction, but he couldn't see her face—she had moved her chair into the shadows so that Oscar wouldn't spot her right away.

Queenie shocked Mozelle right down to her bones. She was a full-figured woman, and looked like she was close to four inches taller than Oscar. And the way she was dressed? Throughout her entire marriage, Oscar had told Mozelle that the clothes she liked to wear were unfit for a decent woman. And if he truly believed that, then what Queenie was wearing should have been an abomination in the sight of God. Mozelle could see straight through Queenie's tight, turquoise fishnet dress to her matching flimsy slip, and right on down to her turquoise bra and bikini panties.

Mozelle leaned over and said to Louise, "What in the world would make a woman want to come out in public dressed like that?"

Louise shook her head and asked, "What in the world would make a man want to come out in public with a woman dressed like that? Girl, she show do look like one of those women who don't wash they behinds good."

Mozelle shook her head in disgust and said, "I was just thinking, Louise, that she making that dress look right funky. Remember what our mamas used to tell us about how some menfolk like to sniff all up on a funky-looking woman, and why?"

Louise laughed. "Honey, don't say another word," she said. It was rumored that such a woman was totally uninhibited in bed with a man, especially if the man belonged to somebody else. She had once overheard her grandmother whisper that one "funky-tail" woman in her town had worked a man over so good that his toes curled up so tight he couldn't get his shoes back on.

"Well," Mozelle said wryly, "look like what our mamas said was true. Don't it?"

Louise said, "Umm-hmm. 'Cause she look like if Oscar sniff too hard, the stuff will clear out his sinuses."

"And," Mozelle added with a touch of sadness in her voice, "I bet he walking 'round thinking he getting the ride of a lifetime."

As soon as Oscar and Queenie got settled near the bar, Christmas left Mozelle and Louise and headed over to their table. Louise figured that he wanted to feel Oscar out, so he could find the best way to let him know Mozelle was at the club. But she was not about to let Christmas get the upper hand in this mess. She whispered to Mozelle, "Get up and go over there and let Oscar know you here."

"He gone be mad. What do you think he'll do?"

"See, that's your problem—always worried about what Oscar'll think and what Oscar'll do. How can he say anything, standing over there all hugged up with that floppy-tailed woman? You get over there before Christmas make his move, and then dare Oscar to say anything to you. It's long past the time, Mozelle, for you to get Oscar Lee straightened out."

Mozelle got up slowly and walked over to her husband and his girlfriend's table. She didn't have the faintest idea what to say. On the one hand, looking at those two together was excruciatingly painful. On the other hand, Mozelle felt bold and excited, knowing that the next few minutes were going to change her life.

Queenie's eyes got big when she saw Mozelle Thomas bearing down on their table. Queenie had only seen Mozelle once, and from a distance. And never in a thousand years would she have expected to see such a proper and ladylike woman as Mozelle Thomas at the Mellow Slick Cougars Club. She looked down at her dress, mentally comparing it to the quality of Mozelle's beautiful suit.

Oscar was just registering Queenie's shock when he felt a tap on his shoulder. As he turned to look into the face of his wife, his heart started pounding like a jackhammer, and he almost hollered out loud. Grabbing his chest, he tried to steady his heart's erratic beat by panting out a few shallow breaths.

Once he could breathe again, he ran his tongue across his dentures, glad that he had added a little cement glue to his adhesive. Oscar needed to get his dentures readjusted because they had started slipping around. Without that extra glue, he knew, the shock of seeing Mozelle would have knocked his teeth right out of his mouth.

Regaining his composure, he angrily demanded, "What do you think you're doing here, Mozelle?"

"I was about to ask you the very same thing, Oscar," Mozelle replied, surprised at how calm her voice came out.

Oscar puffed up and shot her one of his fierce, chastising looks. But instead of lowering her eyes and fidgeting with an apology, Mozelle stood there motionless, just staring him in the eye.

"Who brought you here?" he asked.

"Why you want to know?" she replied.

"What did you say to me, woman?"

"I said, why do you want to know? You ain't never home because you so busy laying up with this trashy woman. So why you want to know, Oscar Lee Thomas?"

Queenie jumped up, towering over Mozelle, and then snapped her head around at Oscar. "I *know* you ain't about to stand here and let this little siddity-tailed woman talk to *me* like that, Oscar Thomas," she hissed.

Oscar opened his mouth to speak, but Mozelle put her hands on her hips and got right up in Queenie's face. "I know you not calling me out of my name," she declared, "standing there looking like some old reject from the Ike and Tina Turner Revue Band. I wasn't talking to you, so just shut your mouth and keep your young self out of grown folks' business."

Queenie raised her hand, open-palmed, to slap Mozelle, but Christmas, who had stepped back from the line of fire, grabbed it. "Now, darling," he said, "ain't no need in you getting all huffed up with Mozelle here. Oscar Lee is her husband."

"Husband? Not for long. Ain't that right, Oscar?" Queenie said smugly.

Oscar bowed his head and stared at his feet, not able to utter one word.

Queenie bent down and stuck her face right in his. "You better TELL her, Oscar Lee Thomas."

"Yeah, Oscar Lee Thomas. *Tell* me," Mozelle said, again amazing herself with the coolness in her voice.

By now everybody in the club was gearing up for a fight.

The DJ had cut the music off so they could all hear better, and those who'd been dancing had cleared the floor to allow unobstructed views. The silence hung heavy until Oscar managed to croak out, "Uhhh, Queenie, there ain't nothing to tell."

"What?"

"There ain't nothing to tell. I ain't leaving Mozelle after six babies and more than forty years."

Queenie stood frozen a few seconds, processing his words, then sprung to life with a roar. Sweating and huffing and puffing, she loomed over Oscar, howling, "Nothing to tell? NOTHING TO TELL? OLD fool, what you mean there ain't nothing to TELL!"

Oscar raised his hands, but before he could explain, Queenie yanked him up by the collar onto his feet. She cocked a big meaty fist covered with mood rings, hauled off, and punched him in the mouth, knocking him sprawling across the floor. He lay there on his back for a moment, then started scuttling around in his pink leisure suit trying to get back up. But with those heavy, four-inch platforms on his shoes, he could barely even lift his skinny little legs.

Queenie grabbed Oscar by the ankles to drag him around the room, intent on doing some real damage to his suit. She started swishing him back and forth like she was sweeping the floor, until some old Cougars pried him loose. But Queenie wasn't through. Blowing air out of her nose like a riled-up bull, she growled, "You kiss my big yellow behind, Oscar Thomas. I thought you was in love with me, always coming to me, telling me that your wife cut off relations with you ever since she gone through the change. Now, Miss

Mozelle don't hardly look like no uptight, no-relations woman. You ain't nothin' but a little black Raisinet-looking, no-good lyin' dawg."

Oscar was still struggling to get up. He looked over at Mozelle for help, but she just stood there, amused. That made Oscar spitting mad—and only spit came out when he tried to give her the tongue-lashing she deserved. His teeth were locked, and he couldn't open his mouth.

Apparently that cement glue he had used had dripped down through his dentures and stuck his top and bottom teeth together. All he could do was writhe on the ground on his back, humiliated to the point of tears, unable to call for help because his mouth was glued shut.

"What you got to say for yourself?" Queenie demanded, then answered, "Nothin'. Because there ain't jack you *can* say."

Watching Oscar flail around enraged Queenie even more, and she aimed a hard kick at one side of his narrow behind. Then she snatched at Christmas so hard, it felt like his arm would pop out of its socket, telling him, "Christmas, take me home." When he hesitated, not yet willing to abandon his plans for Mozelle, Queenie barked, "Now, Christmas, before I knock you down on the floor with Oscar and put my nasty shoe all over your high-priced Mack Daddy suit."

Oscar kept squirming on the floor, sweating and drooling, until it finally occurred to the bartender that he couldn't get up. He dragged Oscar to his feet, then propped him against the bar, where he leaned back breathing hard, pointing to his teeth, and gesturing with his head as if he were trying to say something. That's when Old Daddy, who had been standing off to the side sipping his scotch, recognized Oscar's predicament. Lifting Oscar's head to examine it more closely, he asked, "Oscar Lee, did you put some cement glue on your teeth?"

Oscar nodded vigorously, looking ready to cry, as Old Daddy shook his head in exasperation. "You dummy," he said, then turned to Mozelle. "Babygirl, take this fool to the hospital 'fore he kill his self sweating and spitting, trying to open his mouth."

Mozelle started to refuse, but Old Daddy just raised up his hand. "Little girl, I don't care what you might be feeling 'bout now. You got to take this here fool to the hospital. Oscar don't need to be like this. It ain't safe. You hear me, Mozelle?"

Mozelle sighed and agreed. Oscar, she realized now, had always been a pain. How she had stood him all these years was a mystery. And it was nothing short of an act of God that she had not tried to kill his mean self in his sleep.

Oscar looked around for someone to drive him to the hospital and was relieved when he saw Louise Williams. He got out his keys and jangled them at her, hoping she'd understand his message. But Mozelle grabbed Oscar by his arm and steered him outside to where her car was parked.

"EEEhhhh."

"Shut up, Oscar, and get your butt in this car."

His eyes opened wide. Mozelle had *never* mouthed off like that before.

She opened the back door and told him, "Get in." When Oscar looked at her like she was crazy for putting him in the backseat like a child, Mozelle just put her hands on her hips.

"You better get your tail in this car or I'm leaving you right here," she said.

Oscar raised his hand to slap her, but Mozelle didn't even flinch. She just drew back her fist and hissed, "I wish you would, Oscar Lee."

Grunting in outrage, he crawled into the backseat, and Louise let herself in the passenger door. But when Mozelle got into the driver's seat and started up the car, Oscar sat up straight in terror.

Mozelle peeked at Oscar in the rearview mirror as she asked, "Louise, what is the fastest way to get to Homer G. Phillips? Isn't that the best place in town for some triflin' craziness like this?"

"Umm-hmm," Louise said.

"EEEhhhhhhhhhhheeeehhhhhhh!!!!" Oscar shrieked. "Killer Phillips" was the black hospital in North St. Louis, where folks took you when you were shot, beat up, cut up, or all three. Despite its nickname, Homer G. Phillips provided fine medical care, especially to the poor, but Oscar didn't want to chance it. He kept banging on the backseat, demanding to be taken somewhere else, until Mozelle had finally had enough. She didn't even turn around when she said, "I told you to shut up. They got some good emergency doctors over there—best in the city—especially on a Friday night when some fools like yourself out gluing they dentures together."

Mozelle pulled up to the emergency entrance, where she helped Oscar out of the car, then gave Louise the keys to find a parking space. When they reached the intake desk Mozelle asked the young nurse, "Babygirl, please point me to where I need to go, so that I can get this old pimp-daddy fool's mouth fixed."

"Ma'am, I can start your paperwork, but he'll have to wait. We've had a couple of gunshot wounds and two stabbings come in over the past hour. Anybody with something that won't kill him has to wait."

Mozelle sighed impatiently and said, "Oh, alright."

Louise came in just as they were finishing up the paperwork and helped Mozelle lead Oscar to the waiting area. She could tell that Oscar's mouth and jaw were aching pretty bad—he was sweating heavily and his skin had a grayish cast. As soon as they guided him to a comfortable-looking couch, Oscar snatched his arm out of Mozelle's hand and plopped himself down like an insolent child.

Mozelle took a chair next to Louise and picked up an old issue of *Ebony* magazine. She flipped through the pages, but couldn't concentrate because of Oscar's constant grunting and squirming.

"Will you be still and stop acting like a spoiled brat?" Mozelle snapped at him. "You gone make yourself feel worse than you already do, carrying on like that. You'd think, Oscar, that *I* did something to *you.* All of this is your fault. If you'd been acting like a man with some sense, you wouldn't be sitting up in here mad, with your mouth glued shut, and looking like a fool."

Oscar leaned back and closed his eyes, pretending like he was dozing off, so he didn't have to listen to what Mozelle was saying. But Mozelle didn't buy his act.

"Open your eyes and look at me," she demanded. "You ain't 'sleep. This time you gone listen to me good, Oscar Lee

Thomas. And I am going to talk as long as I want to, because there ain't nothing your little Sammy Davis, Jr.–looking self can do about it."

Oscar' s eyes popped wide open. He knew that behind his back people said he looked like a St. Louis version of Sammy Davis, Jr., but it came as a big surprise that Mozelle was one of them.

Mozelle didn't pay Oscar any mind, just kept talking. She had kept so much bottled up inside her all these years that nothing was going to shut her up now.

"You know something?" she told Oscar. "Almost the whole time we been married, all you've done is find fault with me. You say all kinds of mean things, like, 'Mozelle, this here food ain't hot enough, and it taste nasty—cook it over'; 'Mozelle, you didn't dress the children right'; 'Mozelle, I know you ain't wearing that dress with me, looking all cheap'; 'Mozelle, you need to clean out this refrigerator'; 'Mozelle, you waste your time, always reading all those books when you ought to be out in that garden picking greens for my dinner'; 'Mozelle, you ain't got no discipline.' Mozelle, Mozelle, Mozelle. Negro, that's all your old hateful-acting self knew how to do—criticize, complain, be mean, and call my name until I couldn't stand to hear your voice no more . . .

"And for some reason I just kept taking it, forgiving you, loving you, and hoping the day would finally come when you'd see just how good and smart a woman I am. But what did you do, Oscar? You lay up with a sloppy-tailed heifer. And you know what? If I were a different kind of woman and didn't know Jesus, I'd walk over to your chair and knock the living daylights out of your old, tired, silly-looking, Superfly butt, just the same way Queenie did."

Louise put her magazine up to her face so that Oscar couldn't see her laughing. She'd had a hard enough time keeping her face straight back at the club when Oscar was scrambling on the floor with his shoes too big, his legs too skinny, and his teeth stuck together with cement glue. But *this*? This was priceless. She hadn't known Mozelle had it in her to talk to Oscar like that.

And it was making Oscar furious. It was so clear that he didn't think Mozelle had any right to tell him how she felt, even after six children and forty years. Still, it startled Louise when Oscar tried again to smack Mozelle in the mouth.

And again, Mozelle froze him in his tracks, this time with an icy glare hard enough to pierce holes in Oscar. For a moment he stood still, like he was in suspended animation, before he backed up to his seat and sat down.

"You did right for a change, Oscar Lee," Mozelle said. "Because if you had put your hands on me, the only thing that would have saved you is an angel of the Lord."

Scared as he was of the new Mozelle, being a man Oscar had to save face. He balled up his right fist and shook it at her.

"If you don't want to have to use cement glue to keep your hand attached to your arm, I'd suggest that you not try that again," Mozelle warned. Then she closed her eyes, silently thanking the Lord for giving her the courage to at last recognize who Oscar truly was. And who he truly wasn't—a decent husband. She picked up her purse and turned to Louise. "I'm ready to go."

"But Mozelle, what about Oscar?"

"What *about* Oscar?"

"I mean, he still needs someone with him, to help him with the doctor."

"Maybe so, but it won't be me. I'll explain what happened and tell the nurse we are leaving."

As Mozelle walked to the door, Louise just sat there for a moment, in shock that Mozelle would actually abandon Oscar. All these years Mozelle had let him get away with murder, and now he had used up his last reprieve. But then, Louis had told her, many a day, that the worst thing you could do to people you kept hurting by doing wrong was to keep on acting a fool with them. Louis said those types could go on for what looked like forever, but that then one day they would snap and that was it. You had "tore your draws" with them, and they were through. Watching Mozelle walk out of that waiting room without so much as a backward glance, Louise knew that Oscar had "tore his draws" with her once and for all.

Mozelle had gotten all the way out in the hall when she realized that Louise wasn't with her. "I'm leaving, Louise," she called out. "Now, if you want to sit with Oscar, that's fine by me. But I am leaving."

Louise jumped up. The last thing she wanted to do was sit anywhere with Oscar Lee Thomas.

VIII

Once they got in the car, Mozelle sped home like she was on a raceway. She pulled up in front of the house, then hopped out of the car so fast, she had to dash back and get Louise and lock it up. Then she ran into the house, heading straight for her bedroom. When Louise caught up with her, Mozelle was pulling open drawers and throwing Oscar's stuff into the middle of the floor.

"Louise," she said, making her jump to attention. "Can you help me with the chests?"

Louise followed Mozelle to one of the spare bedrooms, and together they pushed two big cedar chests into her room. When Mozelle opened them, Louise was surprised to find that they were empty, except for some tissue paper in the bottom. She had expected to find them full of the "old-timey" clothes Oscar wore before he turned into Mack Daddy.

"I gave them to Rev. Wilson for that young man who just joined the church," Mozelle said, answering Louise's unspoken question. "You know the one I'm talking about, right?"

Louise nodded. The young man had been to Vietnam and was on drugs for years before he went cold turkey and decided to put his life back together. He was about the only person she knew who was slight enough to wear Oscar Lee's clothes.

"That young man was turning his life over to Christ, and he needed to know that somebody cared enough to give him a helping hand. And here is Oscar Lee running around looking like a broke-down Superfly and don't have a clue as to what real hardship is. That boy couldn't save his best friend in combat—all Oscar couldn't save was the right kind of time for me."

Louise was quiet as she watched Mozelle fold up Oscar's

new clothes, amazed at her friend's strength. Here she was, saying good-bye to the only life she had known for over four decades, and she was doing it with a grace and courage Louise knew she could never muster up in herself. Because if Oscar were her husband, those clothes would be lying on the front lawn, cut to shreds. Louis was right. You didn't mess with people like Mozelle Thomas.

Louise grabbed a handful of the baby blue tissue paper Mozelle had folded up so neatly in the chest, and an old brown envelope dropped on the floor. She laid the tissue paper on the bed and bent over to pick it up.

"Mozelle, did you know you had papers packed down in this chest?"

Mozelle stopped working and held out her hand for the envelope. She turned it over and tried to place it, realizing that she had never seen it before.

"What's wrong?" Louise asked.

"This envelope was put in the chest *after* I gave that boy those clothes. I know that to be a fact. And what's more, if Oscar been up in these chests, then he saw that I had gotten rid of his clothes. I ain't heard a peep from him. And when have you known Oscar Lee Thomas to leave something alone like getting rid of his stuff without permission?"

Louise knew that Mozelle was right. Oscar would show his behind over something like this. She said, "Open that envelope."

Mozelle tore open the envelope, which contained a handwritten letter.

"Louise, this letter was written by the man whose family donated the land for the church."

"Who is he?" Louise asked.

Mozelle squinted as she tried to make out the name. "I can't read the name—the writing is too shaky. But the letter is notarized."

"Can you make out anything, Mozelle?"

Mozelle scanned it and then started reading out loud: " 'And in keeping with my father's wishes for his beloved church, the land he donated on which to build it back in 1876 will remain in its stewardship until such time as I make arrangements for Gethsemane's name and not my family's to be placed on the deed. In the event that I die before making this transaction, the land will pass on to my heirs, who are entrusted with protecting it and ultimately deeding it to Gethsemane Missionary Baptist Church when the hundred-year grant of use expires.' "

"Why would a family donate land and not immediately give the deed to the church? That doesn't make sense to me," Louise said.

Mozelle continued reading aloud through the letter and then said, "I don't think the family ever intended for the church to have a problem with this land. I think this person believed his business would be taken care of before he died. But, Louise, if the church got the land to use for a hundred years back in 1876, then our time is about to run out."

"That's right—this is the hundredth anniversary of the groundbreaking," Louise said. "Mozelle, we need to hold on to this information, because it seems to me that whoever has this letter can either protect the church from the wrong hands or use it to place the church in the wrong hands. I don't even think we should give it to Rev. Wilson, because he's still just the interim pastor. If Cleavon got rid of him somehow, who knows where this letter would turn up?"

"I hear you talking, girl," Mozelle said. "This is serious."

"I bet this why Cleavon broke into the pastor's safe, and then he gave it to Oscar Lee when Phoebe threatened to haul his low-down behind off to court."

"Umm-hmm," Mozelle said. "Only thing, Cleavon outsmarted himself by giving it to Oscar. The Lord is amazing. He be after looking after you when you don't even know He watching."

"Amen," Louise said. "But since these papers are so important to our church, how we gone make it look like we don't have them?"

"Like this," Mozelle answered, as she took great care to put enough sheets of folded tissue paper into the envelope to give it the same weight and look that it had had with the documents enclosed. Then she folded the clothes and put them in the chest, making it look like she had never so much as breathed on that tissue paper.

When she was done, Louise looked at her long and hard and asked, "Girl, where did you learn to be that slick? You could be working for the FBI, doing all this undercover work."

Mozelle just chuckled and said, "Louise, I was married to Oscar Lee Thomas for forty years. I had to be smart enough to get around him sometimes, or else he would have run me clean out of my mind."

When Mozelle was satisfied that all of Oscar's things were packed up, she went over to the telephone.

"Who you calling?" Louise asked her.

"Warlene."

"The Mellow Slick Cougars Club Warlene?"

"How many Warlenes do you know, Louise?"

Louise kind of shrugged, as if to say, "I hear you talkin'."

"I want to give her a message for Queenie Tyler," Mozelle said.

"And the message being?" Louise queried.

"To come and pick up *her* man's stuff, funky draws and all, when she get him home from the hospital."

"Her man?"

"Yeah," Mozelle said with a little attitude in her voice. "*Her* man. 'Cause Oscar Lee Thomas show ain't *my* man anymore. I ain't got no man. I'm a free agent."

Louise couldn't say a word. And when words did come to mind, all she could think was, "Lord, wait till Louis hears about this."

Part 4

All in a Day's Work

I

It was only Tuesday, but as far as George Wilson was concerned, it had already been a very long week. On Saturday he officiated over the funeral of Oscar Lee Thomas, whose death was a surprise and a stark reminder that life was too short to let it pass you by.

It was no secret that Mr. Oscar had gotten down in his health after he moved in with his girlfriend, Queenie Tyler. Still, nobody ever expected him to die. He was just too full of fire and vinegar, even if he had devoted most of that energy to tormenting Miss Mozelle. No matter how bad he could act, and even though lately he had stopped attending Sunday service, Oscar Lee Thomas was an important part of the fabric of Gethsemane Missionary Baptist Church.

On the night Oscar died, Queenie Tyler put in a call to Sheba Cochran, pleading with her to bring the pastor over before it was too late. As soon as Sheba finished talking to Queenie, she hustled over to the church and rolled up in George's office so fast that she skidded across the room and into his arms when he opened the door. When George caught Sheba, he had to wonder what ingredients the Lord used when He made this girl—she was an armful and then some.

He held her for a moment, feeling the rapid beating of her heart, before he said, "Slow down. What could possibly make you rush in here like that?"

"Mr. Oscar is dying, George," Sheba said quietly, inhaling his cologne and fighting the urge to grab a hold of this man. She was not prepared for how good George felt—his warmth alone made her want to swoon.

"Are you serious?" George asked, incredulous. "Oscar Lee Thomas?"

"Yes, George. And you have to hurry. Queenie don't think he has that much time. And she's scared. She don't want—"

"Sweetheart," George said gently, as he put his clerical collar on and grabbed his Bible, "I'm not going to let him leave without coming back to Jesus. Let's go, because time is not on our side."

They pulled up just as Mr. Louis Loomis, Louise, Mozelle, and Joseaphus Cantrell, a church deacon who had been visiting Mozelle when Queenie called, were getting out of Mr. Louis Loomis's car. Queenie, who had been pacing around the house praying that God would wait to take Oscar until Rev. Wilson arrived, felt like shouting when she heard all those church people on her porch. She opened the door and said, "Thank you, thank you," momentarily forgetting herself and grabbing hold of Mozelle's hand. When Mozelle started to pull back, Queenie lowered her head and said, "Oscar Lee back in the bedroom," as she ushered them down the tiny hallway in her small home.

Oscar was sitting up in a gold crushed-velvet recliner chair, fully dressed in a navy blue suit, white shirt, and blue, red, and silver star-print tie. Despite his thinness and pallor, he looked classy, nothing like the "Geritol Pimp-Daddy," as Mr. Louis Loomis called him when he was sporting his Superfly clothes.

Mr. Louis Loomis studied Oscar, fully comprehending why he had used up most of his strength to get out of the bed and dress up for them. A man's pride and dignity would make him want to be at his best on his deathbed.

"Louis," Louise whispered, "Oscar look good. And he don't look like no imitation 'Candy Man,' either."

"Yeah, you right on that account, girl," Mr. Louis Loomis answered, hoping that Oscar didn't hear them. He had always been told that people on their deathbeds had keen senses and didn't miss a thing.

He was right to worry, because Oscar did hear Louise, but at this point he found the Sammy Davis, Jr. reference kind of funny. All these years, he had resented Louise Williams's presence in Mozelle's life, but now he thanked the Lord that she had been there holding Mozelle's hand when he was doing his best to turn her every which way but loose. Christmas Jefferson was dead wrong—Louise was a wonderful woman.

But Oscar could not only hear everything, he could feel everything—every vibe and nuance moving through that room. He felt the Holy Ghost shoot right into his heart as soon as Rev. Wilson put his foot over the threshold, and he sensed it the moment Mozelle stepped onto Queenie's porch. Sadly, he also felt worry and sorrow from all of them, especially Queenie, and that made his heart ache a bit.

Oscar beckoned everyone closer to his easy chair and started talking, his voice weak, but his spirit shining strong. When he reached out for Mozelle with open arms, she resisted his embrace. "Mozelle," he said in the gentlest voice she had ever heard him use, "Mozelle, please don't hold back from me like that. I just called you over here to set things right with you before I left. Don't want to meet my precious Lord with this burden on my heart."

Mozelle didn't move a muscle, and neither did anybody else.

"I never did do right by you. Never once treated you like you deserved to be treated. Never once told you how beautiful you were. Even after six babies and getting old, girl, your beauty just got better and better. And me? Never once had the sense to thank God for making you my wife. And since I been down sick, Mozelle, I been praying about that and the whys and hows of how I acted. Queenie know. Don't you, Queenie?"

Queenie nodded, her eyes full of tears. Oscar had been on his knees a lot lately, despite his weakened state, and he had even talked to her about the importance of having the Lord in your life. Those words had begun to take root in Queenie's heart, and she had started praying and reading Oscar's Bible and Sunday school literature. Queenie was ready to be a "New Creature in Christ," but she didn't know how to get to that point.

Taking her hand, Mr. Oscar patted it and whispered,

"Don't you cry. You know I have to go. But you have made my last days happy."

He got still a moment to catch the tears trying to flow down his cheeks. Oscar loved himself some Queenie Tyler. In fact, if the truth be told, Queenie was Oscar's dream woman. But he let the women like her whom he had loved in his youth slip away because he was a coward, ashamed to admit that he loved a kind of woman considered "not good enough to marry."

It was sad that he had spent a lifetime missing his own blessings because he listened to what folks told him made a woman a suitable wife. And even worse, he had made Mozelle pay for every day he'd spent away from a woman like Queenie.

Oscar looked into Mozelle's eyes and said, "Forgive me. That's all I can dare to ask of you."

Everyone in the room was crying except Mozelle. And then the light dawned in her heart. She realized that she no longer resented Oscar—that all her anger had been lifted from her long before now. Tears came to her at last and she said, "I forgive you, Oscar. I forgave you right after I put you out."

"Good," he said, smiling warmly. Then he looked over at Mr. Joseaphus Cantrell, whom he had known since they were schoolboys. He had always been jealous of Joseaphus, who was everything he was not: tall, brown, and kindly, with a hearty laugh. Back before Oscar and Mozelle were married, Joseaphus had had a crush on Mozelle that Oscar believed had never gone away. Now Joseaphus was a widower, and Oscar had not been surprised to hear that recently he had been keeping Mozelle company.

He took Mozelle's hand, extended it toward Joseaphus, and said, "Take good care of her, man. She had my babies, but she has always had your heart. I know you love her. And I know she needs to love you. Will you do that for me, Joseaphus?"

Mr. Joseaphus Cantrell nodded gravely and took Miss Mozelle's hand gently in his, pulling her over to him, and into his strong arms.

Then Oscar gestured toward George. "Rev. Wilson, I want to rededicate my life to Christ. I want to see my Savior's face when I reach glory, and I want to hear Him say, 'Well done, my good and faithful servant, well done.'"

George squeezed Sheba's shoulder for support. His heart was full of profound emotions—deep sadness over Mr. Oscar, mingled with joy that he had returned to the Lord in time. Then George reached out and took one of Oscar's hands in his; it was so frail that he feared he would break it if he squeezed too hard.

"Oscar Lee, do you acknowledge that you have been a sinner and that Jesus died for those sins and then rose again. And do you accept Jesus as your Lord and Savior?"

"Yes, Reverend."

"Then, Father, in Jesus' name, I ask just this—forgive Oscar Lee Thomas for all of his sins, anoint him with the Holy Ghost, save his soul, and let him dwell in glory with Thee. Just like the thief hanging on the cross, let Oscar see glory hand in hand with Thee. In Jesus' name I pray, amen."

"Amen" echoed around the room.

"You alright, Mr. Thomas?" George asked gently.

"Mighty right, Pastor," Oscar replied, smiling. "But there's just one more thing I need to tend to while I'm still here." He looked at Mr. Louis Loomis and said, "I suspect you have something that belongs to me."

When Mr. Louis Loomis frowned in confusion, Oscar laughed weakly and said, "Louis, I know you have the papers on the church—figured Mozelle here would give them to you for safekeeping. The reason I wanted you here was to tell you face-to-face, man-to-man, that I know."

Rev. Wilson was confused. If there was something this important going on with the church, he should have been told. Why would Mr. Louis Loomis hold out on him? And he almost asked, until he felt Sheba's gentle tug on his sleeve. "Not now, George," she whispered. "Mr. Louis Loomis got your back."

"Louis, hold tight to those papers," Oscar was saying in a raspy voice. "As you already know, it's the key to keeping the church safe." He grimaced and massaged his chest, and Queenie jumped to get his oxygen tank. But he stopped her with a shake of his head and reached for a Kleenex tissue to wipe the sweat off his forehead. Then he took as deep a breath as he dared to, because his heart and chest muscles were awfully weak and tender.

"Look, y'all do whatever you have to do to keep Rev. Earl Hamilton out of our pulpit."

They all looked surprised. Everybody knew that the Cleavon Johnson Faction in the church, as it was now called, didn't want to make Rev. Wilson the permanent pastor. But they had thought that Cleavon was smart enough not to try to pawn Earl Hamilton off on them again. If Cleavon and his folks had secret plans to install Rev. Hamilton, then there was more devilment brewing than anyone had guessed.

Oscar adjusted himself in his chair, gasping for breath, as he tried one last time to explain. "Y'all need to keep quiet on the papers. But pray. Pray for guidance about when you need to use it and how you need to use it. I know the Lord will guide you. I know the Lord will help you keep Earl Hamilton out of my church. 'Cause if he becomes the pastor, he gone—"

All of a sudden, Oscar's eyes rolled back up in his head and there was a guttural, rattling sound coming from down in the back of his throat. Everybody in the room knew what that meant. It was what the old folks used to call the "death rattle."

Mr. Louis Loomis dabbed at his eyes, and Louise wept openly, as George lay his hand on Oscar's head. Mr. Joseaphus Cantrell wrapped his arms protectively around Mozelle to shield her from the pain of Oscar's death. By the time Mozelle turned back around, Oscar was gone, looking more peaceful than he ever had in life.

It took Queenie a moment to understand that Oscar had passed. And even then, she couldn't bear to accept it. She reached down and shook him by the shoulders so hard, she would have given him whiplash if he were alive to feel it. Queenie screamed out, "Oscar! Oscar! Please, please. Open your eyes, baby, squeeze my hand. Don't leave me, baby, don't leave me."

Mozelle pulled away from Joseaphus Cantrell.

"Queenie," she said softly, touching her arm gently. "Baby, it's over now. Oscar Lee is gone."

"But . . . but, Miss Mozelle, I love him. He is everything to me."

"I know, baby," Mozelle said, opening her arms to Queenie, who flew into them like a little girl running to her mother. "But listen, Jesus is your everything. Oscar was your love, your heart. And the Lord gave him to you and to me. But your everything, baby, is the Lord."

Queenie sobbed as Mozelle stroked her hair and whispered, "There, there, baby. It's gone be alright. There ain't no sorrow on this earth that heaven cannot heal."

Louise handed Queenie a handful of tissues. Queenie blew her nose and whimpered, "I know you right, Miss Mozelle. But how am I gone live with this ache in my heart, this hole in my soul?"

At that point, Sheba, who had been fighting tears, broke down sobbing. Sheba knew how much God loved her, but her loneliness was a constant heartache. There were times when she had to get on her knees and beg the Lord's forgiveness for being so sorrowful over being so alone. So she knew better than anyone else in the room what Queenie meant when she asked what God would do with the ache in her heart.

George couldn't stand to see Sheba like that. He pulled her into his arms and held her so close, he could hear her heart beating up against his own.

"Baby, baby," he whispered. "It's okay. I'm here to catch you when you fall. I'm here to catch you when you fall."

Queenie calmed down some when Miss Mozelle kissed

her and said, "Baby, you need to get saved and get right with God. Ain't right for you to be out in this world without the Lord." Then Mozelle turned to George and said, "Reverend, we need to lay hands on Queenie."

George let go of Sheba and took both of Queenie's hands in his, while the rest of the group surrounded her, just like back in the day, when folks used to circle people and tarry with them until they received the Holy Ghost.

"Are you a sinner, Queenie?"

"Yes."

"Do you believe Jesus Christ died for your sins?"

"Yes."

"Do you accept Him as your Lord and Savior, Queenie?"

"Yes, I do."

George took one hand and placed it on Queenie's forehead, and said, "Father, receive Queenie into Your arms and forgive her sins. Save her, Lord. Save her, Lord. In Jesus' name I pray and claim the victory, amen."

Then he tapped Queenie's forehead and she fell back into the arms of Mr. Louis Loomis and Joseaphus Cantrell. The Holy Ghost was so now strong in that room that everybody felt it. Mozelle lifted up her hands and shouted, "You a good God. The alpha and the omega, the beginning and the end." George had to stomp his foot and cry out, "Thank you, Jesus!" Mr. Louis Loomis just waved his hands before grabbing one of Joseaphus Cantrell's, who had tears streaming down his cheeks.

Sheba knelt down and held Queenie's hand, whispering her praises to God, and then shouted out, "Ohhhh, glory" when Queenie opened her eyes.

And after it had all calmed down, Louise said, "Well, I guess we done shouted old Oscar Lee right on up the King's Highway, and he should be pulling up an easy chair to the right of the Lord."

"You know you need to quit, Louise Williams," Mozelle said, as she picked up the church fan on the dresser and then started dialing the number of the funeral home.

II

George thought about that last meeting with Mr. Oscar Thomas and the lesson Miss Mozelle had given them all in the power of love and forgiveness. That Mozelle could come out of such a destructive forty-year marriage and manage both to forgive Oscar and bring his girlfriend Queenie to the Lord seemed almost miraculous. There weren't many worse hells on earth, George knew, than a loveless, abusive marriage, yet Mozelle had emerged from hers stronger than ever in her walk with the Lord. She was truly an inspiration.

Marriage was on George's mind because today he'd had not one but two pastoral marriage sessions scheduled. Just an hour ago, he had finished conducting the first prenuptial meeting with Bertha, Melvin Jr., and both sets of parents.

Bertha, with her spoiled self, wanted a wedding that was big and fancy enough to get a picture in the wedding section of *Jet* magazine. Everybody tried to tell her that a modest ceremony with a big reception would be the way to go, because what Bertha wanted would take months to put in place. That would bring her so close to her due date that

Nettie said she was scared the baby's head would crown before Bertha even got down the aisle good.

But no one could get through to that girl. Bertha was too stubborn to back down, and everybody just got tired of arguing with her. In fact, it was Bert who finally ended the meeting, saying, "Let's quit worrying with this silly girl and go on home." Then he looked over at Melvin Jr. and said, "Boy, you got yourself a handful sitting over there acting like she the only woman in St. Louis to ever get pregnant and married."

As he sat in his office, George thought he heard a soft tap on the door, and then he sat up in his chair, smiling, when he heard Sheba's "Hello?"

"Come on in," he said.

As she entered, she studied his face, then asked, "Are you okay?"

"Tired. Week barely started and I feel like I'm running to meet myself."

Sheba put a plate wrapped in wax paper on George's desk. "What a surprise," he said, then leaned toward it and sniffed. "What's this?"

"Spareribs, cabbage, yams, cornbread, and a piece of German chocolate cake. I brought a rib tip sandwich for myself."

"Hmm," he said, grinning. "I like members like you, girl. Come on over here and shake your pastor's hand."

"George," Sheba said, letting a giggle escape. "You so crazy, boy."

"I'm crazy alright. Crazy 'bout you," he mumbled, not knowing what possessed him to say that, even though it sure did feel good.

Sheba blushed, wondering if she'd heard him right. When she was quiet too long for George's comfort, he grinned at her and said, "What you standing over there like that for? Sit yourself on down, girl, relax, and eat your food with me."

Sheba pulled up a chair and started unwrapping her sandwich, smelling up the office with Pompey Hawkins's signature barbecue sandwich.

"You bring anything to drink?" George asked, biting off a piece of corn bread and sprinkling pepper on his cabbage.

"Yeah," she said, reaching down in her purse and pulling out two cans of Vess Cola, along with two straws.

"Now see," George said, with a twinkle in his eyes, "now see, you slipping in your walk with the Lord."

Sheba looked concerned, until the corners of his mouth turned up in a mannish, flirty grin.

"How am I slippin', Reverend?" she asked with a sly smile tugging at her lips.

"I think you keeping bad company."

"What?"

"Well, you in my office being such a good churchwoman, and all I can think about is what makes you get all fiery and feisty under that sweet churchgirl exterior."

Then he gave Sheba a wink that was so hot and "grown," all she could do was whisper, "My, my, my."

Completely satisfied with Sheba's response, George picked up his fork and dug right into his cabbage and said, "Hmmm. Mr. Pompey know he is so wrong, fixing food that taste so good it make you want to hurt somebody."

"Yeah," Sheba agreed while sucking on a rib tip. "Mr.

Pompey's food so good, it'll make you wanna slap your mama."

George laughed. "That's some show 'nough good food. 'Cause if I ever thought about slapping my mama, I wouldn't even have a head. Be walking 'round this church with a lamp shade or a bucket or something up on my neck."

"I believe it," Sheba said, and reached her hand out for a palm slap. She glanced up at the wall. "George, when are you going to take that thing down?"

"What thing?"

"That thing," Sheba answered, pointing to the portrait of Pastor Clydell Forbes.

"Can't," he said. "Not as long as I'm just the interim pastor."

"Shame," she said. "You know, I don't know how that ugly, cross-eyed, big-black-glasses-wearing, bad-perm-in-his-hair fool got more than a greasy glass of water from a woman, let alone all folks say he got from some silly women in this church. 'Cause that man is so ugly he could make the lights in here start blinking."

George laughed, and they ate in silence for a few minutes, content just being in each other's company. Finally, Sheba said, "A penny for your thoughts," when she saw a pensive expression creep across his face. "George?"

"Yeah, baby," he replied.

That "baby" sounded like music from heaven to Sheba. She sipped on some soda to keep from melting out of the chair and on the floor, but she gulped it too fast and started choking.

It tickled George no end that his calling Sheba "baby"

could send her into such a tailspin. He was beginning to think that her "reputation" was a whole lot more hype than reality and that her knowledge of men arose simply from her very astute sense of people in general. He came over to her chair and gave her his handkerchief, his eyes sparkling with pure mischief. "Hmmmm, baby," he said, "I must be the man. Got this sweet, sexy lady all choked up over me."

Sheba took the handkerchief with shaky hands and wiped at her tears.

"I . . . I," she stammered, desperately trying to come up with a smart retort.

"I . . . I what, baby?" George asked, his voice low, soft, and sexy. "Can't talk, Miss Sheba Loretta Cochran?"

Sheba strained to come up with something to wipe that smug and mannish grin off George's face. But he always befuddled her, looking as good as he did. Today, as usual, the brother was razor-sharp, with his shoulders and biceps bulging in a royal blue silk turtleneck sweater, tucked into finely woven black silk gabardine bell-bottom slacks. His shoes were soft, black leather slip-ons, with a modest stacked sole and heel—just enough of a platform to be stylish but still appropriate. His Afro was perfectly smooth, about three inches high, and his sideburns and mustache were so immaculately trimmed that he put Shaft to shame. He smelled good too, standing there grinning with those almond-shaped eyes and full lips, making her feel as nervous as some fast little teenager wanting to kiss on a boy in the top row of the movie theater.

To hide her discomfort, Sheba started collecting the wax paper and napkins, which reminded George of a conversation he had with his friend, Theophilus Simmons, many years ago. Theophilus said he'd first figured out that his wife-to-be Essie was in love with him when the girl kept fussing around in her mama's kitchen, washing out one glass over and over, until Theophilus put a stop to that nonsense and put something else on her mind. Watching Sheba fuss around his desk, George's heart started to sing as he helped her clean up before his next appointment.

Sheba tried to not stand too close to George, but he wanted her to know that he had discovered her secret. He put his arm around her waist and sank back in his chair, pulling Sheba with him onto his lap. She sat there all stiff and awkward, not knowing how to respond, until George wrapped her up in his arms.

"I won't bite, baby," he said in that low, sexy voice. He ran his finger down the side of her face and cupped her chin in his hand, pulled her face to his, and kissed her softly on the lips.

"See," he whispered, kissing her again, "I told you I wouldn't bite you, baby."

Sheba lowered her eyes, and something in that openly sweet response got next to George. He grabbed the back of Sheba's head and kissed her deeply. Her mouth was warm and soft and delicious.

"I like these lips, baby," he said. "And I like this, too." He began kissing her eyelids, nibbling on her ears, and placing hot kisses on her neck, before moving back to her lips.

"Do these sweet lips belong to me, baby?" George asked.

Sheba said, "Yes," in a barely audible whisper.

"I said, 'Do these sweet lips belong to me, baby?' "

"Yes, George," she replied, meeting his eyes. "They belong to you."

"Don't you give anybody so much as a taste of these lips. These are my lips, Sheba," he said, kissing her with so much passion that Sheba felt like she was going to melt right into that man.

"George," Sheba whispered in his ear, sending a shiver across his shoulders and down his chest.

"Oooh, baby," he said, "heaven must be like this, it must be like this."

Sheba buried her head in George's shoulder. She was so overcome with emotion that a tear trickled down her cheek. No man had ever before touched her so profoundly with just words and a kiss.

George pulled at Sheba's chin and once more captured her mouth with his own, moaning as he kissed her again, his hands roaming over her hips as if they had a mind of their own. Sheba knew she was headed for the danger zone and quickly asked the Lord to help her get out of this pinch. She had been in a pinch of this nature a few times before, and back then she hadn't had sense to ask God for some help. Gerald, Lucille, Carl Lee, and La Sheba were living proof of that.

"George," Sheba whispered, trying to pull away from him.

"Yeah, baby," he murmured, not in the least bit interested in letting go of her. In fact, he wanted to go further, despite the fact that he knew better. He was a pastor, a man of God, and a man with a sincere desire to serve and please the Lord. The last thing he was supposed to want to do was make love to a woman who was not his wife, and especially in the pastor's office. But George couldn't help it. He wanted to make love to Sheba, as he knew in his heart she had never been made love to before.

"George," she said. "Don't you have an appointment?"

Suddenly George remembered that he had to meet with Latham and Rosie Johnson, and looked at his watch. Their meeting was fifteen minutes away, and Latham was always on time, if not a few minutes early. George stood up so fast, he almost dropped Sheba on the floor.

"What are you doing?" Sheba demanded."I know you didn't have the nerve to roll me off of you like that."

George was frustrated. He had not wanted to stop. With his body still racing ahead of his mind, he opted to go into what MamaLouise always called "crazy-man space," pouting and getting all in a huff with her.

Sheba knew George was frustrated, but that didn't excuse him for blaming her for making him do the right thing. She fixed her eyes on him and muttered, "You need to grow up."

"What?" George asked, thinking he was hearing things. Because he just knew that girl didn't have the nerve to tell him to grow up.

"You better get ready to meet with Latham and Rosie," Sheba said, hoping he had heard her loud and clear, but playing dumb, so she could get away with having said it.

"Yeah, I do have to get ready, though I'm not looking forward to this meeting at *all*," he replied with a heavy sigh. "I am hoping I can help those two keep it together. But Sheba, the Lord will have to forgive me. I just don't have anything in me that I can say to help them. Latham Johnson is a piece of work, and I don't have the patience to deal with him."

"So what are you going to do?" she asked.

"Don't know. Unfortunately, I don't even feel led to tell those two to stay together. Rosie seems like she is in so much pain, I can't help but wonder if she would be happier without Latham in her life."

Sheba took a deep breath and spoke from her heart. "George, you can't save this marriage, because Latham doesn't accept Rosie for herself—and he never has, for that matter. He has always believed that he's better than Rosie because Sylvia and Melvin Sr. are caterers and his father is a dentist."

"But—," George began.

"But nothing, George," Sheba said. "I believe the Lord is working in one of His unfathomable ways, moving Latham right out of Rosie's life, and I hope that she will not refuse this blessing in deep disguise that is coming to her."

Sheba could tell George was having trouble accepting the idea that he might be presiding over the inevitable end of a marriage. But she also knew that when a man had trouble digesting a hard truth a woman put in his lap, a wise woman did not try to force the issue, but instead petitioned the Lord to open the man's heart and ears to receive what she had to say.

"I better get going," Sheba said, breaking the tense silence that had descended on the room. "My intercessory prayer meeting with the Prayer Troopers will start soon."

"How is that going?" George asked, glad to focus on something other than Sheba's thoughts about Latham and Rosie Johnson. He had been wondering how Sheba, as the youngest member of the group, was faring among such old-timers as Mr. Louis Loomis, MamaLouise, Miss Mozelle, and Mr. Joseaphus Cantrell.

"I love it," she announced brightly. "It's nice being the youngest in the group. I get a whole lot of attention and I am learning a lot about the power of prayer."

"*And*," she thought, "I am taking notes from some serious prayer warriors on what to do about *your* behind."

"Will you come by the office after prayer meeting?" he asked. When Sheba gave him a sweet smile and nodded, he said, "Lift me up in prayer when you go downstairs."

"Don't you worry none, George. I'll be doing just that very thing."

Sheba opened the door and was about to leave when something occurred to her.

"Why are you meeting with them anyway? With all that is going on with you and Latham's uncle Cleavon, I would think you'd want to steer clear of that family."

"Sylvia asked me to talk to them. She said that things were bad for her daughter and she needed some help in getting through to 'that boy' she was married to. And after watching what Miss Mozelle went through with Mr. Oscar, Sylvia said, she didn't want her babygirl to waste forty years of her life."

"That makes sense," Sheba answered, shaking her head. "Because I don't know *how* Rosie stands that boy. Lord *knows* I don't know how she *stands* him."

III

Barely five minutes after Sheba left, the Johnsons arrived. George opened the door, shook Latham's hand, and told them to come in and sit down. He saw Latham nod at Rosie, indicating where he wanted her to sit.

George couldn't understand why Latham thought he was so much higher than Rosie. The girl had started the city's only black interior-decorating firm on a shoestring budget, and she was making quite a name for herself, helping folks put their houses together at a reasonable price. The two members' homes she decorated that George had seen were beautiful—tasteful, down-home, welcoming, with all kinds of creative black touches in each room.

But it seemed that the more folks sang her praises, the worse Latham treated her. He even had the nerve to walk off from one of the church mothers who told him how good Rosie's work was. And that was the Sunday that Rosie's mother Sylvia had decided to intervene. As soon as church was over, she'd come straight to George's office and said, "I don't know about my daughter. But as for me, I've had enough of Latham Johnson and his jacked-up foolishness."

Now, George started to sit on his desk, something that made most folks he counseled feel more comfortable. But one look at Latham told him to take a more formal approach, if he wanted to make any headway with this man. So he went and sat behind his desk, drew himself up to his full height, and looked right at Dr. Latham Johnson, who was flipping through an appointment book like he had something far better to do with his precious time.

George could see that this was not going to be easy and said a silent prayer, fervently hoping that Sheba was praying for him too. Because he was going to need all the prayer he could get to deal with this pompous-acting fool.

"Latham, I will be honest with you and Rosie. I called you in because Rosie's mother is worried about what's going on with you two. She says things are bad and you-all need some help."

Latham cleared his throat and glared at Rosie as if to say, "I told you not to talk about us to anyone."

She lowered her eyes in an attempt to avoid the anger in his before saying, "I didn't talk to Mama. She talked to me. What was I to do, lie to my own mother?"

"Yes, if that would keep her out of *my* business," he answered nastily. "What goes on with you and me, *between* you and me. I don't know why you can't get that through your big fat head."

"But, Latham," Rosie started to say, then stopped when he held up his hands, making it clear that he didn't want to listen.

"What's wrong with you-all?" George asked. "I wish I could approach you textbook style. But honestly, the friction being displayed here calls for me to put a few things on the line. I—"

"I," Latham interrupted, "I figured that you would ask me about our difficulties, so I wrote out my complaints for you." He pulled a paper out of his briefcase and handed it to George.

"There is a table of contents at the beginning of the paper and an index at the end, if you wish to look up a subject on

Rosie without having to comb your way through the entire paper. I do, however, strongly urge you to read the opening statement, because it articulates my complaints about Rosie's behavior over the past year."

At that point, Latham looked real satisfied with himself, sat back in his chair, and unbuttoned his very expensive brown tweed blazer as if he was relieved that he had regained control over this situation.

George didn't quite know what to do with this turn of events. He couldn't remember ever dealing with such cold and calculated hostility from a man toward his wife. Mr. Oscar had sure showed out with Miss Mozelle, but at his lowest point, he wasn't like this. George eyed Rosie, wondering if she had something in writing for him too. But she was just sitting there trying not to cry and looking like she had been stung by a very angry hornet.

George flipped through the paper to the end of it and read the index. This paper was simply amazing—written in a lofty style, wide-ranging in subject matter, and quite thorough, even if it was a bunch of hincty-fied craziness.

He glanced at the section labeled "Personal Growth and Integrity." Latham had written, "As it relates to the personal growth of my *wife,* I wish to make the following analysis and summation: It appears that Rosie has become too comfortable with her current level of intellectual development. On too many occasions, she has resisted my directives concerning the level of literature she should be reading. And her lack of integrity on the matter was exhibited when the book I purchased for her, *The Psychology of a Dysfunctional Wife,* sat unopened on our dresser while she read magazines on home decor. This reflects a serious intellectual deficit, which makes Rosie dull and prone to acting at a level that is beneath the cognitive functioning I am striving to produce in my home."

George reread that mess to make sure it said what he thought it said. Then, in the most patient and neutral voice that he could muster up, he said, "Latham, I am not in a position to give this paper the response it deserves. All I want to know is what you think the problem is."

Latham sighed in exasperation and said, "Rev. Wilson, there is no one problem. For example, please turn to page eight. It reads," he started quoting himself, " 'On the matter of cleanliness, Rosie has been inconsistent with cleaning the home efficiently. On occasion, there have been dishes in the sink and a full trash can . . .' "

George knew that Rosie's home was immaculate, because her mother always talked about how the girl seemed obsessed with a clean house. He stared at Latham, thinking, "Why can't your lazy, cognitive-functioning behind wash dishes and empty the trash?" He took a deep breath before saying, "Latham, I don't want to go over this paper with you right now. I just want you to tell me what's wrong. I know something has to be eating at you, if you spent time writing this . . . mes—this treatise on your wife."

Latham threw up his hands in frustration. "Rev. Wilson, you called *my* home and asked if you could speak to the two of us," he said angrily. "I have obliged your request for a meeting I wasn't interested in having. And now you are refusing *my* request to deal with this problem in the way that I see best. I wrote this paper to save time and give *you* some direction regarding how you need to deal with my wife. I believe this paper spells out all of the problems we have been experiencing and even offers solutions, on the bottom of page twenty-two."

George sighed, not caring how it looked, and decided to go straight to the heart of the matter. He was not playing any power games with Latham Johnson. Sheba's voice echoed in his mind: "I don't know *how* Rosie stands that boy. Lord *knows* I don't know how she *stands* him." And at that moment, all he could think was "I don't know how she stands him, either. Lord knows, I don't know that."

"Latham, it is a shame before God for you to write something this vicious about Rosie, or anybody else for that matter," George said, holding the paper out toward Latham.

Latham was outraged that a man he viewed as no better than a jackleg country preacher would talk to *him* like that. He jumped up from his chair and was about to snatch the paper out of George's hand when he saw the expression on his face. It was straight up from the street and clearly said, "If you snatch this paper out of my hand, I will forget I'm a preacher."

Latham weighed that look a moment and decided to back down, turning his anger on Rosie instead. "Just look at you," he spat out. "You are far more trouble than you'll ever be worth, Rosie, trying to tear down your husband with the help of this ignorant fool. Women like you do everything in their power to suck a man dry."

George had heard enough. He said, "You are way out of line, Latham. You don't have a right to talk to a rabid dog like that, let alone your wife."

Latham swung around to face George, so full of bitter anger that his face had turned a dark purple.

"What would you know about a wife, George?" he said in a voice so nasty, it sliced through the air like a machete. "From what my good buddy Marmaduke Clark says, you couldn't hold on to your own ex-wife, Glodean Benson. She had to find another man—or should I say, men—to take care of her right."

George, who had long been over his ex-wife, didn't dignify Latham's statement with so much as a blink of his eye. He turned to Rosie, who was sitting there with her head hung in shame over Latham's awful behavior, and said, "Rosie, you don't need to keep taking this off of him. I know I'm the pastor, and it's my job to save marriages, but don't nobody need to take this kind of abuse from another person. I don't care who they are."

George thought of what Sheba had tried to tell him—that Rosie would be better off with Latham out of her life. He had not wanted to hear it at that moment, but he understood now.

"Get up," Latham ordered Rosie. "We are leaving. He," he said, nodding in George's direction, "isn't worthy to advise me—or even someone like *you,* for that matter."

"No, Latham," Rosie said softly but firmly.

He looked at her, eyebrows rising up so far that George thought they were going to fall off of the back of his head.

"Ex-cuse me?"

"No, Latham, I am not leaving here until you apologize to me and to Rev. Wilson. You ought—"

"You ought to kiss my black behind, with your illiterate

self," Latham said, slapping Rosie across her face. George jumped up and grabbed Latham's arm. He started to resist but quickly gave up when he couldn't break George's iron grip. Latham was a surgeon and wasn't going to risk hurting his wrist struggling with Rev. Wilson.

When Latham's arm relaxed, George let it drop. Then Latham snatched away from him and walked to the door, nursing his arm, and taking a few seconds to get his words just right.

"Rev. Wilson, you know nothing about women. You married that Glodean Benson, a known tramp, and now that man-eating hustler Sheba Cochran got you whipped. That hussy will lay up with any man she can, and the whole church knows it. She even chased after my uncle Cleavon till he could get her straight."

George momentarily forgot he was working and stepped toward Latham, who laughed and held up his hand. "No need for violence, Pastor. You, not me, have a . . . hmmm, shall we say, *thing* for women with character flaws—if you know what I mean.

"So, Rev. Wilson," Latham went on haughtily, "normally I find church politics beneath me. But I am going to make an exception in your case. I am going to join my uncle in his campaign to rid *our* church of riffraff, and run you and that tavern wench, Sheba Cochran, clean out of town."

Latham turned back to Rosie, eyes narrowed, and mouth turned down in disgust. "You have one second to get over to this door or we are history."

Rosie made a move to follow after him. But George was quicker than she was. He came around to her, placed a firm hand on her shoulder, and snapped, "Don't you even think about moving."

Latham walked out, slamming the door behind him as hard as he could, and Rosie broke down, sobbing. George handed her the whole box of tissues, feeling that he had failed miserably. He had wanted to help Latham and Rosie, but it seemed that all he had done was help turn a big problem into a big mess. A part of him wanted to start crying with Rosie, but his heartache eased up a bit when he thought about Miss Mozelle and all of those years of unnecessary suffering.

Then, he flashed back to the day Glodean left him for another man. Like Rosie sitting here and practically falling to pieces, he had thought that his heart would disintegrate and never ever be whole again. But after some time passed and he began to heal, he realized that her leaving him was a blessing in disguise. "Rosie," he said, "Latham may have just done you a favor. Anyone with a spouse who spends more time tearing her down than building her up needs that person prayed out of her life. I know that doesn't sound right coming from a pastor. But I just don't think the Lord wants us ripped to shreds in our own homes. Just don't seem right to me.

"So, do yourself a favor and let Latham go for now. Let him go with forgiveness for all the hurt he has caused you and with a prayer that he can turn himself around to become the kind of husband God wants him to be. But if he can't, pray that God will open up the windows of your life and bless you beyond that which you could possibly imagine at this moment. You know, if Latham doesn't turn around, I suspect that in a relatively short time, you will have a completely new life—great career, happiness, peace of mind, and a new man who simply adores you.

"Now, what is your mother's number?" George asked, picking up the phone.

"393-9778."

The phone rang one time and Rosie's father, Melvin Sr., answered, sounding like he was waiting on this call. "You need me to come and get my babygirl, Reverend?"

"Yes," George said.

"That . . . that Negro showed out, didn't he?"

"How'd you know that, Melvin Sr.?"

"Humph" was all that Melvin Sr. said, adding, "Tell Rosie it will be alright and that her daddy is on his way to get his baby."

"Okay, man," George said.

George hung up and told Rosie, "Your daddy is coming to get you. Have him pick up your kids, and all of you should stay with your parents tonight. And then tomorrow, you need to call Phoebe Cates, so she can get busy protecting you."

"My marriage is over, isn't it, Rev. Wilson?" Rosie asked through a sniffle, knowing the answer but needing someone to say what she could barely begin to think about.

George looked at Rosie's tearstained face and took both of her hands in his. He did not understand her soon-to-be ex-husband. This was a good woman, the kind of woman any man with some sense would be proud to call his own.

George thought about what Rosie was asking him. It was a hard question to answer when put in that way. He looked her straight in the eye and said, "It may be, Rosie. Your marriage may have ended when your husband walked out of that door."

IV

As soon as Melvin Sr. left with Rosie, George felt the hard memories of his own bad marriage pushing through. It was a painful day when he came home to find his wife, Glodean Clayton Wilson, packing her clothes. And worse, to find another man, Rev. Teasdale Benson, a prominent pastor in the Gospel United Church, sitting in *his* house, with his feet under *his* kitchen table, eating food *his* wife had cooked for him, and waiting patiently for her to finish packing so they could leave.

Rev. Benson had been a bold so-and-so, too. He didn't even stop eating when George, who had just gotten off his job as a night security guard, walked into that kitchen. When the man didn't have the decency to look uncomfortable, George went straight over to the table and snatched the food he was eating right out of Teasdale Benson's mouth.

"What you doing here, man?" Rev. Benson demanded, mad when collard green juice dripped on his white silk tie and ran down his navy silk suit, ruining the tip of the white silk handkerchief stuffed in his breast pocket. But George didn't give him a chance to think too much on why he was at his own house after working all night. He just grabbed Benson by his tie and lifted him clean out of the chair, holding him by the throat so tight that the man's face started losing its color—and Teasdale Benson was black as ebony wood.

"Let him go," Glodean yelled, looking breathtaking in a pink raw silk suit.

But George was so hurt and angry, he found that he couldn't let go of Rev. Benson's tie. So he pulled on it harder, oblivious to the blue tint on Benson's lips.

At that point Glodean, fearful that her soon-to-be ex-husband was going to kill her husband-to-be—and thus killing as well all of her carefully laid plans—got desperate. She picked up the sterling silver tray George's grandmother had given her and slammed it hard across his back, stunning him long enough to loosen his grip on her lover's necktie.

As soon as George let go, Benson struggled away from him and fell on the floor, gasping for breath. Glodean ran over to him, loosened his tie, and held his head in her lap. When Benson regained a bit of composure, Glodean helped him to his feet and then walked out of George's life without so much as a backward glance.

For many months after that, George hated preachers and refused to set foot in church. But the Lord had other plans for George Wilson. God pulled on him so hard that George had no other recourse but to go to church one Sunday morning, desperate only for peace. And that morning, he not only found peace, he got saved, got baptized, received the Holy Ghost, joined the church, and got a calling to preach before service got started good.

George sat in his chair with his feet up on his desk, eyes closed, listening to the Ohio Players' "Heaven Must Be

Like This" on the radio, thinking that the Lord had brought him a mighty long way from the day he came close to killing another preacher.

Sheba knocked, then pushed at the door, saying, "George?"

"Yeah," he answered, not moving, with his eyes still closed.

"That bad, huh?" she asked, hating to see him so upset.

"Worse," he replied, rubbing the bridge of his nose.

"You couldn't help them, could you?"

"What do you think?" he snapped.

"Is there anything I can do?" she asked softly, hoping to pacify him a bit.

"No, Sheba. There is ab-so-lute-ly nothing you can do for me right now—or for Rosie, or for Cleavon's idiot nephew Latham, for that matter. I guess you know first-hand what the men in that family are like."

"What, did Latham say something about Cleavon?"

"It seems there's a lot 'the whole church,' in his words, knows about you that I don't."

Sheba was very hurt by that statement and, blinking back tears, started for the door. But then she decided that she wasn't letting George Robert Wilson—or anyone else, for that matter—talk to her or treat her like less than what she was. No one but God had the power to judge her, forgive her sins, or redeem her soul, so no man was going to throw stones at her and get away with it.

"George Robert Wilson," Sheba began, in a voice that had "mama" all over it, "most times I let people think what they will about me. One, because I don't give a care about what people think who have never lifted a finger to help me and my children. And two, because I know I am a good woman.

"But I have always believed, George, that you of all people could see the real me and that you knew that I was a good woman who deserved to be treated with respect."

Sheba waited a moment and then, when George didn't respond, continued, "You're absolutely right that I know how difficult a Johnson man can be. And it's no secret at all that my four children have four different daddies. But it's a lie that I just ran out in the streets and got all of those babies because I was hot, fast, and trifling. What I did wrong was to fall in love and believe, like a fool, that those four men knew they had found a treasure and wanted to claim me as their own.

"And I made some other mistakes. Cleavon was a mistake. Just like your first marriage was a mistake."

George sat up in his chair and opened his mouth, but Sheba ignored him and kept right on talking.

"Mr. Louis Loomis told me that you were once married to a woman who was so crazy and fixed on preachers, she was stupid enough to leave a good man like you for a pastor who dumped her for someone else before the ink on the marriage license could dry."

All George could think at that moment was that the CIA didn't have a thing on black church folks' spy network.

"But you know something, George," Sheba went on, "I asked the Lord to forgive me my mistakes. And if the One who made the heavens and the earth could forgive me, surely a mere mortal like yourself could find it in your heart to do the same."

George said nothing, and Sheba bit back another rush of tears. It was a shame and so frustrating that he was being so hardheaded, refusing to see that the Lord had placed her in his path. Because Sheba knew deep down in her heart that she was George's wife. It hurt that he was fighting so hard against himself and his own blessing. Her only comfort was the knowledge that God was in control of this situation, so it would work out as He saw fit. No matter how hopeless it might look to her right now, she had to remember that nothing was impossible with God.

But when George finally spoke, he didn't apologize. Instead, he opted to "put a little tear in his draws" with Sheba. He stood up and in his "preacher voice" said, "I need to address some important church business before I get off work. So," he continued, not having sense enough to pay attention to the expression on Sheba's face, "we'll have to have this little talk later, when I get some free time."

Sheba was so mad at George for that dismissal, she couldn't even cry. Her eyes fell on the piece of German chocolate cake she had brought him, still sitting on his desk. Before George could even blink, she snatched it up and smashed the entire piece of cake right onto his immaculate, carefully groomed, shimmering Afro Sheen–sprayed head.

"Sheba! You, you, you got some nerve, girl. What is wrong with you?" he hollered as a chunk of cake fell off his head and splattered on his expensive turtleneck sweater.

Ignoring George's angry sputtering, Sheba walked over

to the office door, then turned to say one more thing. "George Robert Wilson, you certainly do have a lot of work to do. Because it's gone take you all the rest of this week to work out why you acting like a pure-dee fool and keep running from the Lord. But I have work to do, too. And my work ain't no fancy church work. See, I'm pressed with the task of taking you and your nonsense to a Higher Source. I'm taking it to the One Who can deal with you better than your mama or your daddy or your grandmama or your granddaddy or your auntie or your uncle ever could."

When the door slammed for the second time that evening, George thought that Sheba was going to talk to Mr. Louis Loomis about him. It didn't occur to him that the girl was about to do just what she said—go straight over his head and on up to the Lord, to tell her Father "just what that boy did."

Sheba managed to hold in her tears until she reached the chapel. She made sure there was no one around, then went into a corner, got on her knees, and leaned on her elbows on a pew cushion. She began to pray—that kind of deep praying that gave Bible folks courage, like when Queen Esther prayed up the nerve to walk up to King Xerxes uninvited and unannounced.

"Lord. Lord-Lord-Lord. Lord, that man done worked over my last nerve. You know, Father, that I been praying about this heart/love, man/woman thing for years, and since I have rededicated my life to you, Lord, I have been praying on it hard and ceaselessly.

"Now, Lord, I trust You, I believe in You, and I know You

hear me and that You answer my prayers. But Lord, I'm sick and tired of being all alone.

"Lord, you know the reason there is so much mess about love and sex in folks' lives, is that too many people think those issues don't concern You. They think You don't see our tears of loneliness and feel the painful aching of our needs. But I believe You do. I just know in my soul, Lord, that a God who made beautiful flowers, rainbows, colors, music, and lightning that flashes across the sky is a passionate God, One Who understands the hearts and longings that You Yourself created.

"Even George, for all his faith, his good works, and his dedication to You, doesn't completely trust that You understand that part of him. But You do, I know You do. You even understand how he threw away all the sense You gave him when he married that crazy Glodean woman. You helped that man by letting that woman walk right out of his life. And another thing, Lord—don't that boy know that nobody but You, God, could have conceived of and fashioned something as complicated as what happens to men and women when passion overtakes them and begs to be expressed through physical love?

"Father, I know that some folks would want to run me right out of this church for having a conversation like this with You. But Lord, You know I love George. That's why I didn't snatch a hole out of his behind when I was in his office. But that boy is *Your* chile. And I want You to deal with George Wilson before I have to hurt him. Lord, I am coming to You on this one, and it seems to me, in my humble opinion, that You would want me to be able to testify to the power of prayer and about Your miracle-working in this area of my life. So, please, deal with *Your* chile and help him and help me. Thank You, Lord. In Jesus' name I pray and claim the victory, amen."

Sheba wiped her eyes, checking again to make sure nobody saw her before she left. But Sheba hadn't been alone. Aside from the Lord, Mozelle had heard every single word of her prayer. And when she knew Sheba was gone, Mozelle went to the very spot where Sheba had prayed, knelt down, and offered a supplication prayer for her.

"Lord," she began, "these children need these prayers answered. And those waiting on the answer are tired. Love between a man and a woman is something You need to take care of. It is too precious to be directed by a man or a woman without Your help. You need to give Your children testimonies when they come to You in prayer, asking with heart in hand for the blessings of that kind of precious love in their lives.

"You have blessed me with Joseaphus, Lord, and now I beg You to help Sheba. I been watching the pastor and, Lord, that is one stubborn boy. Scared to death of giving the woman he loves his heart. And that boy know Sheba love him. Umph, Lord. It ain't fair. Deal with that boy, Jesus. Deal with Rev. Wilson and let him know Who running the show."

Part 5

A Love That Only God Can Give

I

Louise was more nervous than the bride. She looked at Bertha Kaye, with that baby just growing, and said, "Girl, hurry up. You not even dressed. Gone hold up the whole ceremony—have everybody sitting out in the sanctuary waiting on you."

"MamaLouise, it takes me longer to go to the bathroom and get myself straight now. I feel like I move like a snail."

"A snail who's about to pop," Phoebe said, laughing as she watched Bertha waddle around the women's lounge where the wedding party was getting dressed.

"Well, you should have thought about that 'fore you laid up with Melvin Jr. and got that baby."

Bertha and Phoebe looked at each other and rolled their eyes when they knew MamaLouise couldn't see their faces. Why did your grandmother always have to say "laying up with" when getting on you about yourself and a man? They just loved to say, "If you hadn't been layin' up . . ."

"She wasn't able to think, Louise," Miss Mozelle said with

a chuckle. "All Bertha Kaye could think of at the time was 'Mel . . . vvvviiinnn . . . oh, Melvin.'"

Bertha's mouth flew open. It had never occurred to her that Miss Mozelle even thought about things like that. And she certainly never imagined her saying anything that fast and frisky.

Louise stopped pacing around, shaking her head at her granddaughter. Young people didn't think that anybody they considered to be "old" knew anything worth knowing about men, love, and lovemaking.

"Close your mouth, Bertha Kaye, and finish dressing," Louise said as she picked up a box of corsages and boutonnieres and started out the door. "Mozelle, you 'bout ready? We need to get these upstairs."

"Okay," she answered, and followed Louise.

"You know you look beautiful," Louise told her.

"Thanks. You don't look so bad yourself," Mozelle countered, grinning.

Louise laughed. "Well then, I guess we two good-lookin' old girls ought to get this show on the road."

Mr. Louis Loomis was waiting for them, looking handsome in a black tuxedo, even if he did have on his trademark brown leather belt. How he got a tuxedo with belt loops was a mystery Louise wasn't so sure she wanted solved.

"I thought I was gone have to stand at the top of these stairs for almost forever," he fussed. "I need to get the boutonnieres to the groom and his party and then take the rest of the flowers to Precious Powers. You know that boy about to worry me and everybody else in the men's parlor to death, wanting the ceremony to get under way."

Mr. Louis Loomis looked down the stairs behind Louise and Mozelle. "And where that Bertha Kaye? If she don't hold up more stuff these days, moving slow as molasses and complaining it's the baby making her that way."

"You know it all ain't that baby, Louis. Bertha Kaye just slow. Ain't she, Mozelle?"

"Umm-hmm. But she'll be along soon," her friend replied.

"Well, you two need to get situated," Mr. Louis Loomis said. "Ceremony starting in about twenty minutes. And if it's late, I'm gone have to take off my belt and use it on the slowpoke."

He started walking off in the direction of the men's parlor, shaking his head, mumbling, "That boy 'bout to bust a vein gettin' to that girl. But he gone have to wait like the rest of us had to wait on our wedding day."

Louise and Mozelle decided to walk outside to get to their places for the ceremony. That way, they wouldn't bump into too many people. This wedding was very simple and sweet, in terms of the ritual itself, but it was turning out to be a three-ring circus, because everybody at Gethsemane Missionary Baptist Church said they were "gone be there."

Louise and Mozelle found their places just in time. Precious Powers, who was making quite a name for herself coordinating weddings, was standing in the vestibule entry at the back of the church, tapping her foot and frowning at them.

"Now, I thought I told you two to be here at least fifteen minutes ago," she said, with a hand on her generous and sexy hip. Precious was splendidly dressed in a gold suit, with a short skirt to show off her shapely legs and the shiny gold, ankle-strap platform sandals she was wearing. "Miss Mozelle, you know better than to run around here like that. Come over here and let me make sure you just right. Gone ruin my reputation."

Louise smiled at Precious. That girl had really come into her own after tearing up the Gospel United Church of America when she caught her old trifling boyfriend, Rev. Marcel Brown, with another woman. If it weren't for Precious Powers, that church would have lost so many members, it would have seriously crippled the denomination and its ministry. Her earrings caught Louise's eye—gold hoops sprinkled with diamond chips.

"Anniversary present from my baby," Precious said, all grinning teeth. "You know he got me so spoiled."

Louise and Mozelle started giggling. It was no secret that Precious Powers's husband, Tyrone, thought the sun rose and set on that girl.

"And where is Tyrone, Miss Lady?" Louise asked.

"Right here," Tyrone said as he came up behind them and kissed both Louise and Mozelle on the cheek.

"Boy, you gone mess up their makeup," Precious admonished.

"Baby, calm down. It's okay. They don't mind. Do you, ladies?"

"No, baby, we don't mind one bit," Mozelle answered, smiling at that ebony-hued boy with the kind of physique that Louise said made his "suits hang on him right."

"Tyrone," Precious said, "I need you to go on out and start

lighting the candles. And tell the musicians to start playing, so we can get this ceremony started."

Tyrone kissed Precious on the cheek, then patted that big behind when he thought Mozelle and Louise weren't looking. Precious was a bossy thing, but he knew how to take the reins. He watched her try not to jump as he gave her a little squeeze, just to let the girl know who really ran things in their family.

Mr. Louis Loomis walked into the vestibule just as Tyrone was signaling to Precious that everything was ready, then he opened the florist box he was holding and presented bouquets to Louise and Mozelle. He gave the empty box to Precious and took Mozelle gently by the arm.

"Is the bride ready?"

Mozelle answered with a breathless yes—as excited at age sixty-six as any bride of twenty-five.

Her gown was breathtaking, an Essie Simmons handcrafted original. At first glance it looked simple—a matching skirt and top made of silver lace. Closer inspection revealed that Essie and her seamstresses had sewn iridescent bugle beads on the shimmering lace fabric, which caught the light and glinted as Mozelle moved. And the lines of the dress were stunning: the top dipped to a deep V in the front and the back, the sleeves a sophisticated elbow length, and the hem of the top trimmed with tiny silver silk bows that gracefully framed Mozelle's hips. The straight skirt, grazing two inches above her ankles to show off her pale silver patent-leather pumps, was cut to mold Mozelle's bottom and emphasize the shape of her hips. As Essie had said,

"Miss Mozelle, you got a cute little butt, and we gone show it off for your new hubby."

But Essie never finished with just the outfit. She had not only chosen Mozelle's dress and shoes but also picked out heart-shaped diamond earrings, set in white gold, and a matching pendant. And for Mozelle's hair, she had the florist make a wreath of pale pink and off-white silk roses. Mozelle was radiant.

Essie had also outdone herself with Louise, the matron of honor. Tall and brown, with lovely dark brown eyes and thick beautiful salt-and-pepper hair framing her slender face, Louise was an older version of her granddaughter, Phoebe. For her, Essie had created the palest blue chiffon suit, cut in a very crisp tailored style, with silk piping on the lapels and cuffs. The long skirt was slit up past Louise's knee, profiling her legs, and showing off her pale blue stockings and pale blue satin sandals. In keeping with the simple elegance of the suit, Essie found Louise a pair of sterling silver hoop earrings sprinkled with semiprecious stones in bluish tones—amethyst, sapphire, and turquoise.

Mr. Louis Loomis, who was about three inches shorter than Louise, looked her up and down, patted his belt, and said. "Girl, you so fine, about to make me whisk you off alone somewhere, so I can get a *good* look at that slit. *Lawd,* ha' mercy!"

Louise blushed and giggled, saying, "Ohhh, Looouuuis, you so baaaad," while Mozelle laughed.

Precious couldn't believe those elders. But she silently thanked God for showing her proof that the fire of life didn't grow cold when the coals were gray. In fact, if her eyes and ears were serving her right, age was making those gray embers glow even hotter. She silently vowed to take very good care of herself, so that she and Tyrone would have it just as good as what she was witnessing in their so-called old age.

Inside the sanctuary, the Holy Rollers were entering the choir loft humming a gospel song by the blues singer Big Johnnie Mae Carter titled, "A Love That Only God Can Give." Then their main soloist, Sister Hershey Jones, came to the microphone and crooned out the words to the beautiful ballad:

"One night I got down on my knees and I prayed and I prayed and I prayed. I buried my head in my arms and I cried and I cried and I cried. And I prayed and I prayed and I prayed. And I asked the Lord to send me a blessing, to send me a love that only God can give . . .

"And on that night, I stayed on my knees, as I prayed and I prayed and I prayed. While I cried and I cried and I cried. The Lord heard my prayer. He heard my cry. And He sent me you. He sent me a love that only God can give . . ."

The melody was so slow and bluesy and the song so sweet and tender that even Sister Hershey Jones started to cry when the Holy Rollers lit into the chorus: "*I prayed and I cried. I cried and I prayed. I prayed and I cried and I cried and I prayed for a love that only God can give.*"

Mr. Louis Loomis wiped at his eyes with a handkerchief and whispered, "You alright, Mozelle?"

She nodded, barely managing to hold back the tears that were threatening to spill down her cheeks and ruin the makeup that Precious had spent so much time applying to perfection.

As the song was ending, Rev. Wilson came in and showed the groom and his son to their places. Mr. Joseaphus Cantrell was *clean,* from his short silver Afro and meticulously groomed sideburns to the white boutonniere, sprayed with a touch of silver, that graced his formal, conservatively cut black tuxedo. With it he wore a white, raw silk shirt, with black studs on it, and a black silk tie and cummerbund shot through with very thin silver stripes. On his feet were soft patent-leather, slip-on shoes with silk bows.

At the sight of the groom and his son, Charlie, who was a forty-six-year-old version of his father, a lot of women, young and old, started using those church fans. Nettie and Viola nudged each other, as if to say, "Umph, umph, umph." Sylvia whispered, "Girl, Mr. Joseaphus Cantrell and Charlie standing up there making Richard Roundtree and Fred Williamson look kind of plain. And you know that is a *hard* thing for them to do."

They all laughed and slapped palms. What Sylvia said was true. Because if Richard Roundtree and Fred Williamson strutted up in church today, nobody would know they were there, for staring at the groom and his best man so hard. This was going to be a good wedding.

Nettie and Viola looked around the church to find Katie Mae. She was up in the balcony with her husband Cleavon and his nephew Latham, who was making it a point to sit as far away from his soon-to-be ex-wife, Rosie, as possible. Nettie felt kind of sorry for Katie Mae, who was looking like she would rather be anywhere but where she was. Lately, every time Cleavon found out that Katie Mae had been hanging out with her friends or talking to them on the telephone, he picked a fight with her, then stayed out all night or slept on the couch—anything to get her back under his control.

About the only woman in church who wasn't drooling over Joseaphus and Charlie Cantrell was Sheba Cochran, who had eyes only for George Wilson. And the harder she looked, the more mad at him she got for so adamantly denying what she just knew were his feelings for her.

"Why does that man have to look so doggone good today?" Sheba thought, wanting to smack George for being *too* fine in his royal blue clerical robe, fashioned out of the finest Ghanaian fabric, with an orange, red, and blue Kente stole around his neck.

Five of Miss Mozelle's six children were sitting in front pews with their spouses and her grandchildren. With the exception of the oldest brother, Oscar Lee Jr., they were overjoyed that their mother had finally found love and happiness. They loved their daddy, but they knew what he was like. When Mozelle had first brought up the subject of marriage to Mr. Joseaphus Cantrell, those five said, "Go for it, Mama."

Oscar Lee Jr., on the other hand, had put on a performance just like his daddy would have done back in the day. He even looked just like Oscar Lee Sr. And he showed out right in his mama's house, carrying on about her being "totally disrespectful" and "desecrating" his father's memory. He insisted she was acting rash and foolish, hopping up and marrying this stranger, when, as he said, "Daddy ain't even cold in his grave."

But what Oscar Lee Jr. had not bargained for was that his

mother had over forty years of experience dealing with a fool. She just kept right on cooking during his tirade and then, when she sensed that Oscar Lee Jr. had used up all his energy and words, she took him on.

"Oscar Lee Jr., you ought to be ashamed of yourself," she told him. "Your daddy gave his blessing for this marriage, and it will happen whether you like it or not. Lord knows I want you there—you, my firstborn, the first baby I ever held in my arms. But if you want to be a fool, then be one. As for me, I am getting married and that's that. I have Oscar Sr.'s blessing on this, and that overrides any objection coming from you."

Oscar Lee Jr. was speechless. But just like his daddy, Oscar Lee Jr. hated losing a fight, and especially to a woman. He snatched his jacket off the back of his chair and started stomping out of the kitchen. But his mother's voice sliced right through him, stopping him dead in his tracks.

"You know, your daddy spent his whole life making everybody miserable. But in the last days of his life, he worked hard to set his wrongs right. I've never seen anybody make amends like your daddy did. So, I know in my heart that he would be disappointed and disgusted with you right now, *Oscar Lee Thomas, Jr.* He didn't set wrong right just for me. He did it for you, too. He did it so you wouldn't have to live the way he did—always needing to get himself right with God.

"Now, son, you can leave my house. And don't you come back until you have an apology on your lips, and you got sense enough to show the proper respect to me. 'Cause the next time you walk up in *my house* cuttin' the fool, you gone need the ambulance people to get you out."

Louise took her place at the front of the altar to await the entrance of the bride. She could see Bertha positioned at the back of the church, glowing and so pretty in a pale blue chiffon A-line "hostess" gown that flowed gracefully from her shoulders. Beside her stood Melvin Jr., watching Bertha with the special pride and love of a man who is crazy about the woman carrying his baby. Louise would be happy and relieved when those two finally got married—people that much in love *needed* to be married. Plus, she could tell, just by Bertha's cravings and how that baby was sitting, the baby was a boy—Melvin Vicks, III.

On the other side of Melvin Jr. stood Phoebe, her cautious tomboy grandbaby, statuesque in a short pale blue chiffon shift that hugged all her curves and emphasized her long legs. Her beautiful, thick hair, swept off her face with pale blue jeweled hairpins, hung soft and heavy down her back. Louise watched as Phoebe fussed with her corsage a moment before Jackson Williams rushed over to help her with it. If her old-lady eyes weren't playing tricks on her, Louise would have sworn that Jackson stroked Phoebe's cheek for a second after fixing her flowers.

"Umph, umph, umph," Louise thought. "All this time I been thinking Miss Phoebe Josephine Cates been all by her little lonesome, and Miss Lady got that ole long sip of Pepsi-Cola being all attentive to her self."

The organist struck up the first chords of the traditional bridal march. Phoebe and Bertha opened the church doors and rolled a white paper runner down the aisle, sprinkling it with pale pink rose petals. Then Mozelle appeared at the door, arm-in-arm with Mr. Louis Loomis, looking like an angel in her silver lace dress, holding a large spray of pale pink and ivory roses.

"Girl, this show 'nough your day," Mr. Louis Loomis whispered. "You been waiting all your life for it, haven't you?"

Mozelle could only nod, and seeing tears gathering in her eyes, Mr. Louis Loomis handed her his handkerchief. "I *thought* something was missing," he said. "I knew you had something old, something new, and a blue garter. 'Cause you ladies love those blue garters. But I wondered if you had something borrowed, and now you do."

Mozelle took the handkerchief gratefully. Then they started moving slowly down the aisle to a soulful version of the wedding march, rendered on organ and piano, drums, and lead and bass guitars.

"You know, black folks can really work over white folks' songs, can't they?" Mr. Loomis murmured.

Mozelle chuckled, saying, "Louis Loomis, you a mess." When they reached the altar, Rev. Wilson greeted them, beaming, feeling so blessed at conducting this wedding and marveling at how much the Lord loved folks in love. He took Mozelle's pretty little hand and placed it in the strong outstretched one of Joseaphus Cantrell, who was glowing with joy.

Mozelle smiled into the eyes of the man who was about to become her husband. Then she bowed her head for a second in memory of Oscar Lee. She felt thankful that Queenie Tyler had blessed him with true love before he died. It was a miracle how God had worked all that out, despite how Queenie and Oscar came together. Through the grace of God, Oscar got the kind of love he had wanted all his life, and so did Mozelle, when the Lord gave her Joseaphus.

And the power of the Father's love was so supreme that it had inspired Mozelle to insist that Queenie, who had recently joined the church, sit in the family pew alongside her children. Mozelle was glad that God had opened her heart in forgiveness, for the love Queenie showered on her and her children was so sweet and sincere that it was a blessing in itself. Mozelle could understand why Oscar loved Queenie Tyler so much. Even with those gruff street ways, the girl was one of the kindest and most generous people Mozelle had ever met.

Queenie caught her gaze and winked over the head of the grandbaby she was holding in her lap. Then she turned and smiled at her best friend, mean old Warlene, who was huddled up under Old Daddy like she was scared he would slip away from her. As usual, Old Daddy was sharp as a tack in a lime green silk leisure suit with a matching lime green silk derby, a pale turquoise silk shirt with a big collar, turquoise gators, and a sterling silver cane. Since getting saved, Queenie had been desperately wanting her friend to share in the joy she got from the Lord, and she didn't want Old Daddy to reach death's door before rededicating his life to Christ. But Queenie also knew that Warlene had something that could be helpful to her new church, should Cleavon Johnson try once more to force Rev. Earl Hamilton into that pulpit.

And if Warlene got saved, it was a certainty that she would share what she had with the church.

Queenie thought it best to entice Warlene and Old Daddy to church with an invitation to the wedding and reception. Those two liked to party, and she knew that was about the only way they would come to church. When Miss Mozelle called Warlene, at Queenie's request, to personally invite her to the wedding, both Warlene and Old Daddy replied that they were tickled pink and couldn't wait to come.

With a light brush of his fingers on her bare wrist, Joseaphus drew Mozelle's attention away from Queenie and Warlene. His eyes were loving and tender, but in them she saw a passion so intense, it made her have a hot flash. Her reaction brought a rumble of pleasure from her groom that set Mozelle's heart to racing. She had to clutch her bouquet of roses to steady herself as Rev. Wilson began their wedding.

II

The Soul Train line was long—twenty-five people on each side, from little kids standing across from their mamas and daddies, to teens who couldn't wait to "get down" the way they saw the *Soul Train* dancers do it on television, to Rev. Wilson, Sheba Cochran, Bertha waddling across from Melvin Jr., Bert and Nettie, Phoebe and Jackson Williams, MamaLouise and Mr. Louis Loomis, Warlene and Old Daddy, and, of course, the bride and groom.

George was happy to be standing across from Sheba in

the line. It had taken quite a bit of maneuvering to get this spot. And everything would be perfect if Sheba would stop glaring in his direction like she was ready to do him some damage.

The music changed from the O'Jays' "Love Train" to James Brown's "We Gone Have a Funky Good Time." George, who *loved* James Brown, jumped out in the center of the line before his turn, threw a hump in his back, and started Camel Walking to the beat and the claps of the other folks in the line.

The teens laughed, and one of the boys shouted out, "Pastor, you look like Shaft, one baaaaad—"

"Hush yo' mouf," his friend chimed in. "You ain't talkin' 'bout Shaft."

"And," the second teen's mother said from her spot farther down the line, "yo' li'l narrow, mannish behind better hush *yo'* mouf, talking grown enough to get it washed out with some soap!" The teen bent his head down in embarrassment, as his friends snickered and poked at each other, glad that it wasn't one of them.

George stepped up the pace of his movements and then lunged to yank Sheba from the line and into the center with him. But she pulled back, saying, "I'll wait this one out and let you carry the show yourself, Reverend." Again George, who had been trying his best to get back in Sheba's good graces, grabbed her hand, and this time he wouldn't let go. "You scared to dance in this line," he challenged, " 'cause you know you can't do nothing with me."

Sheba couldn't believe that boy. He had the nerve of a brass monkey drinking Brass Monkey, talking that trash about how *she* couldn't handle *him.* She sucked on her teeth and started moving to the music, acting like he wasn't even standing there.

George was not about to let Sheba play him off like that. He got right in front of her and started doing a series of dance steps, spinning around, while his congregation egged him on.

"Pastor, you know you ought to quit."

"Gone 'head with your superbad self."

"Sheba, girl, you better work it a little harder, 'cause that boy gettin' ready to take it to the *bridge.*"

And when George got to dancing harder after that last comment, somebody said, "You know I'm gone pray for you, Pastor. 'Cause you gone need some prayer and laying on of hands, when you wake up all stiff and sore in the morning."

George moved in closer to Sheba. "You ready to be turned every which-a-way but loose?" he demanded. "Or are you too chicken for that?"

"Chicken?" Sheba snapped.

"Yeah," George retorted. "Chicken—*bawk, bawk, bawk-bawk-bawk,*" he cackled, laughing and doing the Funky Chicken.

Sheba wanted to *hurt* George Wilson, and she was not about to let this think-he-God's-gift-to-the-Missionary-Baptist-Church boy get the best of her. She stared at him with what was clearly an I-ain't-a-bit-more-playin'-with-you-than-I-am-the-man-in-the-moon expression and stepped into the clear. In one smooth move, she slid down into a split with such grace that her lavender silk hat didn't even budge on her head. Only a taste of thigh showed when her lavender silk maxi coat swung back to reveal the matching short dress beneath it. Then, without missing a beat, she jumped back up on her feet, breaking into the Crazy Legs, and then the Robot.

"Some smart-mouth Negro who shall remain unnamed in front of *his* parishioners need to shut up and take some notes on this lesson," Sheba said as she bent back into a Parliament-Funkadelic version of the Limbo. She eased back up and then slipped into a Camel Walk that had everybody looking at the wooden floor of the Masonic Lodge as if it had turned into the hot sands of the Sahara Desert. "Ooooh, Rev. Wilson," someone said, "Sheba Cochran just capped on you good!" Folks started clapping and calling out, "Go on, girl, 'cause you know your self is just as bad as that Foxy Brown."

George stopped dancing and was just moving from side to side with the beat, unable to tear his eyes away from Sheba. Those moves on that girl made him wonder, when he knew better than to, what kind of moves Sheba could put on him in private—and to make matters worse, she had the nerve to look breathtaking in that lavender suit. George glanced upward for a second and made a silent plea: "Help me, Father."

Sheba danced right out of the Camel Walk and spun around so fast, she looked like she was doing a *Soul Train* pirouette. Then she stopped spinning, purposefully landed right in front of George, stared him dead in the eye, and stated "So, you were saying that I couldn't handle you? What about you handling me?"

"You can handle me in a Soul Train line, Miss Sheba Loretta Cochran," George whispered in his I-ain't-in-the-pulpit-now voice. "But there's just some situations where you wouldn't be able to do a thing with me, girl."

Sheba narrowed his eyes at George, thinking that he had more nerve than Goliath when he *thought* he was going to whip little David's tail. She said, "Yeah, right, and the world was not created in seven days, *Pastor.* It took eight."

Mr. Louis Loomis and Louise, who were watching those two fuss and dance down the Soul Train line, kept signaling each other to mark the progress of George and Sheba's tiff. Leaning over to Louise, Mr. Louis Loomis whispered, "That boy don't always make the best use of that connection he got with the Lord."

Then he pulled back, grabbing the belt hoops on his tuxedo pants, and started dancing like Cab Calloway did when he sang "Minnie the Moocher."

Katie Mae was stuck at one of the large banquet tables with Cleavon, Latham, and the rest of the Johnson clan, wishing she could yank that mink stole off Cleavon's mother's neck and choke the living daylights out of her. If that woman didn't get on her nerves, she didn't know who did. Besides, she wanted to get in the Soul Train line and dance with everybody else so bad that she could practically taste the music. And she would have gone over there and done just that, had Cleavon not picked that horrible fight with her before they left, threatening separation if she didn't do his bidding at the wedding and reception.

When Cleavon saw George and Sheba dancing down the Soul Train, and Katie Mae looking like she was praying to get over there, he said in a disgusted voice, "And that's who you want to install as the permanent pastor of this church?"

Then he pointed to Mr. Louis Loomis, dancing like Cab Calloway, and shook his head. "This church is going straight to the dogs."

"Naw, Uncle Cleavon," Latham replied. "From the looks of things, I'd say it was going to the goats—the *old* goats."

Everyone at the table started laughing—everyone except Cleavon. Both the hundredth anniversary and the date that George's interim pastorship expired were almost upon them. There was nothing funny about the adversaries Cleavon would have to face in the battle he was about to wage. That old Cab-Calloway-dancing goat over there was the kind who could pack dirt under his feet faster than the speed of light, and then walk right out of any hole you tried to throw him in. And Lord help you when he finally got out and snatched on that big Sears belt.

III

Mozelle sat in a white brocade chair in the bridal suite at the Chase Park Plaza Hotel, arranging her pale silver nightgown and not knowing quite what to do with herself. She was amazed at the fancy room, with its white and gold decor, huge crystal vase filled with long-stemmed white roses, and expensive champagne, chilling in an ornate sterling silver bucket. Years ago, when they were younger, the only room she and Joseaphus would have been welcome in at the Chase Park Plaza was the one where they stored the mops and brooms for the maids and janitors.

Her new husband had gone out to get some ice and, she

suspected, to give her time to get ready for him. It was a strange feeling, being a bride again after all of these years. She got up and went to check herself out in the mirror. Her gown was very pretty—a gift from Sheba Cochran. It was made of the finest silver silk, with spaghetti straps and it clung too close for her comfort, even if it did look real good on her.

She sprayed on some more Estée Lauder perfume and went back to sit in the chair, wondering what she was supposed to do when Joseaphus came in. Oscar hadn't been very romantic, and she was pretty dumb about men when she married him. And if the truth be told, she was *still* kind of dumb about men and the way they were with their natures. But she suspected this wedding night would be very different from her first one—or at least she hoped so.

Mozelle started to get up again and sip on some of the expensive champagne the members of the Mellow Slick Cougars Club, of all people, had given to her and Joseaphus as a wedding gift. She thought about how Old Daddy had come strutting up to them at the reception, with Warlene on his arm and a fancy bottle in his hand. Smiling, he'd said to Joseaphus, "Man, I never thought you needed an invitation to join the club because you were not the kind of man who would really take to being a Mellow Slick Cougar. But you were always one cool brother, Joseaphus. And to honor you and this day, and this lovely little lady here, the club brought this for you. It's two hundred fifty dollars a bottle—top of the line."

Joseaphus said, "Thank you, Old Daddy. And you right—I never was a Cougar type, so no harm done by me."

Old Daddy gave Joseaphus the "Black Power" sign, like he'd been watching all the young bloods do, and then held out his palm. Joseaphus slapped it and gave Old Daddy a firm handshake. Then Old Daddy leaned down and kissed Mozelle softly on the cheek. He said, "You be good. You hear me, babygirl? 'Cause I think you gone get a taste of a *real* man tonight."

Mozelle was deeply embarrassed, but Joseaphus calmed her with a gentle pat on the hand. He knew how bashful and nervous Mozelle was about their wedding night.

The door opened, and Joseaphus strolled in with ice bucket in hand, which he set down on top of a towel on the dresser. He walked over to where she was sitting and bent over, hands on either arm of her chair. Then he lifted one of her hands to his lips.

"I would get down on my knees and kiss on you a bit, Mozie," he said, "but I don't think that is such a good idea at my age."

Mozelle giggled and didn't pull back when Joseaphus drew her up and took her in his arms, tracing soft circles on her bare shoulders. He leaned down and kissed one of those shoulders and let his fingers slip under one of the straps. Mozelle stood perfectly still, holding her breath.

Joseaphus knew he was getting to her, which was what he'd planned. He slid his fingers over her shoulder, up her neck, and on to her chin, lifting her lips to his for a deep, soulful kiss. When he felt her relax and let out a breath, he slid his hand to the back of her head, luxuriating in the silky softness of her hair. Still kissing her, he edged toward the bed, where he sat down and pulled her in close to him. She looked so shy, it made him laugh out loud.

"Baby, it's okay," he said, with his eyes soft and the corner of his mouth turned up in a slight grin. Then he frowned. "This is in the way," he said as he slowly pulled her night-gown down to her feet.

Mozelle gasped and said, "Oh, Joseaphus, I . . . "

"Look like heaven," he said, holding her at arm's length. Mozelle's skin was satiny and radiant, with barely a stretch mark or an age spot. Her little tummy tooted out just enough to be cute. Joseaphus ran his hands over her hips, getting a little squeeze right at the dimpled part of the top of her thighs. He liked her thighs. They were full, round, and soft—a woman's thighs.

Joseaphus stopped and gazed into Mozelle's face. She was softening under his touch. He liked that. "Baby, let me get undressed," he whispered.

Mozelle gave Joseaphus a shy smile and slipped under the covers as he stood up and started taking off his clothes. Beneath his wedding garb, he had on a white undershirt and a pair of white silk boxers with tiny blue moons and stars. Mozelle tried to peek through the slit in those white boxers to see the rest of her husband, which tickled Joseaphus no end. But he didn't let on. He just calmly removed his socks and shoes, stood up and took off his undershirt, then walked over to the bed.

Mozelle loved the sight of Joseaphus. He had a handsome face, smooth, even skin, and strong, nicely shaped legs—not big and muscled but not all skinny and dry and scaly like Oscar's, either. His butt was nice and "toochie," not falling up under his legs like she saw on some men his age. And his chest was beautiful, not hard or superdeveloped but just comfortably firm, with fuzzy gray hair trailing down to his stomach.

When Joseaphus knew Mozelle had gotten herself an eyeful, he slipped out of his boxers and stood there, not in the least bashful. Mozelle's eyes got so big and round, Joseaphus laughed and said, "Baby, don't you worry none. Daddy got it *all* under control."

Mozelle scooted deeper under the covers and pulled the quilt up to her nose like it was zero degrees in the room. Joseaphus loosened the bedclothes and slipped in beside her, pulling her close so he could feel her warm skin next to his. He sighed softly and said, "Baby, I think you're trembling. You have to know that I love you, Mozie."

"I love you, Joe," she whispered back in a husky and sexy voice that came as a surprise to her, let alone Joseaphus.

"And you know something, baby," he whispered in her ear, "God is truly amazing to have created something this good and make it so that folks as old as us can still enjoy it."

Mozie giggled and whispered back, "He truly is an amazing God. Because only the Lord could have given me you."

"Ohhhh, thank you, baby," Joseaphus breathed, as he held tight to his wife and the two of them became one flesh.

IV

Sheba pulled up in front of her house, relieved that the couple that lived across the street wasn't having a card game tonight. She was not in the mood to bang on their front door and make whoever had the nerve to park in her space get his sorry behind outside to move his car.

"Gerald, baby," Sheba said to her oldest, "as soon as we get in the house, I want you and Lucille to help Carl Lee and La Sheba get ready for bed. l am so tired that I can hardly see straight."

"Okay, Mama," Gerald answered.

As soon as Sheba put the car in park, Gerald and Lucille grabbed hold of their sleeping brother and sister and helped them up to the house. Sheba followed and went straight to her room, kicked off her shoes, removed her hat—massaging her head to relieve some of the tension she was feeling—took off her clothes, put on her robe, picked up her favorite pajamas, then headed to the bathroom for a long hot soak.

As soon as the tub was full of bubbly water, Sheba eased down and let it embrace her tired body, as she closed her eyes. Miss Mozelle's wedding was the most beautiful wedding she had ever attended. It was fun, sweet, loving, and full of the Holy Ghost. And it was exactly her own heart's desire to get married to a man who loved her and who knew in his heart that the Lord had been their Supreme Matchmaker. Tears streamed down her face as Sheba thought about George and how much she loved him, much as she sometimes wished she didn't. "Lord," she whispered through her tears, "will You please let that be me one day? Bless with me a husband and make me a bride."

Then a soothing thought eased its way into her soul: "This battle is not yours, Sheba. It's the Lord's."

* * *

Ever since the reception had ended, George had been driving around feeling sad and torn up inside. He longed to have Sheba in his heart, in his arms, in his life. But he was stubborn to a fault and, to tell the truth, afraid what would happen if he gave his heart to Sheba—and just as scared of what would happen if he didn't.

It was after eleven at night when he finally pulled up in front of Sheba's house, parking and sitting in the car, wrestling with himself, listening to Ann Peebles sing, "I'm Gone Tear Your Playhouse Down." Sheba might not have gone after his playhouse, but she sure was tearing down the fortress walls around his heart.

The house was completely dark, so when the song ended, with a mixture of relief and disappointment George restarted the car. But then the porch light snapped on, and when he saw the door open, he cut off the motor again. Sheba was standing in the doorway in white pajamas, trimmed with soft lavender ribbon, and a bright purple satin wrap on her head. She looked so adorable that, before he knew it, George was out of his car and standing on her front steps.

"Can I help you, Pastor?" Sheba asked in what he always called her you-don't-know-who-you-messin'-with voice.

She was shocked to see George at her house—he'd never come by at night like this. But she would have rather snatched Mr. Louis Loomis's brown leather belt out of his hand than let George know how stunned—and pleased—she was to see him.

"You could let me in," he said, trying his best to stay in charge of the situation. Because he felt so out of control, about the only thing he could do was be bossy and not let Sheba get to him.

"Why?" Sheba demanded, a hand on her hip.

"We need to talk to each other."

"Do we?"

George came closer. "Girl, let me in this house," he said gruffly, trying to hide his anxiety. "You know we need to talk."

Sheba stepped aside and waved him in, with a little attitude in her demeanor.

"Hurry up, I'm sleepy," she snapped.

Ignoring her tone, George walked into the house like he felt he was welcome. He sat down on Sheba's white couch, wondering how she kept it so clean with no plastic on it and all those kids.

Sheba claimed a position in the doorway leading to the living room.

"Come here, Sheba," he ordered. "I can't talk to you right with you all the way over there."

She walked over to him real slow, dragging her feet and pouting, reminding George of the way her baby girl, La Sheba, acted. He patted the sofa and said, "You need to sit your surly self down. I always wondered where Miss La Sheba got her little ways from. Now I know—her mama."

Sheba rolled her eyes at George as if to say, "Boy, you ain't gone worry my soul." She did sit down, but all the way on the other side of the couch.

If the situation wasn't so serious, George would have laughed. "Baby—," he began.

"I ain't your baby."

George slid over to Sheba and took her hand in his. Looking into her eyes, he said, "Girl, quit trying to shut me out. 'Cause you know that is not what you really want."

"You *got* some nerve, Rev. George Robert Wilson. It's you, not me, who all up in the open-shut-case business."

"Yeah, baby. I do have some nerve," he whispered, and scooted closer to her. "But if I didn't have some nerve, I would not be sitting here, trying to get next to you. Look, I know how I have hurt you. At first, I was put off knowing you once dated my worst adversary, Cleavon Johnson. Maybe that was wrong—"

Sheba had started softening at his words, but then bristled when she heard him say "maybe." She started to jump up, but George grabbed her wrist.

"You sit right down."

Sheba was scared, glad that he was there, and mad all at the same time. Just the sheer frustration of the situation filled her eyes with tears. And when one crept down her cheek, George wiped it away with his fingertip.

"Sheba, baby, I also think I pushed you away because I have been so scared at the thought of falling in love with you."

"George," Sheba said with some impatience in her voice. "You are already in love, just too stupid to accept it. Why else would you need to run from something, unless it already existed?"

George chose to ignore her and continued, "Baby, last time I fell in love, it happened too fast and it was a disaster. I was devastated by Glodean."

"Look, George Wilson," Sheba said with exasperation.

"We all make mistakes like that. But unlike *you,* most of us don't waste our time being scared and second-guessing ourselves when love finds us again. We thank the Lord for a second chance.

"Now," she said, starting to get up, "I want to go to sleep, so you gone have to go."

But George snatched Sheba back down and drew her close to him. As she tried to pull away, he held on tight.

"Sheba," he said, "don't leave. You know, it's been rough settling into this church, dealing with Cleavon and everything else. Falling in love on top of that just seemed like too much pressure. It's been hard for me to stay away from you, but it has also been hard on me to cope with what I feel for you."

Sheba sniffled and then said, "George, if you think it makes sense to run from love, then I think you ain't *never* truly had it hard enough."

He pulled back and looked at her, surprised. He opened his mouth to reply, but she held up her hand and kept talking. "Oh, for sure you have had heartache, disappointment, and struggle. But anybody who has really had a hard time of it—and especially a hard time they couldn't easily overcome—doesn't stare a blessing in the face. Even if it comes in an unusual package, like me with all of these babies and baby daddies, they just grab at it and be thankful the Lord thought enough of them to send it in the first place. Don't matter what that blessing looks like. A person who has had it hard knows that if the Lord sees fit to send a blessing their way, then He will just see fit to make it all work out alright."

George kept silent, his heart convicted by her words, but waiting to hear the rest.

"And you know something, George? I don't think that you have good sense. All those excuses you are using to keep me at bay are nothing but smoke screens from the devil. He doesn't want you to see past your fears and your heartaches long enough to recognize the blessings God has placed right in your lap. And you letting the devil *keep* you blind."

"Are you through?" he snapped at her.

"As a matter of fact I am," she answered him calmly.

"Now *you're* the one with the open-shut case. You won't even try to understand. I try to apologize and you throw it back in my face. You know, a man has his pride, Sheba—"

"All I need to know is one thing," Sheba broke in. "Are you gone stay blind, George?"

George jumped up with fury in his eyes and his mouth all tight. He glared at Sheba, threw his shoulders back, and then, with long deliberate steps, started for the door.

On any other day, Sheba would have fallen apart if George tried to walk out on her. But tonight, the Lord held her hand and wouldn't let her succumb to being upset over his mess. Staring holes in his back, she said, "George, it ain't my fault that the good Lord saw fit to make me the woman for you, even if you are too stupid to accept it. So I rebuke you in the name of Jesus. God ought to reach down and slap you clear across this room."

George was about to storm out and slam the door on Sheba for good. But when he turned around and saw her standing there, all prissy in white pajamas with that fancy purple rag on her head, with her hands on her hips and trying to be

"Big Mama," his heart just melted. She was right—the Lord did make her just for him. Who else but Sheba Loretta Cochran could have stood up to him like that, working his nerves to the bone, if nerves had bones. The girl had guts, not to mention faith like Job.

George walked over to Sheba, grabbed her wrist, and snatched her up into his embrace. When she tried to pull away, he held on, saying, "If you made just for me, you better keep still, girl, so I can see how well you fit into my arms."

"Stop holding on me like that, boy."

"Okay," he answered. "I won't hold you like that 'cause here's how I really want to hold you." George grabbed the back of Sheba's head with one hand, tightened his grip on her waist with the other, and kissed her deeply and passionately.

"Was that stupid and stubborn enough for you, baby?" he whispered, while planting soft hot kisses on her nose and forehead, then at the nape of her neck. "Mmmmm. You show is right, 'cause God definitely had me in mind when he made your sweet, fine self."

Sheba was having trouble reconciling his words with the fact that her children might be awake and stirring. Nothing like being soft-eyed and mushy over a man to make your kids feel the need to wake up and check things out.

"They are sound asleep," George whispered, mischief lighting up his eyes.

"How you know?" Sheba asked.

"Been keeping an eye out since I've been here."

"Oh?" she said, lowering her eyes.

"You see," George said, "I'm practicing keeping an eye out for the Brady Bunch when I want to get busy with they little grown mama."

"Is that so?" Sheba said, feeling a little bolder.

"Yeah, baby," he murmured through another kiss, then ran his hands up and down the length of her back.

"Uhh, George, we . . ."

"For a lifetime, Sheba."

"Huh?"

George laughed. He was loving this. Even if he was asking the girl to be his wife, he was still controlling it. It was hard enough to ask.

"You gone marry me, little sweet, saved grown girl?"

Sheba was in shock. She had been praying for this very thing for months on end, wearing God's ears out with her tearful pleas to bring her husband into her life. But this prayer had been answered so unexpectedly, she didn't know what to make of it.

"Baby, when God sends you a blessing, you better seize it. Or is it that you haven't had it hard enough," he teased.

"Oh, no you don't," Sheba said, trying to act bad with that big man all over her.

"Oh, yes I do," he whispered. "You call Precious Powers and Essie Simmons and get your wedding stuff fixed up. And do it fast. I'm not a patient man, and I don't know how much longer I can keep my hands off you.

"Now, I'm going home," George announced, as he kissed Sheba's hand and left before he forgot that he was a preacher and that the woman he loved was saved and doing her best to be a dedicated woman of God.

Part 6

God Ain't Playin' with You People

1

Ray Lyles paced around his office, biting his bottom lip to contain the expletives that were threatening to spew forth from his mouth. He had made a promise to himself to never curse in public, but the two men seated before him were making that promise near to impossible to keep. This had not been a good meeting for Ray. In fact, the meeting had not gone well for any of the men present—Ray Lyles, Rev. Earl Hamilton, or Cleavon Johnson.

As the meeting had progressed from bad to worse, Cleavon felt less confident with each passing minute that Ray Lyles could be trusted to follow through with his plan. It was 1976, the country's Bicentennial for liberation from tyranny and oppression, and white men *still* hated taking directions from a Brother. And especially guys like Ray Lyles, the ones with a foot in the door of a house in an all-white and very expensive suburb, while the other foot was dragging off the metal steps of a trailer.

He should have pulled the plug on this thing when Lyles tried to weasel out of the original plan to put Earl Hamilton in Gethsemane's pulpit and instead bully his own assistant pastor at the American Worship Center into that spot. When Ray first put that trash on the table, Cleavon looked at him like he was crazy and said, "This is a *Missionary* Baptist Church, which means it's black—all black. That Opie Taylor assistant pastor of yours wouldn't even be able to sneak in through a side window, let alone walk in through the front door, talking some junk about being the pastor of *my* church. I don't know why you white people have such a problem understanding that black folks like their pastor just like their coffee—hot and some shade of black."

Cleavon studied Earl Hamilton for a moment. He wasn't so sure about that tight-acting, tight-lipped-talking fool, either. Every time Cleavon saw Hamilton, he kept seeing a bigger and bigger "Bought and Sold for Massa" sign on him. And to make matters worse, Hamilton, who supposedly knew better, didn't so much as open his mouth to yawn when Ray Lyles had the audacity to say that they would change the church's name from Gethsemane Missionary Baptist Church to the American Worship Center Auxiliary Congregation. "What Negro in his right mind," Cleavon thought "would even *want* to pastor a no-denomination church like that?"

Cleavon watched Lyles pacing behind his desk and thought that this *Dragnet*-looking, plaid-polyester, light-blue-patent-leather-shoes-wearing, no-preaching white man was bad news. He was beginning to regret that he had ever struck up a deal with him. It had seemed like a good idea after Pastor Forbes's death, when Cleavon had intercepted Lyles's notice of intent to repossess the church's land, effective June 1, 1976, just twelve days before the anniversary. He had told himself back then that he was doing it to help the church—to prevent its demolition and buy time to find the heir who was supposed to give Gethsemane the land, according to that letter in the safe. To get Lyles to play ball, Cleavon claimed to have the actual deed, confident that it would really be in his possession when push finally came to shove. But however the game played out—whether Lyles thought he was getting a satellite American Worship Center, with Cleavon's man in the pulpit, or whether Cleavon saved the day by producing that heir, who would run Lyles off—Cleavon would hold the winning hand.

Except now, his trump card—the letter in the safe on which his whole scheme rested—was lost.

"How could you be so stupid as to let that deed slip right through your fingers? I—" Ray Lyles blew air out of his mouth, trying to calm down. Blacks! Why had he ever thought he could work with these people? According to his lawyers, his wife's document granting Gethsemane the use of the land for a hundred years could be executed as long as the land hadn't been deeded to someone else. So having that deed floating around was not good—not good at all.

But Lyles was determined to get what was rightfully his, both that land and control over the church that would be his first foothold in North St. Louis. And if he had to stomach the likes of Cleavon Johnson and that weak-kneed patsy Earl Hamilton to get what he wanted, then so be it.

Ray bore his eyes into Earl Hamilton, who flinched. He couldn't understand why Hamilton couldn't control Cleavon Johnson. The man was a black preacher, and anybody with half a brainful of information knew that black preachers had a lot of clout and power. What Earl stood to gain from this deal should have made him doubly conniving and forceful in getting total control of this situation at Gethsemane.

Ray never doubted that the way to any man's heart was through his wallet. So unbeknownst to Cleavon, once Earl took charge of Gethsemane, he would get a hefty off-the-record check for working with Ray each and every month. After Ray bulldozed that old church into the ground and built a new, modern satellite American Worship Center, he would allow Hamilton to serve as its pastor for as long as he followed orders from the central office. And the very first order he was giving Earl was to eliminate all that shouting, dancing, and just plain out-of-control black frenzied craziness from the Sunday service. Sometimes Ray secretly hoped that heaven was segregated, because he knew he couldn't stand listening to all that noise and "mumbo jumbo" throughout eternity. And he certainly wasn't going to stand for it in a branch of his own church.

"Earl, do you have any idea where that deed is?"

Earl had been watching the other two men in quiet desperation. Neither Ray nor Cleavon knew that his current church was working feverishly to get rid of him. So if this plan fell through, Earl Hamilton was going to be out of a job. He shifted his eyes to Cleavon, who was digging dirt from under his nails with a pearl-handled pocketknife, wondering why the man couldn't put his hands on that deed.

Cleavon looked up from cleaning his nails and said, "What? Y'all staring holes in me like I lost the deed on purpose. Ain't my fault that doggone thing disappeared."

"What I don't understand," Ray spat out, "is how you could entrust something that important to some old black janitor."

Cleavon sat up straight and glared at Ray Lyles. "For your information, *Ray*," he said evenly, watching Lyles turn red because he called him by his first name, "Mr. Oscar Thomas was a respected member of Gethsemane Missionary Baptist Church. He didn't like where the church was going, and he was one of the people in my camp working to turn things around."

Ray Lyles wanted to punch Cleavon Johnson. He could tell that Cleavon didn't believe that nonsense he was handing him.

"Respected member or not," Ray said in a hard voice that made Cleavon think of a slave driver, "he was just an ignorant Negro janitor who probably didn't even know the meaning of the word *deed*."

Earl looked at Lyles, wondering if he had the good sense to remember that he was alone in a room with two black men. He hoped the man stayed out in St. Charles when he finally took over the church. Because if Ray Lyles waltzed up in Gethsemane talking that talk, one of those "ignorant Negro janitors" was going to whip his tail and then lead the charge to run Earl out.

Cleavon stood up and leaned on Ray Lyles's desk, staring him down. "You may have money and connections and be white," he said, "but if you ain't itching to take this up outside, I'd recommend that you think twice about talking trash about my people in front of me."

Ray Lyles squared off his shoulders, trying not to flinch

under Cleavon's street-hard gaze. He reached for the green security button under his desk and was about to push it when the intercom beeped.

"Ray dear," his wife Betsy's voice rang out. "Are you still in that meeting?"

"Yes, darling," Ray answered. "What are you up to?"

"Honey, I was just about to do a new song," she answered brightly. In the background the pianist was playing what Cleavon thought was a very familiar-sounding tune, only the beat was kind of stiff and off.

Betsy Lyles coughed, cleared her throat, and started in on the song that Sister Hershey Jones sang at Miss Mozelle Thomas and Mr. Joseaphus Cantrell's wedding. Her voice was real high, thin-sounding, and somewhat off-key, in contrast to Sister Hershey's rich and beautiful mezzo-soprano voice. Cleavon happened to glance over at Earl Hamilton and noticed that he was wiping sweat off his brow and grimacing in pain. Cleavon was forced to close his eyes and massage his forehead when she hit a high note that almost made him cry out, "Help me, Jesus."

While Earl and Cleavon were suffering, Ray Lyles was sitting back in his chair with his eyes closed, listening to his wife like Cleavon listened to Gladys Knight. When the song finally ended, he said, "Betsy, darling, that was absolutely beautiful."

"I am so delighted that you liked it, Ray."

"Loved it," he answered with a big smile on his face, momentarily forgetting the two black men sitting in his office.

Cleavon stared at the intercom, wondering how in the world a Beaver Cleaver white woman like Mrs. Lyles got her hands on that song. It was on the only gospel album ever recorded by the blues singer Big Johnnie Mae. No one but a real blues lover would even know about Big Johnnie Mae, and then would have to find a record store in the black community to get the album.

Once the intercom was off, Ray Lyles went from smiling to scowling in a matter of seconds. "Now about that deed," he continued.

Cleavon sat there thinking up a kiss-my-black-behind, boldface lie. The truth was, he had given the letter to Mr. Oscar so Katie Mae wouldn't find it when she went snooping through his things looking for evidence of other women. And the deed, of course, might well not even exist.

Luckily, a plausible explanation popped into Cleavon's head. He looked at Ray Lyles, stroked his chin, and said, "Well, I thought it best to keep the deed out of my hands because I wanted to avoid facing a court order demanding that I turn over any church documents in my possession to the pastor. I didn't want to give it to the current pastor. And I didn't want the Deacon Board to know about it, either."

Ray studied Cleavon's face a moment and then said, "That was a smart move, Cleavon. But that doesn't make me worry any less that the deed may fall into the wrong hands."

"Raaay," Cleavon answered, drawing it out, again enjoying how Lyles's face flushed at the sound of his name in a lowly Negro's mouth, "the possessors of the wrong hands at my church also possess very big mouths. They would never be able to sit tight and keep quiet this long if they had that deed. We're black, Ray. Don't you know how black people can't keep secrets?"

Ray Lyles gave what Cleavon and Earl Hamilton called his "white man laugh"—a hearty chuckle lodged in the back of the throat, with very little emotion—followed by a crisp, "You're a riot, buddy," to drive the point of the laugh home. "Well, buddy. I'll bet you're right. And if the deceased man's widow does find it, I doubt that she'll have any idea what to do with it. Maybe when Earl gets in here he can smoke it out with a little pastoral counseling, eh, Earl?"

Cleavon fought to keep his temper in check. He was sick of sitting up here trying to look like a "safe Negro" with Lyles. As far as Cleavon was concerned, Gethsemane was *his* church, and it would remain his church after any pastor they hired was long gone. Up until today, he hadn't possessed any qualms about doing a shuffle dance with the devil to regain what he considered his right to control his church. Cleavon Johnson was not a man with a secret desire to be a preacher. Instead, he was a layman run amok—one who was determined that no preacher ever gained full control over what he believed belonged to him and his family.

Earl responded to Lyles's suggestion with a weak laugh, knowing full well that Cleavon was trying to play them both for fools. And as for Ray Lyles, if getting this church wasn't so important to him, he would have gone over to that hyena-laughing white boy and beat him like a slave. Ray Lyles didn't have a clue about black church people. They were not about to let a white boy come up in their church thinking he was going to run it. They would burn it to the ground first.

"Prayer Changes Things," the motto for Gethsemane's Prayer Troopers Intercessory Prayer Group, kept nagging at

Miss Mozelle, causing her to toss and turn so in her sleep that Joseaphus shook her hard to wake her up, so he could get some rest himself.

"Mozie, what did you eat before you went to bed?"

"Nothing."

Joseaphus eyed her suspiciously, saying, "You sure about that?" Mozelle loved to sneak and eat hand-packed chocolate Velvet Freeze ice cream late in the evening, when she knew that it would give her indigestion, crazy dreams, and a restless night.

"You think I'm lying?"

"About chocolate, maybe yes." Joseaphus sat up in bed. "But if you ain't, why you tossing and turning so, Mozie?"

"I'm just so worried about that letter Cleavon gave Oscar for safekeeping. The hundred years the church got to use the land is just about up, and we haven't heard one peep about it. Cleavon never even came looking for that letter after Oscar died. And remember Oscar's last words, telling us to keep Earl Hamilton out of the church?"

Joseaphus nodded.

"Well, I just know in my heart that snake in the grass Cleavon Johnson is in cahoots with that serpent Earl Hamilton, and they are getting ready to spring some poison on us."

"I think you're right, Mozie," he said.

"But, Joe, I don't know what I should do about it."

Joseaphus reached out and stroked her cheek. His Mozie was such a busy little thing. Always had to be doing something—cooking, cleaning, working in the yard, washing her car. Even when she got in the bed at night, the girl had to squirm and fidget for a few minutes before she could get still long enough to fall asleep.

"What was running through your head in your dreams, Mozie?"

Mozelle thought hard and then said, "I kept dreaming the words *Prayer Changes Things.*"

"Then, Mozie, I think the Lord is telling you to come to Him with the problem, reminding you that He is in control. And when the Lord has given you some answers and His direction, you can tell the rest of us Prayer Troopers what we need to do."

"Yeah, I'll do just that," she said.

"And now, get some sleep. Remember, we have a big day tomorrow."

"Oh, that's right."

"Don't know how you could forget, as much as you been praying on it, girl," Joseaphus said, smiling and then pinching her on the thigh.

"What was that for?"

"I just remembered that I'm still on my honeymoon," Joseaphus said, grinning and pulling Mozelle close to him.

"You so grown, Joseaphus Cantrell."

"I know that's right, baby," he answered with a sexy laugh running all through his voice.

II

Mr. Louis Loomis stood next to Sheba, who was radiant in a pale peach two-piece ensemble designed by Essie Simmons. Sheba had seen the fabric in Essie's shop when she was there to buy the lavender suit she wore to Miss Mozelle's wedding. And as soon as she saw it, she said, "Essie, hold on to that material. Don't know why I'm thinking this. But I know that's what you gone make my wedding dress out of. Hope I don't sound like I'm crazy, seeing that I ain't even got a man."

All Essie did was laugh and say, "Girl, I will put this away for you. If you feel strong enough to risk asking about it, then you know in your heart that you need it. You just have to have enough faith to sit back and let the Lord work it all out."

And in only two weeks, Sheba ran back into the shop hardly able to contain herself, breathlessly blurting out, "Essie, you'd never believe it but—"

"You need your peach wedding dress."

When Sheba nodded, Essie embraced her, then immediately set out to fashion a Ghanaian-inspired gown that had Precious Powers drooling over it when Sheba came in for her final fitting. The fabric alone was breathtaking, a rich brocade pattern on handwoven cotton, so soft and delicate that it looked like silk. The ensemble had a peplum top with cream-colored silk braiding on the collar and edges of the sleeves, and a long, straight skirt with a slit high up the side. For the wedding, Sheba's hair was wrapped in a headpiece made of the same material as the dress, and she wore white gold hoop earrings, engraved white gold bracelets on each arm, and cream satin platform pumps. Her bouquet was a large assortment of bright colors and shades—oranges, reds, hot pinks, and sunshine yellows.

This was the second time that Mr. Louis Loomis had to give a bride away in a month, and he was starting to feel like "Marryin' Sam." He was so proud of Sheba—ever since she'd joined the church, she had grown more and more into a godly woman on the order of that described in Proverbs 31. And he had to hand it to Louise, Mozelle, Nettie, Viola, and Sylvia for pulling together a wedding in less than one week's time. The tiny side chapel at Freedom Temple Gospel United Church looked beautiful decorated with fresh flowers and ribbons in the same reds, oranges, pinks, and yellows as Sheba's bouquet.

George and Sheba had picked a popular gospel love song by Elroy Thorn and the Gospel Songbirds for her entrance, played on the small stereo Rev. Simmons kept in his office. The song was so perfect for the two of them—with lyrics stating so loud and clear what George and Sheba had secretly felt from the moment they first met:

"*I took a walk with God one morning, and on that day I asked Him to send me someone just like you. On that morning while I prayed, I didn't even know if it were meant for me to have a love so true. But God was with me on that day. He listened to my heart and sent you my way. I said, my God, He truly heard me pray, and sent me one as wonderful as you—my blessing in the form of you . . .*"

As the song faded, Sheba took her place beside George, with her children standing behind her, along with her closest friends. She had always dreamed of having a big, fancy wedding. But never had she imagined that her real wedding would be as beautiful and spiritual as the one the Lord had given her today.

When Sheba got saved, she understood that she had been looking for love the wrong way, partying at the Mothership Club all Saturday night and coming home so early on Sunday morning that the thought of going to church made her head hurt worse than the drinking, hours of dancing, and lack of sleep ever did. And on the day she accepted Christ in her life, she had gotten down on her knees, praying, "I tried it my way, Jesus, and we both know it didn't work. Now I want to do it Your way. Deliver me from this aching loneliness and give me a witness to the power of God to answer our deepest prayers, especially when we pray for love to come our way." And the Lord granted her that witness, with today shouting out her testimony.

George was so regal he made Sheba think of an African king—*her* African king. He was wearing a pale blue Ghanaian tunic with silver braiding around the neckline and sleeves, as well as on the edges of his matching pants and hat. When George looked deeply into Sheba's eyes, whispering, without moving a muscle in his face, "You are my queen, Sheba," she reached out toward Mr. Louis Loomis for a handkerchief.

Rev. Theophilus Simmons, who was conducting the ceremony, was overjoyed for his friend on this glad day. George Wilson was the first friend he'd made when he was appointed the pastor of Greater Hope Gospel United Church in Memphis. It was George who had let him talk out his grief when Theophilus was healing from being tangled up with a woman he would discover was George's own ex-wife, Glodean Benson. Only a man who had been whipped down by Glodean could understand the pain and torment that woman could inflict.

From the beginning, George had been as loyal and good a friend as Theophilus's buddy, Rev. Eddie Tate, who had flown down from Chicago with his wife, Johnnie, to attend this wedding. When Theophilus told Eddie that George had finally gotten some sense and was going to marry Sheba Cochran, all Eddie could do was say, "God is good. 'Cause Theo, man, some of the sweetest and most virtuous women can come in the most controversial and unusual packages, like Sheba and my wife, Johnnie."

As the guests formed a semicircle around the bride and groom, Eddie wrapped his arm around Johnnie, kissed her on the cheek, and whispered, "You know I love you, girl—with your ole sapphire-tooth-wearing self."

Johnnie, looking good in a pastel pink dress that hugged every voluptuous curve, smiled and sucked on that sapphire and gold tooth she was so famous for. She loved her some Eddie Tate. And she worked hard by his side as the first lady of Mount Zion Gospel United Church. Of all of the people in this chapel, Johnnie Tate was the most joyful for Sheba. Because when she fell in love with Eddie, he was just as stubborn and running as fast from love as George Wilson. When she first heard about Sheba, she started praying on that hardheaded George right then and there.

The wedding was very small—just MamaLouise, Mr. Louis Loomis, Bert and Nettie, Viola and Wendell, Sylvia and Melvin Sr., the Tates, the Cantrells, and Theophilus and Essie Simmons—but it was perfect as far as George was concerned. His first wedding had been a major production, and being merely the groom, he was assigned only a walk-on role in the extravaganza. But this wedding was different—it was not about the show, it was about the Lord and the marriage.

Sheba and George exchanged their simple white gold wedding bands amid loved ones gathered in one accord, all rejoicing over this union. And when Theophilus pronounced George and Sheba "husband and wife," he could barely get "And now you may kiss the bride" out of his mouth before George had Sheba wrapped up in a deeply passionate kiss.

At first Sheba was embarrassed by her husband's display of affection. But when she felt his heart beating in the same rhythm as hers, she relaxed and embraced him, losing herself in his kisses. Then George put his cheek next to hers, closed his eyes with the pleasure of the softness of it, and whispered, "I love you, baby."

Sheba blushed and lowered her eyes. George held his wife and breathed to her in a voice so soft that it made Sheba feel like he was making love to her, "Can you feel me, girl?"

When she gave him a shy and self-conscious smile, he said, "Can you handle me, baby?"

"Time for y'all to leave," Mr. Louis Loomis said, to diffuse some of that heat, because those two didn't even know there was anybody else in the chapel at the moment. Folks like that needed to handle their business so that they could come back to earth with the rest of the people. But then again, as far as Mr. Louis Loomis was concerned, it was a mighty beautiful and blessed thing for two people to feel that way about each other.

III

The parsonage looked beautiful, decked out in flowers and ribbons for the pastor and his new First Lady by Nettie, Viola, Sylvia, MamaLouise, and Miss Mozelle. It was a lovely classic two-story house with large, high-ceilinged rooms painted a soft cream with a hint of sunset pink, which was echoed in the sand-colored hardwood floors. It had gracious bay windows with comfy window seats, overlooking a well-manicured lawn and flowers in the front yard and a tiny vegetable garden in the back.

George took Sheba's hand and guided her upstairs, then opened the door to the master bedroom. He couldn't help but smile as he witnessed the pure delight on his wife's face at seeing the inviting room for the very first time. It had pale violet walls, a large sleigh bed with a pale gray satin comforter, and large soft pillows in violet, pink, white, and gray.

"Your wedding gift, baby," George said. "You like it?"

Sheba's eyes shone. "It's perfect. Thank you, George. I've never had anybody give me a gift like this."

George took Sheba's bouquet, placed it on the dresser, and kissed her hand. "You deserve it, sweetheart," he said, kissing each of her fingertips. He reached up and unwrapped her headdress to reveal beautiful cornrowed braids swept up into a French roll, which glistened in the light. He ran his fingers over those braids and said, "Baby, who did your hair? I've never seen this kind of braided hair."

"Sylvia."

"I love it."

Sheba's eyes filled with tears, as she whispered again,

"Thank you, George." Nobody had ever told her that she had beautiful hair.

George kissed Sheba with such love and tenderness, the tears fell down her cheeks. He bent down and tasted them, taking her chin in both hands, and kissed her on the lips, first softly and gently, then more urgently. She felt the heat coming from that kiss all over her body and pulled her husband in closer.

"Baby," he said, "you just hold on to me to your heart's content."

George let his hands slip down to cup Sheba's behind. It felt good. He pressed her to him and did a slow grind, slipping his foot between hers, letting Sheba feel as much of him as she could. When she jumped and said, "*George,*" he just laughed. "What's wrong, girl?"

"Nothing. But you . . ."

"I'm what, baby? Tell me what I am," he asked, with mischief running in his voice.

"Uhh, never mind."

"Sheba," George said, unbuttoning the top of her dress, "how did you get those four babies?"

"The regular way," she answered bashfully, eyes closed, as he slid her top from her shoulders, put it on a chair, and slipped off her skirt.

"Hmm . . . I'm not so sure about those," George muttered, tugging at her stubborn panty hose. "Help me with these things, Sheba."

Sheba took off her panty hose and shoes. She was standing in front of her husband wearing only a baby blue lace bra and matching panties. Her figure wasn't curvy, just nice, and cute, and so firm that it didn't look like she had one baby, let alone four.

"I thought brides were supposed to wear white."

"You once told me that blue was your favorite color," she pointed out. "So I thought I'd wear something you liked on your wedding day."

"Oh really?" George said, and eased Sheba over to the bed, standing in front of her and removing his clothes down to the pale blue cotton boxers he was wearing. Then he slipped her out of the rest of her clothes and lay her gently on the bed.

"I'm cold, George."

"No you're not—you are embarrassed," he said, lying beside his wife and wrapping his arms tightly around her. "Now, is that better?"

Sheba nestled up in George's arms and whispered, "Yes."

"Well, then," he said, planting a hot kiss on her lips, "this should be even better. What you think, girl?" George rolled Sheba on her back and let her feel his full weight, looking deep into her eyes, before kissing her again. He kissed her lips, each cheek, her earlobes, her jawbone, and nibbled at the hollow of her neck, then moved down to her collarbone and planted a soft kiss right on the spot where he could feel Sheba's heart beating hard and fast. George sighed and kept kissing his wife—her stomach, the sides of her hips, and on down.

Sheba lay perfectly still, almost afraid that if she moved this moment would evaporate. Her husband kept blazing his hot trail of kisses until, all of a sudden, Sheba jumped and said, "*George?*"

All he did was chuckle and kiss his way back north, not stopping until he was looking in her eyes once more. "I love you, my bodacious, bashful-with-a-man, little North St. Louis girl," he said.

"And I love you with all my heart," Sheba replied.

They rested in each other's arms, luxuriating in the closeness of their bodies, for a moment until Sheba said, "I feel like we should have some music."

"Umm-hmm," George answered lazily, and reached over to the radio on the nightstand.

He flipped it on, and Betty Wright's "Tonight Is the Night That You Make Me a Woman" filled the air.

"What a perfect song," George murmured, and set out to finish what he had started—making his woman, Sheba Cochran Wilson, his wife.

IV

Unfortunately for the newlyweds, their honeymoon bliss was short-lived. Just ten days after the wedding, Ray Lyles sent George a certified letter officially laying claim to the land under the church. It began, "Pursuant to my letter of October 13, 1975, we intend to reclaim possession of the land granted to Gethsemane Missionary Baptist Church upon expiration of the 100-year term on June 1, 1976. Inasmuch as there has been no response or counter to our claim, my wife, Betsy Ashton Lyles, the sole living heir of the grantor, is prepared to assert her right of ownership . . ."

Reading the letter, George was aghast. "How could the

church receive a claim like this back in October and not act on it?" he said. "Who would have gotten it?" Then it struck him. "Cleavon!"

George jumped up from the table so fast that he knocked over his soda and a chair.

"Wait!" Sheba said. "What's going on?"

"Whatever Cleavon was after in the safe has something to do with this," George fumed. "And I aim to find out what if I have to beat it out of him."

"Baby, you ain't going nowhere in this state," Sheba insisted, "especially not over something this big. You can't deal with that fool without an attorney and a clear head. We need to call Phoebe right now."

George called her, and when he finished reading her the letter, all she said was "Hmmm, interesting, very interesting."

"What do you mean by 'interesting, very interesting,' girl? This is serious," George insisted.

"Pastor, you need to calm down, so that you can handle this like you do everything else—with smooth, prayerful, street-brotha finesse. Now, that has always been a winning combination in my book."

George relaxed and said, "I hear you, Miss Lady. Gone 'head and do your thing, and then come back and tell your pastor what he need to know."

"I'm coming by to get the letter, then heading on over to Mr. Louis Loomis's house to get some information that might turn this thing all the way around."

Mr. Louis Loomis answered his door wiping his mouth with a napkin in the way that only black men can do. He brushed it across his mouth, his mustache, and then both hands, patting each one several times before he was through.

"Come on in, baby," he said. "Just got off the phone with Sheba, who gave me the news. You know that white boy done lost his mind. And I'd bet some money that Cleavon is somehow tied up in this mess."

"Yeah, Rev. Wilson and I were thinking that very same thing," Phoebe said as she followed Mr. Louis Loomis into the kitchen. She liked his house. Mr. Louis Loomis was a carpenter before he retired, and he could do just about anything with his hands. And she especially liked his handmade kitchen set. The wooden table was painted bright blue, and it was surrounded by four chairs in bright green, yellow, red, and orange.

Her grandmother was sitting in the yellow chair, her favorite color, eating a bowl of red beans and rice like it tasted so good she wanted to cry. She smiled at Phoebe and asked, "Baby, you hungry?"

"Yes, ma'am." Phoebe smirked at MamaLouise as if to say, "You ain't foolin' nobody with your slick self."

MamaLouise looked back at Phoebe, eyes twinkling, as if to reply, "You don't stop being a woman just 'cause you get old."

Phoebe sat down in the red chair as Mr. Louis Loomis handed her a bowl of red beans and rice. Then he refilled his own and, sitting back down, dipped up a big spoonful and blew on it a few seconds before pulling it in his mouth. MamaLouise poured Phoebe some iced tea and added a little more to her own glass. Then Mr. Louis Loomis put on his reading glasses and perused the letter, chewing and sucking on his teeth. "Oooh, babygirl," he exclaimed, "this boy is plumb crazy. Do they have a case they can take to court?"

"Maybe," Phoebe answered him evenly, "but I have a workable plan. I just need your help to set it up. And I'm going to ask Miss Mozelle to call Queenie Tyler."

"Queenie Tyler?" Mr. Louis Loomis and MamaLouise both said, looking perplexed.

"I can't go into it right now," Phoebe said, "but Queenie Tyler has access to something that can help the church and eliminate a bunch of foolishness once and for all."

Mr. Louis Loomis, doing exactly as Phoebe had instructed, put out the word: "You better be at church on Wednesday night, unless you want your church torn all up by a pack of wolves."

Wednesday night prayer meeting had been suspended for the emergency, and George walked up into the pulpit not knowing what he was going to say. He glanced at Sheba, who was wearing a stunning cotton candy pink knit suit, with black rhinestone buttons and black braided silk trim on the collar, the cuffs, and the bottom edge of the jacket, along with black patent-leather pumps and a matching envelope shoulder bag. The outfit came from Essie Lee Clothiers, and it had "First Lady" written all over it.

But as good as Sheba was looking tonight, George knew she was very nervous. This was her first official appearance as the First Lady of the church. George winked at her to let her know how proud he was of her, then grinned at his four stepchildren, drawing strength from their answering smiles.

"Church," he began, "it is no secret that this congregation

has been in turmoil since the day Rev. Clydell Forbes died. But now it is imperative that we come together to deal with a serious threat.

"I don't know if any of you know this, but the land this church sits on was loaned to the church by a dedicated member for one century. And frankly, church, I don't believe for one minute that this man meant for any of his descendants to try to do us harm. But sadly, one of them has surfaced and wants to take our church right from under our feet without a thought or care, just weeks before we are to celebrate our hundredth anniversary."

The congregation erupted in cries of outrage and horror. George gave them a few minutes to absorb the shock before he resumed. "Brothers and Sisters in the Lord, you know that I am only the interim pastor and that my term will end around the time this crisis comes to a head. But I am as committed to this church as if I were baptized in it. I want to stand by you and help to guide you through this storm, and I hope that you will give me the authority to do so. See, I know that the Lord has called me to be the permanent pastor of his church. And I have perfect peace that He is going to work it all out."

"Yes, Lawd," Queenie Tyler shouted out. "We the bread and you the butter, Pastor. Just spread the word right on over us."

A ripple of laughter ran through the congregation, easing the anxiety caused by the announcement. "Thank you, Sister Tyler," George said. "I don't think anybody in this church could have put it better than that."

"I know that's right," Sister Hershey Jones called out.

"To show you the depth of my commitment to Gethsemane, let me introduce you to one of your Sisters in the Lord who has become my wife, the First Lady of my life, Sheba Cochran Wilson."

Folks began to applaud, until Cleavon's voice rang out from the balcony, "Man, you have the nerve to stand up there and ask to be our permanent pastor, when you bringing along Jezebel as our First Lady?"

"What did you just say?" George asked Cleavon, unbuttoning his robe.

"Negro, you heard exactly what he said," Latham joined in. "This whole church knows that Sheba Cochran is not, nor will she ever, be a decent woman, a woman of God, or the First Lady of our church."

George laid his robe neatly on the pastor's chair and removed his clerical collar, so as not to insult the Lord too much, then stormed out of the pulpit, heading for the balcony. Sheba coughed to get his attention, frantically shaking her head, but George shot her a look saying "I'll handle this as I see fit . . . "

All Sheba could do was acquiesce to her husband's silent command, fold her hands in her lap, and turn the matter over to the Lord.

At that point, Katie Mae stood up, loudly gathering her things and her children. Embarrassed, Cleavon grabbed her wrist with such force that she could feel the bruises form.

"You need to sit your butt down," he hissed.

Katie Mae didn't say a word. She just wrestled her wrist out of Cleavon's grip, then headed her children down to sit with Bert and Nettie. After waiting at the bottom of the stairs to let them pass, George was about to bound up and whip Cleavon's tail when he heard a commotion at the back of the church.

As if on cue, the television minister, Ray Lyles, and Rev. Earl Hamilton came strutting in, with Lyles's wife trailing behind them.

"What the . . . ," Bert murmured, and got up to investigate. He advanced on the intruders with Wendell, Melvin Sr., Mr. Louis Loomis, Joseaphus Cantrell, Melvin Jr., and Jackson Williams on his heels. George remembered Mr. Louis Loomis's story of how Ray Lyles's men had come at him, and wanted to avert the same kind of free-for-all. Stepping out into the sanctuary, he held up his hand to signal the men to hold their peace.

Ray Lyles kept walking, making a beeline for the pulpit. But George blocked his path, warning, "You better stop right there unless you want to feel the real black hand of fellowship."

Lyles halted, but stood his ground and addressed the congregation. "Children of God, we are here to announce the dawning of a new day at Gethsemane Baptist Church—now the Auxiliary American Worship Center."

Up in the balcony, Cleavon sat looking smug, as the rest of the congregation began buzzing: "Who that man think he is, comin' up in here like this? That white boy must be on drugs."

Lyles removed a paper from his pocket and prepared to read it, until he saw George staring him straight in the eye, saying in a low and very deadly-sounding tone, "Get out."

Lyles hesitated, and then a woman's voice called from the

side door of the sanctuary, "Didn't you hear the man tell you to get out?"

There stood Warlene, hanging on Old Daddy's arm. "Thank you, Jesus," Queenie and Phoebe whispered.

"Rev. Wilson," Warlene said, "I have something that will put a stop to this mess. Ain't that right, Osceola?" she added, looking right at Betty Lyles.

All eyes tracked her glare to the back of the church, where Ray Lyles's wife was still lurking, looking like she wished she could disappear.

"Who are you?" Ray Lyles demanded.

"Ask *her,* if you wanna know so bad," Warlene snarled, digging in her purse. She pulled out a document, which she placed in George's hand, saying, "Read it, Rev. Wilson."

Flipping through the pages, George began to smile, while Warlene kept after Lyles's wife: "I can't believe you and that jacked-up, money-begging, sorry-excuse-for-a-preacher white boy you married would try to game on this church. All you got is our grandpappy's old grant to use the land—land that he left to our daddy, Osceola. And our daddy—our black daddy, Mrs. Lyles—died and willed it to me. That's his will that Rev. Wilson reading right now.

"You left and never came back, Osceola. I was only ten years old. We never even knew where to find you until we started seeing you on TV, up at that American Worship Center—and passing for white. That's when Daddy knew you had run off for good, just like our mama. You never even came when he was dying."

All the congregation members were craning their necks to look at the women, and a few of them even stood up to get a better look. The resemblance between Warlene and Mrs. Lyles was uncanny once you saw them side by side. The only difference between them was their skin color. Warlene was pale ivory brown, with a shot of redbone in her skin, and Mrs. Lyles was ivory, with just a hint of olive. But they both had thick, short, dark red curly hair, very dark blue eyes, round faces, and stocky builds with big feet and large breasts. They even looked like they wore the same kind of bras, the stiff cone-shaped ones that made their breasts look like torpedoes.

"Now, just a doggone minute," Lyles huffed, starting to move in on Warlene with a raised, clenched fist. That made the entire church sit up, eager to see Warlene whip the man, as they knew she surely would. But then a gunshot stopped Ray Lyles in his tracks and sent everybody else hopping out of their pews and onto the floor, dusting off the plaster the bullet dislodged when it hit the ceiling.

"The next bullet will go right up in your behind, if it don't ricochet off of your big head and hit somebody else first," Old Daddy said, as he cocked a pistol with garnet and topaz stones embedded in its glistening mother-of-pearl handle.

Ray Lyles reluctantly backed away from Warlene and turned toward his wife. He felt sick. The resemblance between his Betsy and that crude-acting black woman could not be denied.

"Ray," Betsy/Osceola pleaded, starting toward her husband until Old Daddy stopped her by brandishing his pistol. He had never liked Osceola, with her phony, lying, and greedy self. Warlene hadn't spoken to her sister in thirty years, but Old Daddy had seen the heifer a number of times when she sneaked down into North St. Louis to buy music or get some rib tips and chitlins and a fried tripe sandwich. But she never even sent her family any money, rich as she was.

"Stay right there, Osceola," he said. "Stand there and explain why you'd sell out your own kind and try to steal their property. I knew your grandpappy, and I know he'd rather wear a cheap suit and run-over shoes than see you and your okey-doke husband run this church."

"Now, see here," said Earl Hamilton, crawling out from behind a pew, where he'd taken refuge when the gun had been fired. He could hear the lonesome whistle of his gravy train pulling out and leaving him behind. "Let Mrs. Lyles alone. Remember that you are in God's house and should refrain from the lull of heathenism."

Old Daddy pointed the pistol in Hamilton's direction, taking pleasure in the fear that flickered in the man's eyes. "That's right, son—I am still a heathen. So it ain't gone bother me none if I need to shoot you."

Lyles stared at his wife, his eyes hard and accusatory. "How could you do this to me, Betsy?"

"I love you, Ray. You wanted the land so much that I . . ."

"I mean, how could you be a nig . . . a black?" He scoffed and laughed in disbelief at the same time. "And for nineteen years you've been in my church, in my house, in my bed, the mother of my—oh my God, my children are black. I am the only white person in my home."

Lyles threw up his hands in horror, then pushed past his wife, heading for the back doors. She grabbed at him, begging, "Ray, don't be angry. Don't go, please. Please, you are my whole life, you are my family—"

"You said your family was dead. Get those lying black hands off me, you spawn of Satan." Yanking his arm out of her grip, Lyles shoved Betsy so hard that she fell to the floor, sliding clean across the rug. Then he spun around, standing over her to spit out a final question. "But Betsy, if you're black," he said, with venom in his voice, "why can't you sing?"

Then he stormed out, as his wife picked herself up off the rug and ran after him.

Earl Hamilton was furious. If that big red woman had not come up in this church today, he would have had a sweet job and a whole lot of money. Now he had absolutely nothing, along with a name that was sure to be slandered throughout St. Louis. He walked right up to Warlene and slapped her so hard, his hand left dark red marks across her face.

"Oh, no," Old Daddy said, waving his pistol. And as everybody dove for cover, he squeezed off two more shots, grazing Earl Hamilton's behind.

Earl grabbed at the seat of his pants—which were now on fire—hardly able to grasp what had just happened. When he saw the blood on his hand, he cried, "Why, you infidel, you . . . "

"You the devil, boy," said Old Daddy. "So I know the Lord don't mind me shooting you in His house."

"Amen," Queenie Tyler shouted out. Sister Hershey Jones, who was becoming fast friends with Queenie, who had an incredible bluesy voice, added, "Hallelujah and thank you, Jesus."

"Now, you have just eight seconds to get out of my church," Old Daddy told Earl Hamilton.

"Eight seconds?" he asked, still in shock. "What—"

"Seven now" was all Old Daddy said, watching with satisfaction as Earl Hamilton hobbled out in pain. "Hold it there, boy," he called after him, "don't you go wasting any blood in here, neither."

Looking behind him, Earl saw a splash of blood on the walnut floor and desperately wished it had hit the deep red carpet. Bending down with a squeal of anguish, he mopped up the spot with a starched white handkerchief.

After the shooting Phoebe reached down to help Bertha back up onto the pew and got concerned when she saw that her cousin was sweating and looking sick. "Go get Aunt Nettie and Melvin Jr.," she told an usher.

Melvin Jr. rushed back to their pew and, quickly sliding in next to Bertha, asked anxiously, "Baby, what's happening?"

"My water just broke. You better marry me now, before I have this baby!"

Phoebe stared at Bertha's soaked dress and said, "I am so glad I made your butt get that marriage license. I told you, told you this would happen. Come on, Melvin Jr., let's get this girl to the hospital."

As they struggled to help Bertha stand, Jackson Williams rushed over to lend an extra hand. The three of them had just gotten her into the center aisle and started to walk her out of the sanctuary when a contraction hit Bertha so hard that it put her on her knees.

Nettie, Bert, Sylvia, and Melvin Sr. came running over, as

Phoebe looked frantically for Karen, the other doctor in the congregation. Knowing Bertha would never let Latham lay a hand on her, she sighed with pure relief when she spotted Karen heading their way. "Call an ambulance," Karen was saying. "What hospital you want her to go to?"

"Her doctor is on staff at St. Luke's," Nettie said.

Bertha was down on her hands and knees crying. With some effort, Melvin Jr., Jackson, and Bert managed to get her up and carry her to the ladies' parlor. When they got there, Rev. Wilson was waiting on them, Bible in hand, with Sheba standing by as a witness, ready to perform the marriage ceremony in between Bertha's labor pains.

"Dearly beloved," he began.

"Ohhh, Melvin Jr."

"We are gathered here in the sight of God—"

"JESUZZZ!!! JESUZZZ!!!" Bertha hollered, crying and pulling on Melvin Jr. "Why did you do this to me? I am hurting so bad, I could kill you. You knocked me up and made me have all of this pain."

"Baby, baby please, calm down. I can't stand to see you like this."

"I ain't marrying you!"

"Bertha, baby, please," Melvin Jr. pleaded.

"Bertha Kaye," MamaLouise snapped. "You gone marry Melvin Jr. right now! Don't go blaming him like you had nothing to do with getting that baby. Didn't nobody tell you to go and lay up with that man."

George said, "Bertha, do you—"

"YES! YES! Ahhh . . . MamaLouise. It feels like the baby is kicking me in the back!"

"Bertha," Karen asked, with a worried look on her face, "can you close your legs?"

"No, stupid!" Bertha sobbed, sweating and panting.

"Hmm, I'd say this baby is coming. Lay Bertha down on the floor. Melvin Jr., sit behind her. And I want you to grab her under her knees and hold them up for me."

Karen dug around in her black bag for some surgical scissors. When she pulled them out, Bertha managed to say, "What you gone do with those?"

"Cut your panty hose and underwear off."

"In front of everybody? Ohhhh, Lawd."

Karen waved the men off to a corner, while MamaLouise and Nettie came over to shield Bertha's body from view. As she cut off Bertha's underclothes, Karen told Phoebe, "Go and boil some water so I can sterilize my scalpel and scissors." Then she asked, "Miss Sheba, are there towels here?"

"Yeah," MamaLouise piped up. "We have some clean towels and white sheets that we use for Communion Sunday."

"Melvin Jr.!!!" Bertha hollered out.

"Yeah, baby. What you want, baby? Tell me, baby!"

"It feels like a big watermelon."

"What?" Melvin Jr. said.

"The baby?" Karen asked. She put on her rubber gloves and took a look.

"Mama, Mama," Bertha cried.

"Mama's here, Sweet Potato," Nettie crooned, as she stroked her daughter's forehead with a cool towel. Poor Bert was pacing in the corner with the men, almost having a heart attack at seeing his little girl in so much pain.

"The baby's head has crowned," Karen said. "She's not going to last until the ambulance comes. Where is Phoebe?"

"Right here," Phoebe answered as if on cue, carrying the pot of boiling water.

Karen dropped her tools in the pot while Sheba pinned a big sheet around her to protect her clothes. Then Karen said, "Bertha, I need for you to push when I tell you to. And Rev. Wilson, you have very little if any time left to marry them."

"Do you?" George began again.

"Lawd," Bertha hollered.

". . . Melvin Earl Vicks, Jr."

"LAWD."

"Push, Bertha," Karen commanded.

"I can't. It hurts."

"You better."

". . . take this woman to be your lawfully wedded wife in all ways . . ."

"Lawd!"

"I do, Pastor. I do," Melvin Jr. said hurriedly.

"The baby's head," Karen said.

"JEEESUZZZ!"

"Now his shoulder."

"HEELLLPPPP!!!!!!!!!!!!"

"Rev. Wilson, hurry," Nettie and MamaLouise exclaimed together.

"By the power . . ."

"JESUS! JUST KILL ME!"

"Y'all married. In Jesus' name. Y'all married. Amen."

"It's a boy," Karen said brightly, smiling and holding up a screaming, mad, big, fat, healthy little baby boy.

Melvin Jr. started to cry. He held his wife close, gazing at his bellowing son, sounding just like his mama, and said, "You a good God! Thank you, Lord. Thank you, Lord."

George grabbed Sheba's hand and pulled her along as he made his way back to the sanctuary.

"Baby, we need to get back in church," he said. "I just hope Old Daddy hasn't shot anybody else while I was gone. I'm not looking to perform a wedding and funeral in an hour's time."

As they hurried into the sanctuary, Sheba realized why she had been so nervous about being introduced as the new First Lady. With Lyles's attempted takeover, Old Daddy shooting Rev. Hamilton, Warlene exposing her crazy sister, and Bertha getting married and giving birth at the same time, being First Lady was a job that no thinking woman would attempt to do alone. It was the kind of job that only the Lord could help you handle.

The sanctuary was in complete chaos. Now it was Cleavon and Latham who were the center of controversy, surrounded by a ring of angry church members, who were all up in their faces, shouting and shaking their fists. Mr. Louis Loomis and Joseaphus Cantrell had grabbed hold of Cleavon's mother, Vernine, who was pushing folks to get to her son, and carried her to the door, opened it, and put her out.

Two older deaconesses in the church had set upon Latham and proceeded to beat him in the direction of the door. One was armed with a big, ugly, pea green pocketbook and the other with two church fans—one in each hand.

George tried to subdue his unruly flock, waving his arms to get their attention, but his voice was all but drowned out in the commotion. He looked for Sheba and found her up in the pulpit, down on her knees, starting to pray. George ran to join her, on the way grabbing the organist and steering her toward the instrument.

As the chords of "My Heavenly Father Watches over Me" rang out in the sanctuary, folks realized that their pastor and First Lady were not caught up in the fracas. Instead, they were on their knees, calling on the Lord to bring healing to the church. Some of the scufflers immediately dropped to their knees, while others made their way to the altar. Within minutes, the tension and anger that had gripped the church had begun to fade, replaced by an air of warmth and peace.

When George and Sheba stood and faced the congregation, they saw Cleavon sitting in the back of the church with his face all twisted up. George just stared at him, astonished at his nerve, but Sheba left her husband's side to confront him. She said, "You punk. You get on your knees and pray for your church, or take yourself and the mess you made on out of here."

Cleavon had stood up defiantly and was ready to walk out, when it struck him that Sheba had called him out of his name.

"My name ain't 'You punk.' Sheba, you better use my name when you talk to me."

"Can't do that."

"What?" Cleavon said, as George eyed his wife curiously, wondering what was up.

"You punk, I once overheard you bragging to Latham that Rev. Earl Hamilton would be the pastor of this church, or your name was not Cleavon O'Rell Johnson. Well, he's not the pastor of this church. So I guess Cleavon is not your name."

Epilogue

On the Second Sunday in June, Gethsemane Missionary Baptist Church celebrated its hundred-year anniversary. Over the past nine months, it had been nearly devastated by a raging storm of trial and tribulation. But thanks to the faith of its steadfast members, the church had emerged from that storm not only intact but with a rainbow of blessings curved over it.

Folks came to church on the anniversary dressed like it was Easter Sunday. The morning service was so hot that it left some members shouting and praising the Lord all the way to their cars. Thirteen people, including Warlene and Old Daddy, got saved and became candidates for Baptism. Seven more people came up to be baptized on the spot. Nine rededicated their lives to Christ. Twenty-eight people received the Holy Ghost and the gift of tongues. And so many people got anointed and slain in the Spirit, there were folks laying out on the floor all over the sanctuary.

The afternoon service, with its special hundred-year-celebration concert, promised to be even more spirit-filled—"a hot Holy Ghost good time," in Mozelle's words. The concert was the debut of the church's newest choir, the King's Men, or as they called themselves, the KMs. The KMs had been founded by Jackson Williams, who felt the church needed a chorus to showcase its best male singers—with himself being one of them, a tenor who could put Dennis Edwards of the Temptations to shame.

For this special day, Sheba was elegant in a violet silk suit, with her hair done in the same French roll of cornrowed braids that Sylvia had designed for her wedding. Her makeup was natural and sweet—soft gray shadow on her eyelids, glowing blush on her cheeks, and rich pink lipstick specially selected by Precious to complement her outfit.

George looked down at Sheba from the pulpit and gave his First Lady a sexy wink. He loved the way she always grinned and lowered her eyes when he did it. Then he gazed out over the congregation, lifting up his hands to declare, "God is a good God. Say 'Amen,' church."

"Amen, Pastor."

"Say 'Hallelujah,' church!"

"Hallelujah!"

"Say 'Praise the Lord,' church!"

"Praise the Lord!"

"Now look at the person next to you and say, 'Neighbor, my God don't play. That's why I trust in Him each and every day.' "

Everybody looked to their right or left and repeated, "Neighbor, my God don't play. That's why I trust in Him each and every day."

"Y'all ready to have some more church?"

"Yes, Lawd," some folks hollered out.

"Well, let's get this show on the road. Church, the King's Men."

George took his seat beside Sheba, enjoying the chance to do something a pastor rarely could—sit with his wife in church. Taking her hand, George wondered again why it had taken him so long to understand that this woman was the answer to his prayers—all he could ever want in a wife and helpmeet.

The musicians came out first. There were twelve of them, nine men and three women, dressed in black tuxedos and black formal gowns—pianist, organist, bass player, lead guitar, conga drummer, drummer, trumpet and French horn player, tenor and alto saxophonists, flutist, and violinist. Tuning their instruments, they struck up the chords of the first song, a funky gospel-blues piece.

Two ushers opened the double doors at the back of the church, revealing the KMs in formation, with Mr. Louis Loomis leading the pack. He led them down the center aisle to the halfway point, where they stopped and stood rocking from side to side, just feeling the rhythm and letting everybody get a good look at them. Each KM was wearing a powder blue leisure suit, a black silk big-collared shirt, a silver chain, and a black suede hat; and each carried a black cane.

Mr. Louis Loomis searched the sanctuary for Louise, who was sitting with Bertha, holding her new great-grandson. When he caught her eye and saw her smile, he broke into a rhythmic strut down the aisle, with the rest of the choir behind him. Then, one by one, each KM removed his hat to the beat of the music, from the oldest members—Mr. Louis

Loomis and Joseaphus Cantrell—down to the youngest—Melvin Jr. and Jackson Williams.

When they reached the choir stand, they laid their hats on the seats behind them, handed their canes to waiting ushers, and started moving with the music. Then Mr. Louis Loomis stepped up to the microphone. With the funky beat of the song going *whommp de whommp, de whommp whommp whommp whommp,* Mr. Louis Loomis started singing, like a raspy James Cleveland:

"The devil gone try and keep you all down. But like that old goat in a story, every time that old devil throw dirt on your head, pack it down with your feet and come out ahead. 'Cause God's got your back, when you down in a hole, He'll get you out, if the story be told . . ."

The chorus joined in on the vamp, "*He'll get you out, if the story be told, if the story be told.*"

As their voices soared across the sanctuary, wrapping the church up in their powerful and anointed music, the KMs started clapping and stomping, and the congregation joined in. You couldn't just hear this song, it ran all through you, and it felt good. Mr. Louis Loomis repeated the verse, then effortlessly ran a smooth ad-lib around the chorus. As the choir sang, "*He'll get you out,*" Mr. Louis Loomis intoned, between the lines, "*If the story be told. If the story be told . . .*"

Immersed in the music, Mr. Louis Loomis started getting happy. Grabbing the microphone off the stand, he danced down to the front of the altar and leaped high in the air. As he landed, he kicked out a leg, clutching his infamous belt, and called out "Laaawwwwd" in a shout-scream. Already at a fever pitch from the singing, the crowd matched the shout with their own praise, calling out, "Sang, sang, sang," "God is up in here *today*," "Praise the Lord," and even one "Don't hurt yourself now."

After one more verse and a final holler from Mr. Louis Loomis, the song came to an abrupt end, with that cutoff that gospel choirs have down to an art form. But the congregation, still clapping, stomping, and dancing in place, couldn't let go of the song. Miss Mozelle started singing the verse in her rich contralto until another woman and then a man joined in. They were sounding too good, and the KMs had to rise to that challenge and start singing again. They sang a cappella at first, and then the musicians got happy and lit into the song, sparking a Holy Ghost fire in the church.

And that was all it took for the rest of the congregation to get happy and cut loose shouting, spilling from the pews into the aisles to work out. Sheba hopped up and started dancing right at the altar with such fervor that Louise leaned over and whispered to Mozelle, who was now seated, "Girl, King David didn't have nothing on that chile."

As the music broke over her like a wave, Sheba lost herself in the rhythm, dancing so fast that her feet were a dizzying blur. The whole church was lit up, the air electric with calls and cries of praise to God. Phoebe searched for Jackson in the sea of dancing, shouting folk but didn't see him until he sprinted past her, breathlessly shouting, "Jesus!"

The Holy Ghost was shooting through George, filling his heart with praise and rejoicing. He had been through a storm, and the Lord had brought him out with such a mighty victory, his clothes didn't even get wet. As the Holy

Ghost slammed down on him, he fell in step with his wife up in front of the church, dancing with all his heart, and all his soul, and all his might. They were husband and wife, deeply in love, coming together before the Lord, giving up the praise to the Heavenly Father and worshiping Him as one.

But no one forgot that the Gethsemane Missionary Baptist Church Centennial Celebration almost didn't happen. When Clydell Forbes died, the church came close to dying itself, almost losing the spiritual fortitude to get back up and walk on faith. It had learned—at times, the hard way—that God don't play, and that if He is for you, can't nobody even think about standing against you. And that was definitely a reason to dance and shout and keep the songs ringing out, and the high praise going late into the night of that Second Sunday. For as Nettie told Bert, "If the celebration keep on going like this, we gone walk out this church and step right on up to glory."